THE CABIN BELOW

A PSYCHOLOGICAL SUSPENSE THRILLER

N. L. HINKENS

This is a work of fiction. Names, characters, organizations, places, events and incidents are either products of the author's imagination or are used fictitiously. For more information about the author, please visit **www.normahinkens.com**

Published by Dunecadia Publishing, California

ISBN: 978-1-947890-23-7

Cover by: **www.derangeddoctordesign.com**

Editing by: **www.jeanette-morris.com/first-impressions-writing**

1

ALLISON

Allison Robinson ripped open the luxurious crested envelope that her husband, Doug, handed her and stared at the contents in confusion. "What is this?" She wrinkled her forehead and waited for him to explain.

A mischievous grin softened his chiseled jawline, lending him that brooding air that effortlessly arrested female attention wherever he went. "I booked a Caribbean cruise to celebrate our wedding anniversary next month. Ten years is worth celebrating in style, baby, don't you think?" He threw his six-foot-two frame down in the chair next to her at the kitchen table and reached for her hands, rubbing his thumbs back-and-forth over her knuckles. A familiar gesture that had once ignited passion inside her, but that she now found mildly irritating. A lot of things about Doug irritated her of late. He was too close to the nucleus of her pain. Every time she looked into his eyes, it was a stark reminder of just how much she'd lost—how much they'd both lost, although he seemed to have forgotten that.

Jerking her hands away, she shook her head. "I don't understand. How is a cruise supposed to change anything?

And why now, all of a sudden? You've barely shown up to any of our marriage counseling sessions. You're always gone on some business trip or another."

Doug leaned back in his chair, closing his eyes momentarily as if searching for the right words to break down something complex in understandable terms. Allison hated it when he masked his condescension in exaggerated patience.

"We both know the therapy isn't helping, Ally. We keep churning up the same conversation again and again. And you know what happens when you churn butter too long—it curdles." He cupped a hand over the nape of his neck. "This cruise is a chance for us to get away from everyone, and the same four walls that are closing in on us. A change of scene will do us more good than a thousand hours in a therapist's chair." He hesitated, pulling his full lips into a winsome smile. "Don't you want to get away from where it happened—just for a little while? Focus on the two of us again?"

Allison dropped her gaze, crushing the envelope in her hand with shaking fingers. How could he even suggest such a thing? It could never be just the two of them again. What was he thinking? They had shared their history, albeit it ever so briefly, with someone else. And that was never going to go away no matter how much Doug wanted it to.

He got to his feet and reached for a Neiman Marcus shopping bag on the kitchen counter. With an elaborate flourish, he presented it to Allison. "I got you a little something for the trip."

With an air of trepidation, she peered into the bag and extracted a wide-brimmed floppy sun hat with a Gigi Burris designer sticker securing the tissue paper it was wrapped in.

Doug's eyes raked over her face for approval. "I hope you like it. I couldn't resist it. You'll look like my very own Jackie O in it with your oversized sunglasses."

Allison angled her face away from him in an effort to

mask her displeasure. She didn't like it when Doug compared her to Jackie O. It felt like he was mocking her. They shared the same thick, dark hair and curves, but Allison's eyes were too wide set and her lips too full. They both knew she wasn't half as attractive as the world's most beloved widow had been, but what disturbed Allison more was the subtle underlying assumption that she was a kept woman. Granted, Doug ran his own successful financial planning company, but she worked full-time too as an executive assistant in a commercial real estate office.

"It's exactly what our marriage needs, Ally," Doug plowed on, either oblivious to her hesitation about the trip he'd sprung on her, or eager not to acknowledge it. "It's a seven-day western Caribbean extravaganza. I even splurged on an open-view balcony cabin."

Allison threw him an alarmed look, before checking the date on the crumpled tickets in her hands. February 09-16. Only a few weeks away. Would they even be able to get a refund this late in the day? Regardless, she had no intention of going. "How much did this set us back?"

Doug raised his hand in a placating manner. "Don't worry about the cost. Trust me, it's nothing compared to what we've chalked up in counseling hours."

Allison tensed at the backhanded rebuke. That was the way Doug operated—striking in such a charming manner that you were left teetering, never quite sure how to take it. She traced her fingers distractedly over her forehead. Julia, her therapist, had cautioned her against being hypersensitive to every comment her husband made. Truth be told, she had a hard time knowing when she'd crossed that line. Months of medication had turned her brain to mush.

Doug raised his brows expectantly. "So, are you in?" He leaned closer and added softly. "I want to make things better between us, baby. I really do. Just not the way we've been trying. Everything's always so serious at the therapist's office. You come out of there more down than you go in. It's time to switch gears—try having some fun together again."

Allison held her husband's gaze for a long moment. She didn't blame him for ditching their last few sessions. If she was being honest, she was burned out on it all herself—Julia's maddeningly calm voice, the water trickling in the background that was supposed to soothe her emotions, the steady stream of *how do you feel about this or that* questions that never seemed to resolve anything. Maybe there was a better way to go about rehabilitating their marriage. It wasn't as if she didn't love her husband anymore, she just didn't feel much of anything anymore. With a resigned sigh, she straightened out the scrunched-up tickets and gave a half-hearted nod. "Okay, let's do it. Let's take a cruise together."

Doug's face lit up with such a flash of exuberance that Allison felt momentarily stricken with guilt. His boyish optimism had been one of the things that had attracted her to him when they'd first met at a mutual friend's wedding over a decade earlier. That, and his dark, espresso-brown eyes that had made her chest constrict the first time they'd settled on her. She still couldn't fathom why he'd fallen for her. He was outgoing and entertaining, a crowd-pleasing storyteller at every party. She was more introverted, better suited to conversation one-on-one. But he seemed to like that about her—that she was content to let him soak up all the attention.

Over the years, she'd remained more than a little insecure of the obvious fact that Doug continued to turn heads wherever they went. Despite his assurances that he found her the most attractive woman on earth, she knew by the pointed glances shot her way that she was not in the same league as her husband when it came to looks. She knew what the women observing them together were thinking. She'd probably have thought the same thing in their shoes. *How does a woman like her score a ten like him?* Allison fought down the wave of unease roiling around in the pit of her stomach as she pictured the upcoming cruise, and the social interactions it would entail. Other than going to work, she'd barely left the house in the past six months. Her heart was still broken and her brain still grieving. But if she didn't make an effort to move past what had happened, Doug might not stick around. He was right. They needed to get out of the rut they were in. And what better way to do it than on an all-inclusive cruise where they could kick back and not have to worry about a thing, other than enjoying each other's company?

With a goofy smile, she placed the floppy sun hat on her head where it promptly slipped down over her eyes. She tilted the brim up with one finger and peered seductively at Doug from beneath it. "Well? What do you think?"

He gave an approving whistle. "Styling on the seas, Jackie O."

"Thank you, honey. It's a tad on the big side, but I love it." Allison plucked the hat from her head and carefully replaced it in the Neiman Marcus shopping bag. "Now I'll have to find a sundress to go with it."

Doug rewarded her with a broad smile. "Take the credit card and go shop your heart out. Get whatever you want and have fun doing it." He paused before adding, "Maybe you should refill your antidepressant prescription before we go, just in case. I know you're not taking it anymore, but you never know how you might feel in a new environment. I'd hate for us to be caught off guard."

Allison frowned at him. "I don't need it."

"No, of course not. But it would give me more peace of mind to know it's available if you do end up needing it. It's like bringing Advil—you don't take it unless you have to."

"I hated being on those pills. I was out of it all the time."

Doug reached for her hands again and this time she didn't pull away. "I'm just covering all our bases, baby. I want this trip on *Diamond of the Waves* to be perfect."

Allison gave an acquiescing shrug. "Okay. If it makes you feel any better, I'll refill it."

Doug brushed his lips gently to her cheek. "We're going to have a fabulous trip making brand new memories. This will be our fresh start. And I'm going to do whatever it takes to make sure you're never depressed again."

2

ALLISON

Three weeks later, Allison settled into the passenger seat of Doug's black BMW SUV while he loaded their suitcases into the back. Climbing into the driver's seat, he laid a hand casually on Allison's leg and squeezed it. "Thanks for going along with this. I know I kind of sprung the trip on you, but sometimes that's the best way to get unstuck."

Allison flicked a smile across at him. "True. If you'd asked me before you bought the tickets, I'd have turned you down flat. But now that we're actually leaving, I realize you were right. I do need a change of scene. It's hard being here … where it happened."

Doug's eyes clouded over as he started up the engine. "We're not going to talk about that, remember? If anyone asks, stick to what we agreed to say."

Allison turned to look out the window. It wouldn't be a lie, per se. They'd just be obscuring the ugly truth. And for good reason. Despite the progress she'd made in therapy, she wasn't at a point where she would be able to talk with strangers about the awful events of that day without breaking down.

Excitement frothed inside her when they turned off the freeway at the sign for the cruise terminal. It had been a long time since she'd felt that flutter of anticipation in her stomach. It unnerved her slightly—that uncanny capacity human beings had to live and laugh again no matter the extent of the tragedies they endured. Today, she welcomed it. There had been far too many days when she'd felt nothing—wondered indeed if she'd ever feel anything again. She couldn't undo what had happened, but she could still work on her marriage. Despite his shortcomings, her husband loved her, and he'd put up with an awful lot in the past six months.

"Wait here. I'll grab our bags." Doug sprang from the car, barely able to tamp down his excitement. Allison smiled to herself. He was like a kid who'd just got released from school for the summer. And his enthusiasm was starting to rub off on her. She pulled out her phone and snapped a quick selfie before uploading it to her long-neglected Facebook page, adding a caption: *Setting sail on Diamond of the Waves today on a long overdue vacation! Life is good.*

After unloading their cases curbside and handing them off to a porter, Doug and Allison drove to the Bella Oceania cruise line parking garage. They rode the elevator down to cruise terminal one and joined the throng of eager vacationers juggling wide-eyed kids and overstuffed bags as they wound their way to the embarkation and security screening hall. Most of the men were dressed for Caribbean fun in baggy shorts and flip-flops, the women furtively comparing pedicures while their kids fidgeted in line, clutching stuffed animals and iPads in heavy duty protective cases.

For her part, Allison carried a striped beach bag which contained a few essentials along with the Gigi Burris sun hat that Doug had gifted her. She'd wanted to exchange it for a smaller size, but Doug hadn't been able to find the receipt, so she hadn't bothered pursuing it—a decision she would probably regret. It was annoying having to constantly adjust a hat that didn't fit properly. She'd considered pretending to forget it but had ultimately decided against it. She would wear it one day during the cruise to keep him happy. After that, she would leave it in the cabin.

"Doing okay?" Doug asked, adjusting the strap of his black laptop backpack.

Allison nodded, smiling uncertainly back at him as she tried to block out the women around them sneaking a second glance his way. She'd forgotten just how disconcerting it could be walking around in public with him—being checked out and found wanting in comparison.

Uniformed Bella Oceania staff with lanyards hanging around their necks directed them left and right at every turn, ensuring that no one wandered off the path on their way to the ship. The tiled floors echoed with the communal rumble of wheeled carry-on cases as the line of people snaked forward under the watchful eye of security guards scattered throughout the terminal, monitoring the proceedings for any sign of trouble or medical emergency. Allison had already spotted a couple of inebriated passengers jostling their neighbors as they struggled to stay upright. Why anyone would want to start drinking this early in the day was beyond her comprehension. She hated that feeling of being out of control—which was another reason she'd stopped taking the antidepressants. In fact, she regretted ever starting them in the first place. Things could have been so different right now.

After showing their tickets to an agent at the check-in booth, Doug and Allison were directed to a separate area for the priority passenger program, far removed from the masses zig-zagging across the convention-sized space to the security screening area. As they joined the smaller line, it came to an abrupt standstill, and Allison inadvertently bumped the woman in front of her with her beach bag. She turned around, a quizzical look on her face, and Allison hastily mumbled an apology. "I'm so sorry! I didn't expect everyone to stop moving all at once."

The woman let out an infectious laugh and tucked a strand of chestnut hair behind one ear, unabashedly throwing an admiring eye over Doug. "No kidding! Just when I thought we were getting somewhere. So much for priority boarding. I'm Sophia Clark by the way." She jabbed a polished fingernail in the back of the man standing next to her, hunched over his phone. He spun around, brows steepled, before it dawned on him that she was trying to introduce him to someone. "This is my husband, Cody."

He yanked out his earbuds and gave a curt nod, hitching his lips into a chagrined smile. "Nice to meet you."

Doug and Allison introduced themselves, and the two men shook hands.

"Is this your first cruise?" Allison asked.

Sophia gave an enthusiastic nod. "I've always wanted to take a cruise, but Cody's been so busy building up the business all these years. All we've ever been able to manage is a weekend away here and there. We're finally at a place where we can afford to take a real vacation and celebrate our success a little. What about you two—celebrating anything in particular?"

"As a matter of fact, it's our wedding anniversary today," Doug announced, a current of pride in his voice as he slipped a protective arm around Allison's shoulders. "We've been married a whole blissful decade."

"You're kidding!" Sophia blurted out, throwing an astonished look at her husband. "It's our wedding anniversary tomorrow. Fourteen years for us."

"What are the odds—that's crazy!" Doug exclaimed.

"Hey, we should get together for dinner later on and have a toast to married life," Sophia suggested.

There was a beat of silence before Doug responded, "Allison and I have a reservation at The Chophouse Grille at seven. I'm sure they could add a couple of seats to our table."

"That sounds like a blast," Sophia was quick to reply. "We'd love that, wouldn't we, Cody?"

"Absolutely," he agreed, sounding as if he usually concurred with whatever Sophia said. He shot a dubious look Allison's way. "So long as we're not … intruding."

"Not at all," Allison assured him, as she placed her bag on the security belt. She quashed down the niggling feeling of annoyance that arose as Sophia and Doug exchanged phone numbers. This wasn't just any old wedding anniversary they were celebrating. She and Doug were supposed to be working on their marriage. That would be hard to do with another couple—strangers, no less—participating in their anniversary dinner. Still, they had seven days to talk things over. It wasn't as if they had to dive right into a marital root canal on their very first night. As Doug liked to remind her, she needed to be more spontaneous. She might as well start practicing now.

After retrieving their bags from the security scanner, they made their way along a winding corridor to the gangway. Right before they boarded, an exuberant photographer snapped their picture in front of a decorative life ring backdrop embossed with the ship's name, *Diamond of the Waves.*

"No doubt that precious memory will be available for the price of a small island by the end of the cruise." Sophia chuckled. "I can't believe people actually buy those overpriced photos. I'd rather take my own—I prefer more impromptu shots anyway."

"She's not kidding," Cody piped up. "She takes a shot a minute. Brace yourself."

Allison suppressed a smile, anticipating how the conversation would go down between her and Doug when they viewed the overpriced official cruise photos available for purchase at a kiosk. She would gasp at the outrageous price, and he would fork it over, insisting it was a memory worth paying for. He'd always been more of a spendthrift than her, but then, as he liked to point out, he made most of the money. He'd conveniently forgotten that it was her inheritance he had used to start the company.

"I guess we'll catch up with you two at dinner," Sophia said, after they'd crossed the skywalk and entered the ship's foyer.

"Sounds good," Doug replied. "Enjoy the rest of your day on board."

With a parting wave, Sophia tucked her arm into Cody's and steered him off in the direction of the elevators.

Doug glanced at his watch. "Our cabin won't be ready for another hour or two. How about we grab some lunch before the masses scramble aboard? Then we can explore the ship at our leisure."

"I'm up for that," Allison said. "I'm a little hungry."

After perusing their restaurant choices for lunch on the ship's app, they made their way up to Balera Bistro on deck six.

The hostess escorted them to a corner booth and handed them each a menu. When their waiter appeared a few minutes later, Doug ordered an aged steak burger on a brioche bun with melted Gruyere and smoked bacon, while Allison settled on tropical ceviche with arugula.

"Wow! The food here's excellent," she raved after a few bites.

"Culinary perfection," Doug agreed. "Not sure how dinner's going to top this."

"I still can't get over the fact that Sophia and Cody have almost the same wedding anniversary as us," Allison mused. "What are the odds that we'd end up next to them in line?"

Doug wiped his lips on his napkin. "I have a good feeling about this trip, baby. It's only just begun and we're already meeting people and having fun. Sophia's a hoot."

Allison sipped her iced tea. "Cody seems more reserved."

Doug waved a hand dismissively. "He'll loosen up. You watch, he'll be doing belly flops into the pool after a couple of cocktails by tomorrow afternoon."

Allison chuckled. "Promise me you won't participate in that birdbrained spectacle. Otherwise, I'll post your unflattering moves on Facebook."

Doug winked at her. "Hey, what happens on the water stays on the water."

3

ALLISON

Inside their cabin later that afternoon, Doug and Allison unpacked their bags and then checked the sign on the back of the door to find out when and where they needed to go for the obligatory muster drill. After dutifully donning their unflattering life vests, they gathered with their fellow passengers on the appointed deck.

"Look! There's Cody and Sophia," Allison said, waving at the couple through the assembled crowd. Sophia put a hand on her hip and twirled left and then right in an exaggerated fashion, showing off the gaudy orange life vest atop her floral sundress.

"You're right about her. She's a real character. I wonder if she's always that upbeat." Allison turned to Doug, but he wasn't paying her any attention.

His gaze was riveted on the leggy blonde crew member striding across the deck in tight white shorts, clutching a microphone. With a flick of her waist-length hair, she introduced herself as Misty and announced she would be demonstrating the proper use of a life vest in the unlikely event of an emergency. Allison gave her her begrudging attention as she began her safety talk, intermittently flashing her flawless smile at the crowd. Casting a quick glance around, Allison doubted any male between puberty and ninety in the captive audience was actually absorbing Misty's instructions—more likely imagining helping her out of her life vest.

After what seemed like an interminable amount of time, the drill finally ended. "That's all from me for now, folks. Enjoy your cruise," Misty gushed into the microphone. "And don't forget to come hear me sing tonight in the Slow Vibes piano bar on deck seven."

The crowd immediately began to disperse, eager to make the most of their first afternoon aboard *Diamond of the Waves,* and Allison soon lost sight of Sophia and Cody.

"I have a hankering to go up on the back deck and watch the ship leave port, before we go hang out by the pool and relax," Doug said. "Or is there something else you'd rather do?"

"A little poolside relaxation sounds good to me," Allison agreed, inwardly dreading the thought of bikini-clad women preening as Doug walked by. But she was determined not to let her insecurities get the better of her. Besides, it wasn't as if that leggy blonde crew member, Misty, would be kicking back by the pool. She was on duty.

They made their way to the top deck and hung over the railing, watching the ship depart port for the open sea as Fort Lauderdale shrank into the horizon behind them like a deflating mirage. Allison took a few pictures and uploaded them to Facebook. Documenting their trip felt like a necessary step in her healing. That's what people did when they went on vacation—they shared photos with friends and preserved the memories to look back over later. If nothing else, the pictures would serve as proof that she'd actually tried to enjoy herself.

"There you have it," Doug announced, gripping the railing. "We're officially en route to the Caribbean." He pulled Allison in close and kissed her. "Even you have to admit this is better than sitting in a therapist's office playing pass the parcel with a box of tissues."

"That muster drill was quite something," Allison remarked, as they went back down to their cabin to change. "I've never seen a crowd so enthralled by a safety demonstration before."

Doug threw her a quizzical look. "What do you mean?"

"Misty—the beguiling blonde who sings in the piano bar in the evenings. Don't pretend you weren't held captive by her charms along with every other male with a pulse." Allison cringed as the words flew from her mouth, immediately regretting exposing her petty jealousy.

Doug's lips curved into a playful smile. "It does help with the boring parts of the drill when you have a little eye candy demoing the moves." He reached for Allison's hand and interlaced his fingers in hers. "You're not jealous, are you? Actually, I hope you are. That would be a good thing. It means you're taking an interest in me again. Trust me, you're my only priority on this trip."

Allison gave him a hollow smile, feeling like a heel for opening her mouth against her better judgement. "I know. I'm just teasing you."

It was only halfway true. There was a part of her that had always struggled to believe her handsome husband only had eyes for her. Being out of their usual environment and seeing all the attention he was garnering from female passengers—some half his age—was more than a little unsettling. Restless whisperings of insecurity were always there, like a cancerous choir deep inside her. But she knew they were unfounded. It was her hand he was holding, her bed he was sharing, her name on his lips. Her jealousy would destroy all they had left if she didn't get a grip.

Up on the pool deck, Doug and Allison settled into a pair of sun loungers in a quiet corner away from the slides where most of the action was centered. Spread out on his towel with a piña colada at hand, Doug sighed contentedly as he admired the view. "This is exactly how I envisioned things. Just me and my lovely wife chilling out without a care in the world."

"Just you, me, and five thousand others," Allison corrected him.

"Yeah, but they don't count," Doug said sleepily, closing his eyes. Within minutes, the all-too-familiar drone of his snores filled the air. Allison set down her book and reached for the pineapple slice garnish on her cocktail. Her eyes wandered in the direction of the colorful water park at the other end of the deck where chubby-legged toddlers in swim diapers trotted squealing through the fountains, their protective parents hovering a step or two behind them, ready to swoop them up at the first tumble. Allison tried not to resent their happiness. It wasn't as if it had come at her expense. Still, it was a painful reminder of what had been snatched from her. She could never have imagined that she and Doug would be celebrating their tenth wedding anniversary as a party of two.

A short time later, she woke with a start to see Doug grinning down at her, his damp hair glistening in the sun. She rubbed her eyes as she sat up. "Did you go swimming without me?"

"Had to cool off. That was quite the power nap you took. I guess your book wasn't all that interesting, after all."

Allison stifled a yawn. "What time is it?"

"Time to hit the showers." Doug reached for her bag and swung it over his shoulder. "I called the restaurant and added Sophia and Doug to our reservation."

. . .

ALLISON SAT in front of the vanity in the cabin and studied her face appraisingly as she carefully applied her make up before dinner. She hadn't missed the fact that Sophia had cast an approving eye over Doug when they'd met during the embarkation process. Still, she wasn't concerned about her making a pass at him. As looks went, she'd rate Sophia as average—her personality being her biggest selling point. Allison had liked her from the get-go. She seemed like the type of woman who made everything fun. And Allison desperately needed to learn how to have fun again. She couldn't expect Doug to be patient with her forever. But it was easier for him to move past what had happened. It hadn't been his fault.

"Ready?" Her husband rested a hand casually on her shoulder. "You look beautiful tonight."

Allison forced herself not to roll her eyes. The therapist had explained that it undermined Doug when she did that. "Thank you," she replied, getting to her feet. "You don't look too shabby yourself for a man who's been married for ten years."

Hand-in-hand, they strolled along the opulent esplanade to The Chophouse Grille, admiring the glittering array of entertainment choices along the way. "I can't wait to check out all the shows," Allison said.

"Don't forget we have tickets for the headliner act tonight," Doug reminded her. "The music's supposed to be first class."

"There's the restaurant up ahead," Allison said, pointing to the white marble entryway with Chophouse Grille in gold lettering over the arched doorway.

Inside, the hostess guided them to an intimate leather booth set for four. Their server had just finished pouring them some water when Sophia and Cody arrived. Sophia was dressed in a red wraparound dress and strappy, silver heels, her hair piled high on top of her head. "Happy Anniversary, you two lovebirds," she said blowing them air kisses, as she wiggled into the booth next to Cody. "This place looks amazing. How was your afternoon?"

"I'm not sure Allison remembers much about it, do you, baby?" Doug quipped. "We kicked back by the pool with a cocktail and she slept through most of it—one drink and she's out cold. I took a quick dip. What did you two get up to?"

"I had the most amazing facial," Sophia raved, patting her cheeks.

"I can tell. You're glowing," Allison responded, trying not to sound irritated that she'd somehow ended up as the butt of the first joke of the evening. A not-so-subtle dig at the many afternoons she'd wasted sleeping off her depression.

"I tried to talk Cody into getting a massage," Sophia gibbered on, "but he insisted on taking his laptop to an internet station." She pulled a face. "He can't ever disconnect from that work thing."

"What do you work at, Cody?" Doug inquired.

"I have an online affiliate marketing company. I promote insurance commodities for companies to consumers—mostly commercial, some life insurance packages. It's a huge time suck."

"Pretty boring stuff," Sophia broke in, rolling her eyes in dramatic fashion. "But he's done well at it. Too well in fact. He never takes a break. Which is why we're here. I booked this cruise to force him to relax and celebrate his success a little. And our anniversary, of course." She grinned at Cody. "I enlisted the help of his parents behind his back to take our twins, Gavin and Will, for the week. After that, he couldn't refuse me."

Cody gave a tight smile as he reached for his water glass.

Allison recognized that smile. It was one she often

reverted to herself when she was trying to hide what was really going on inside.

"I feel your pain, man," Doug piped up, after an awkward silence. "It's hard to tear yourself away when you run your own business."

The waiter interrupted them with a basket of freshly baked bread and a recitation of the specials, before taking their wine order.

"So tell me about you two," Sophia said, shooting another of her disarming smiles across the table after they'd studied the menu and made their selections. "What do you do when you're not chugging down cocktails on cruise ships?"

Allison laughed. "This is our first cruise too. Doug runs his own financial planning company, and I'm an executive assistant in a commercial real estate office."

"Any kids?" Sophia went on, tearing off a hunk of bread and dipping it in oil and balsamic.

Allison swallowed and shook her head. "No kids."

"Allison had a miscarriage last year," Doug added. "It's been a rough road for her ever since."

Cody reached for his wine glass and took a large swig, clearly uncomfortable with the heavy topic.

Sophia leaned across the table and placed her hand on Allison's. "I am so, so sorry. That must have been devastating for you."

Allison withdrew her hand and lifted her wine glass to her lips. "Yes it was, but we're here to celebrate. Let's toast our joint wedding anniversaries."

"Wait just a minute!" Sophia cried, scrabbling around in her purse for her phone. "I need to capture this moment."

They all raised their glasses and clinked them, while Sophia snapped a picture.

Allison hoped no one noticed how badly her hand was shaking. A miscarriage always elicited sympathy, which is why she and Doug had settled on that version of events. The truth was a whole lot harder to hear.

All at once, she became aware of Doug talking to her. She blinked, bringing herself back to the moment, her wine glass reflecting the light from the fixture overhead.

"... and so, Allison, baby, I want to thank you for being everything I could ever have dreamed of in a partner," Doug said, as he got down on one knee and set a beautifully-wrapped gift on the table in front of her. "Happy Anniversary!"

Before she had a chance to say anything, Sophia let out a delighted squeal. "Oh, that is so romantic! Cody, you need to up your game!" She giggled and then added, "He gave me a Macy's gift certificate before we left the house. Can you believe it? Our most successful year in business and the best he can come up with is a gift certificate."

A dark look crossed Cody's face, before he forced his lips into a tight grin and shrugged.

"Go on," Doug urged Allison as he nudged the package toward her. "Open it."

"Oh, yes, please do!" Sophia rubbed her hands together excitedly. "I'm a hopeless romantic. I can't wait to see what's inside."

Allison's face flushed as all eyes turned to her. Why did Doug have to be so pretentious and do this in public? Trying to mask her reluctance at being compelled to open the gift in front of virtual strangers, she picked up the foil package and slipped off the luxurious ribbon. Inside a blue velvet box lay an exquisite sapphire-and-diamond necklace. She stared down at the glittering pendant, too shocked to speak.

"Do you like it?" Doug asked, one corner of his mouth curled into a hopeful grin.

"I ... yes ... I love it. It's gorgeous, but it's too much," Allison sputtered.

"Nonsense," Doug retorted, lifting the necklace out of the box. He undid the clasp and placed it around her neck. "Nothing's too much for you."

"That is a stunning piece of jewelry!" Sophia raved. She snapped a picture and then flipped the camera so Allison could see how the necklace looked on her.

She stared at her reflection in Sophia's camera. "I don't know what to say. I'm speechless." She smiled tentatively at Doug. "Thank you, honey. It's beautiful."

He slid back into the booth next to her. "Only the best for my own Jackie O."

"Oh my goodness! You do look like her!" Sophia exclaimed, her mouth falling open.

All of a sudden, the necklace felt unbearably cold and heavy around Allison's neck. With a frozen smile on her face, she carefully unclasped it and laid it back on its bed of crushed velvet.

She glanced across at Cody, but he avoided her gaze and drained the rest of his wine. Guilt pricked at her. She suspected Doug had made him feel equally as inadequate as Sophia had. A Macy's gift certificate didn't hold a candle to a necklace of this caliber.

Out of nowhere, their waiter swooped in and refilled Cody's glass, dissolving the awkward atmosphere. "Congratulations," the waiter said with a wink. "A very romantic gesture. Half the restaurant's captivated."

Allison threw a sidelong glance around, flushing when she caught a glimpse of a blonde-haired woman peering out from a corner booth, her features obscured in the subdued lighting.

To Allison's relief, their food arrived a moment later, diverting the attention away from her.

"This is amazing!" Sophia moaned, waving her fork in the

air after the first bite of her Asian crispy goat cheese salad. "The cheese melts in your mouth like a savory candy floss."

With the awkward topic of their childlessness safely behind them, Allison started to relax and enjoy the company of their new acquaintances. Unsurprisingly, Sophia proved to be an excellent storyteller and soon had them in stitches. As the evening wore on, and the wine flowed more freely, even Cody's walls began to come down.

"I need to use the rest room," Allison said, after they had split a chocolate mud pie for dessert. Doug lifted her purse from the seat between them and placed it on the table as he slid out of the booth to let her go by.

"Any idea where the restrooms are?" Allison asked, feeling slightly tipsy as she got to her feet.

Doug swung around to hail a waiter, knocking her purse to the ground in the process.

The contents scattered and a prescription bottle rolled beneath the table next to Sophia's foot. She picked it up and, after a furtive glance at the label, handed it to Allison. A deep flush crept over her cheeks when she saw what it was. She hardly wanted to advertise the fact that she had a prescription for antidepressants. But what bothered her more was that she didn't remember putting the pills in her purse. Her head was a tad foggy from the wine, but she was almost certain she'd left them in her toiletry bag in their cabin. So how had they ended up in her purse?

4

ALLISON

Judging by the fleeting glance Doug and Sophia exchanged when Allison returned from the restroom, she guessed they had been talking about her—more to the point, the antidepressants, and her *miscarriage*. Doug better not have breached their agreement and told the Clarks the truth about that awful day.

As she slid back into her seat, she noticed her purse stowed in the corner of the booth, presumably with the prescription bottle safely back inside. She hoped Doug had explained that she wasn't taking the antidepressants anymore, that she'd only refilled the prescription as a precaution. The last thing she wanted was for Sophia and Cody to think she was some kind of basket case.

"I was just asking Doug if you were on Facebook," Sophia said cheerily, pulling out her phone and grinning at Allison. "I can send you a friend request and then we can see each other's cruise pictures."

"I have a profile under Allison Lundberg-Robinson. To be honest, I haven't posted anything much on there recently."

Sophia gave her an elaborate wink. "A lurker, eh?"

Allison cracked a smile. "Guilty as charged. I'm trying to do better on this trip though."

"There you go!" Sophia said, tapping her screen. "I just sent you a friend request."

Allison fished in her purse for her phone and opened up the Facebook app. She accepted Sophia's request and studied the close-up photo of their hands clinking sparkling wine glasses that popped up. Below it, Sophia had written: *First night with new friends. #CruisingIsTheLifeForMe #MakingMemories #NewAdventures.*

"That's a clever angle. You take great pictures," Allison commented, clicking the *like* icon below the post. "I'm not much of an artist when it comes to composition. And I haven't got the whole hashtag thing down yet either." Her eye traveled farther up the screen to the header photo with Sophia and Cody leaning back against an oak tree while two curly-haired, identical twin boys balanced on a branch above them. "Cute kids!" Allison said, trying to nail a cheery tone.

"Thanks, I like to think they take after their mother," Sophia answered with a mischievous grin. "This is the longest we've ever been away from them but, like I said, Cody really needed this break. He *earned* it." She arched a brow at her husband as if waiting on him to back her up, but he merely shrugged and reached for his wine glass again. It hadn't escaped Allison's notice that he'd consumed twice as much alcohol as the rest of them over the course of the evening. A functioning alcoholic? Or maybe he hadn't quite forgiven Sophia for forcing him to take this cruise and was overindulging in retaliation. Whatever it was, something was bothering Cody. He wasn't the carefree cruiser his wife was. Perhaps he was having a harder time tearing himself away from his work than Sophia realized.

Allison's mind drifted back to the suspicions she'd had about Doug in the months before he'd booked the cruise.

He'd been traveling more than usual, gone for a week at a time on several occasions. It had crossed her mind at one point that he might be having an affair. Unbeknownst to him, she'd gone through his receipts after a couple of out-of-state trips. But there was no indication that he'd been making new memories with a love interest at some upscale hotel. He'd always been where he'd said he was going to be, and he only ever ordered room service for one person. Deep down, she knew her suspicions stemmed from her own deep-rooted insecurities. It was time to take a leaf out of Sophia's playbook and make *#NewAdventures* the theme for the week.

Sophia glanced at her phone. "You guys! The headliner show starts in thirty minutes. I need to run back to my cabin and ditch these heels. They're pinching my toes."

"I think I'll do the same, freshen up a little beforehand," Allison said. "How about we meet you in the theater foyer in twenty minutes?"

"Sounds good. See you there," Cody replied, getting to his feet and following his wife out of the restaurant.

"Baby, do you really like the necklace?" Doug asked, peering anxiously at Allison as they left together. "I can exchange it for something else if you want."

"Don't be silly! It's gorgeous," she assured him. "I just feel guilty that you spent so much on me. The cruise was supposed to be our anniversary gift to each other."

"I don't want you to feel guilty," Doug admonished, tugging her closer. "You've been through more than most women could bear. I want this to be a fresh start—a reset. From now on, we're going to live like we mean it."

Allison grimaced inwardly. It wasn't that simple. The truth was, she wasn't sure if she'd ever be able to stop analyzing her actions that day. If only she could go back in time and do things differently. The *what ifs* paraded endlessly through her mind, Molotov cocktails of pain threatening to ignite all over again. She shook her head free of her downward-spiraling thoughts. Not tonight. She wouldn't allow herself to go there. She couldn't keep doing this to Doug.

Back in their cabin, Allison opened the safe in the closet and followed the instructions to reset the password. To her frustration, the lock wouldn't activate. "Doug! Can you come here and take a look at this? Am I doing something wrong?"

He wandered over in his boxers and followed the same set of instructions with the same result. "That's weird. Not sure what's going on with it. We can have maintenance take a look at it in the morning. Just stash the necklace out of sight for now. It'll be fine 'till we get back from the show."

Allison ran a finger over the soft velvet box, a furrow forming on her forehead. Doug was probably right, but she was reluctant to tempt fate with such an expensive item. "Why don't you call maintenance and see if they can come up right now?"

Doug threw her a look of reproof. "This is a huge ship. They can't magically appear the minute we call them. It's not like we have a burst pipe or something critical."

"Still, it's worth a try," Allison insisted.

With an air of reluctance, Doug picked up the phone and explained the situation to the maintenance department before hanging up. "They'll send someone up as soon as they can. In the meantime, we need to get going or we're going to miss the start of the show."

He disappeared into the bathroom and closed the door behind him.

After a quick look around the cabin to assess her options, Allison placed the velvet box in her suitcase and threw a hoodie over it before zipping the case up and shoving it to the back of the closet.

. . .

ONCE THEY'D LOCATED Sophia and Cody in the foyer, the two couples made their way to their seats and sank down to enjoy the headliner show *Spellbound: A History of Magic.* As the lights dimmed and the music crescendoed, Doug wrapped an arm around Allison's shoulders. She leaned into him, giving herself permission to relax—more important—to be happy. For now, she was as contented as a woman could possibly be—loved, cherished, spoiled rotten, full of good food and wine, and about to enjoy a spectacular show.

Before long, she lost herself in the extravaganza, marveling at the agility of the acrobats descending onto the stage, attired in various costumes depicting magic through the decades. Even Houdini had his moment in the production, suspended by his ankles above the stage as he freed himself from a straitjacket.

Sophia intermittently gripped Allison by the arm, gasping at some intricate aerial stunt or inexplicable disappearing feat that defied all natural laws. Allison couldn't help but notice that Sophia and Cody barely interacted with one another the entire evening. Despite all the talk of celebrating the success of their business, Cody seemed worried and edgy, unable to stop checking his phone.

"That was incredible!" Doug raved, when the lights came up after the grand finale.

"Anyone up for a nightcap?" Sophia asked, as they followed the throng of people inching their way to the exits.

Allison shook her head. "I'm going to have to bow out. I've had a fabulous evening, but I'm exhausted."

"How about we catch up with you guys again tomorrow instead?" Doug suggested.

"Sounds good," Sophia said as they hugged goodbye.

Allison tucked her hand into Doug's arm as they exited the theater and merged with the crowd strolling along the esplanade. They took the elevator up to deck ten, trying not to laugh at the inebriated, red-faced couple who were arguing heatedly over which end of the ship their room was at.

"Hey! Look! It's Cody and Sophia!" Allison exclaimed as they stepped out of the elevator.

Sophia spun around at the mention of her name, and then laughed. "Long time, no see! Is this your floor?"

"Yeah, we're right over there, 10664," Doug answered, gesturing to their cabin.

Cody threw him a bemused look. "We're directly above you in 11664. We weren't paying attention and got off on the wrong floor."

Sophia gave one of her elaborate winks. "If someone hadn't had his nose in his phone, he might have pressed the right button."

Allison chuckled. "If you hear Doug snoring, feel free to thump on the floor. He can shake a house off its foundations when he gets going."

Sophia laughed and blew her a kiss as she stepped into the elevator. "Sea day tomorrow. Poolside cocktails are on the agenda."

Allison and Doug walked across the hall to their cabin. Doug waved his sea pass card and opened the door, then placed the card in the slot to activate the lights.

"I haven't had that much fun in a long time," Allison said tossing her purse on the nightstand. She sank down on the bed, throwing her arms out to the sides as she fell backward. "You were right, honey. I needed a change of scene."

"Told you. Hey, there's a note here from maintenance," Doug remarked. "Our safe's working now."

"Very efficient service. I'm impressed with Bella Oceania already, and it's only day one." Allison dragged herself to her feet and made her way over to the closet. She tugged the zipper on her case partway open and reached inside for the velvet box, wiggling her fingers around in vain to locate it.

With a groan of frustration, she yanked her suitcase out of the closet. After laying it flat on the floor, she unzipped it fully, and lifted out her hoodie. Sinking back on her heels, her muscles locked as she stared in disbelief at the empty interior.

5

ALLISON

Allison's heart pattered erratically, a sick feeling flooding her system. It had to be here. The wine must be muddling her memory. Had she hidden the necklace someplace else? Her thoughts flitted to and fro as she mentally tried to retrace her steps. No! She definitely remembered throwing her hoodie over the box to hide it. She'd even zipped up her suitcase. Maybe Doug had locked it away already. "Doug, honey," she called over her shoulder. "Did you put my necklace in the safe?"

"No, I haven't touched it."

"I can't find it!"

Doug popped his head out of the bathroom, clutching his toothbrush in one hand. "Where did you leave it?"

"Right here," Allison answered, unable to quell the hint of hysteria in her voice as she jabbed a finger at the empty case. "I stashed it under my hoodie. It's gone!" She fastened a stricken gaze on Doug. "The maintenance guy must have taken it."

Doug strode over to her. "I doubt it. Those guys value

their jobs too much. It must be around here somewhere. Are you sure you didn't put it in a drawer or something?"

Allison shot him a dark look. "I'm sure I put it in my suitcase. You were right here. Don't you remember?"

He dragged his fingers distractedly across his brow. "I didn't see you put it away. I was in the bathroom."

"We need to call security right away." Allison jumped to her feet and began pacing, hands pressed flat to her cheeks. "I can't believe this is happening. I haven't even had a chance to wear it yet."

Doug rested his hands on her shoulders. "Calm down and take a deep breath. There's no need to panic. I bet it's here someplace. You probably forgot where you put it. You know how you've been lately."

Allison tensed, narrowing her eyes at him. "What's that supposed to mean?"

Doug blinked rapidly, his lips partway open as if searching for a safe way to backpedal. "Nothing. It's just that you've had a rough few months trying to hold it together. This isn't the first time you've been confused about something." His hands slid from her shoulders. "It's okay, baby. It's perfectly understandable. Those antidepressants have side effects, after all."

"But I'm not on antidepressants, am I?" Allison ducked out from beneath him and stomped back to the closet. She sank to her knees and patted all around the carpeted area inside the door on the off chance that the box had fallen out of her case. Next, she got back to her feet and opened and closed all the drawers before checking the nightstands.

Still fuming, she twirled around to face Doug. "And that reminds me. How did those antidepressants get into my purse? Because I know for a fact I left them in my toiletry bag in the bathroom."

Doug studied her with a circumspect look for a long moment. "Baby, how would I know what you keep in your purse or your toiletry bag, for that matter? Can we just stay focused for a minute? Before we go raising the alarm, let's search the room thoroughly together. Maybe the necklace fell down the side of the bed or something."

Allison let out a derisive humph and folded her arms in front of her. "Search all you want. I'm telling you it's not here. Someone took it."

Ignoring her defiant stance, Doug threw back the covers on the bed and checked all around the mattress and underneath. Next, he went into the bathroom and moved aside the rolled towels and rummaged through their toiletries. He came back out and went through the closet drawers again, even opening the minibar—which irritated Allison no end—a not-so-subtle reminder of her bad days when she'd leave a coffee mug in the refrigerator, or put a bag of chips in the microwave. Did he really think she was losing it enough to mistake the minibar for the safe?

"See?" she fumed. "I told you it's gone. *Now* do you believe me?"

Doug rubbed the stubble on his jaw and gave an unconvincing nod.

Rolling her eyes, Allison snatched up the phone and dialed security. "Yes, I need to report a theft. I'm in 10664. My husband and I just got back from a show and a valuable piece of jewelry is missing from our cabin."

Balancing the receiver between her cheek and shoulder, she twisted her wedding ring on her finger, fighting to keep from bursting into tears in front of Doug. He already thought she was an emotional wreck; she had no desire to prove his point. "It was in my case, in the closet," she explained to the person on the other end of the line. "The lock on our safe wasn't working so we had maintenance come in while we went to the show."

Doug smoothed a hand over his hair, sinking down on the bed with an air of forbearance.

"Yes, we'll be here," Allison affirmed. "Thank you. I appreciate that." She hung up and turned to Doug. "The chief security officer's on his way up now to take a statement. He's going to check which maintenance worker serviced the safe and have someone talk to him."

"Good," Doug said warily, as he scratched the back of his neck. "I'm sure they'll get to the bottom of it."

"I hope so. I know you must have paid a small fortune for that necklace." Allison wandered into the bathroom and splashed some cold water on her face. What had started out as a fun-filled first day had deteriorated into a train wreck. She stretched her fingers around the rim of the sink and stared at them for a moment. She was shaking uncontrollably. It wasn't just about the money. It was disconcerting to think that someone had come into their cabin and robbed them while they were off enjoying themselves with friends in another part of the ship. A violation of sorts. Sophia would be shocked when she heard what had happened. Allison was half-tempted to text her but decided against it. She and Cody might be asleep by now. Hopefully, by tomorrow security would have tracked down her necklace and it would be a moot point anyway. After all, it was on the ship somewhere.

A sharp rap on the cabin door startled her. She hurriedly dried off her hands and exited the bathroom in time to see Doug opening the door to a smartly dressed man in a white uniform with an embroidered black patch labeled security on each shoulder. He introduced himself as Chief Security Officer Rob Benson and shook hands with both of them. "I understand you're missing some expensive jewelry?"

"Yes," Allison confirmed. "A sapphire-and-diamond necklace that my husband gave me at dinner tonight for our anniversary. It's brand new, still in the box."

"I'm truly sorry to hear that," Officer Benson said. "Let me assure you, Mrs. Robinson, I'm going to do everything in my power to help you locate it." He pulled out a notebook and jotted something down. "Where did you have dinner tonight?"

"At The Chophouse Grille," Allison replied.

"And can I ask where you last saw the necklace?"

"I put it in my suitcase beneath a hoodie before we went to the show."

"Is there anything else missing from your room?"

"Not that we're aware of," Doug interjected. "Have you tracked down the maintenance worker who fixed the safe?"

"Yes, we did. Let me check with my colleague for an update. He called him in to the office to interview him." Officer Benson reached for the radio on his hip. "Dave, do you copy?"

The radio crackled to life and a voice said, "Charlie two, go ahead."

"Have you spoken to Kabul yet?"

"Yeah, he's here with me now. Says he was in and out of 10664 in under five minutes. It was only a matter of resetting the code on the safe. He didn't notice any jewelry sitting around."

Officer Benson's expression didn't change. "Did anyone else enter the cabin while he was there, the steward perhaps?"

There was a muffled conversation on the other end and then Dave said, "That's a negative."

"Copy that. Go ahead and conduct a search of Kabul's cabin. I'm taking a statement from our guests right now. I'll touch base with you later." Officer Benson clipped his radio back on his belt and turned to Allison. "Do you mind showing me the suitcase the necklace was in?"

Allison walked over to the closet, pulled her case back out and flipped open the lid. "Feel free to take a look inside for yourself. There's nothing in there but a hoodie."

Officer Benson lifted the hoodie out and felt around the interior of the case, before carefully inspecting the outer pockets. When he was done, he made a couple of notes and took a picture of the case. "All right, I'm going back to my office to pull a key card report on everyone who entered your room while you were at the show. Rest assured, if a member of our staff is found with your property on their person, or in their cabin, they'll be handed over to the authorities at the next port. It's unlikely I'll have any more information for you tonight, but I'll check back with you tomorrow." He pulled out a card and gave it to Allison. "This is my direct line in case you think of anything else in the meantime. Do you have any questions for me?"

Allison shook her head. "Not that I can think of."

"Thank you, officer," Doug said, pumping his hand. "We appreciate you jumping on this right away."

"That's what we're here for," Officer Benson replied, tipping his cap to them as he exited the room.

When the door closed behind him, Doug turned to Allison, a deflated look in his eyes. "I don't want this to spoil our trip, baby. Please don't worry about the necklace. If it doesn't show up, I'll buy you another one."

"Let's not go there yet," Allison responded tersely. "I'm tired. I want to go to bed."

She undressed and crawled beneath the covers, but sleep eluded her. It wasn't only the missing necklace that was preying on her mind as she tossed and turned. It was also the fact that her antidepressant prescription had somehow found its way into her purse. That wasn't something she could pin on Kabul, the maintenance guy. In fact, there were really only two explanations. Either she was losing it again, or Doug had put it in her purse and lied about it.

Neither scenario gave her a warm and fuzzy feeling.

6

ROB

Back in the office he shared with his Deputy Security Officer, Dave O'Reilly, Rob Benson slurped from the paper cup of coffee he'd brought back from the mess hall. With a few clicks of his keyboard, he pulled up the key card report on room 10664 on his computer screen. He prided himself on running a smooth operation when it came to ship security—his reputation for being a bit of a control freak didn't faze him in the least. What bothered him was that he already had an incident to investigate this early on in the cruise—theft, no less. Judging by the designer belongings scattered around the Robinsons' cabin, they weren't hurting for money. Still, it didn't rule out the possibility that this was some kind of insurance scam. He'd seen it all before.

He opened the report and noted the time Kabul had checked in and out of the Robinsons' state room. It jived with what the maintenance worker had told Dave earlier. According to the report, Kabul had spent exactly four minutes and thirty-seven seconds in the cabin. Rob scrolled further down the screen, frowning when he noticed a second staff key card entry to the room less than thirty minutes after Kabul had left.

Rob cross-referenced the key card with the staff directory and saw that it belonged to a cabin steward by the name of Brezina Novak. He pulled up her photo ID and studied the head shot of the young blonde briefly before perusing her personnel file. He took another swig of coffee as he scanned through her details. A new recruit—this was only her sixth week working on board *Diamond of the Waves*. Croatian, single, twenty-two years old—the young ones were always the most trouble. Rob gritted his teeth. There was a chance they had a petty thief on board. Not a particularly bright one. The smarter ones waited until the last day to pick off the items they had their eye on.

Rob leaned back in his chair and cupped his hands behind his head. He'd have to find some time later to review the corresponding CCTV footage and confirm that it was actually Brezina Novak who had entered cabin 10664, and not someone else using her key card, before he pulled her in for an interview. If it turned out that she had helped herself to the necklace, he would have no option but to turn her over to the Haitian National Police as soon as they reached Labadee in the morning. An unpleasant task, and not one that he relished. It always made him feel like he had lost control in the captain's eyes.

He tapped his fingers on the desk, his thoughts momentarily drifting off in another more pleasant direction. He liked working the night shift. Mostly because it gave him the chance to wander freely around the ship on the pretext of dealing with problem passengers—which was rarely the case. But it did present him with ample opportunity to stop by the piano bar and listen to Misty Murano perform. The minute she opened her mouth to sing, he turned to mush.

His lips twitched into a smile at the thought of the sultry

blonde he'd first met at a Bella Oceania staff party on another ship almost a year-and-a-half ago. He'd never fallen for anyone so hard before. And she'd been equally enamored with him—at least at first. He rubbed a hand over his jaw. It troubled him that Misty had been increasingly flippant about their relationship of late. In fact, she'd been downright evasive over the past few weeks. Something was amiss. It was time he had it out with her. He was tired of being in limbo regarding their relationship. He was ready to take it to the next level—had been for some time now. But she was unwilling to commit.

Rob glanced at the clock on his computer screen. 11:45 p.m. Misty would be finishing up in the piano bar in a few more minutes. He would take an early break and catch her before she left. She wasn't going to shake him off this time. Committed to his course of action, he tossed the paper cup in the trashcan at his feet and stood.

Downstairs in the opulent Slow Vibes piano bar, Rob stood off to one side of the cream-colored leather seating area filled with jovial passengers. He leaned against a chrome railing and watched discreetly as Misty threw back her head and laughed at something one of the passengers said to her. She flung out a hand coquettishly, palm upraised, as though she were dangling a purse in the crook of her arm—a quirky little habit she had that Rob found especially endearing. He wished she were wrapped in his arms right now instead of stuck making small talk with the overweight, middle-aged passenger currently enthralled with her charms.

Everyone instantly fell in love with Misty. It was a rare night when she wasn't propositioned by at least one infatuated guest. Rob didn't blame them for trying. In her shimmering green, beaded evening dress, Misty positively glowed—looking every bit as fresh as if the night had just begun. She hadn't noticed him yet, which was fine with him. He enjoyed observing her when she didn't know she was being watched, drinking her in like a vampire craves blood. She was an elixir he couldn't live without.

He waited patiently on the periphery until all the passengers had dispersed before making his move. Sensing him approach, Misty glanced in his direction. Rob caught a momentary flicker of vexation in her eyes before she quickly altered her expression.

"Robbie! I didn't expect to see you here tonight. Slacking off again, are we?" She wagged a polished fingernail at him, a tantalizing pout on her full lips that sweetened her mocking tone.

"How am I supposed to work when you're glittering like an uncut emerald in that dress?" Rob whispered to her as he leaned over and brazenly stole a kiss.

"That wasn't very discreet, Officer Benson," Misty admonished him, retreating a step in her satin heels.

For the most part, the band members packing up around them ignored the banter. It wasn't as if their relationship was a secret. Everyone knew Misty and Rob were an item. Only the elderly Russian bass player, Dimitri, looked directly at Rob, eying him like he was Misty's surrogate father and would like nothing more than to break his arms and legs. Misty insisted he was harmless, *a Siberian teddy bear*, but Rob wasn't so sure.

He caught Misty by the hand and drew her to him again. "I'm on break. Let's grab a drink together. I've barely set eyes on you in weeks. You're always either busy practicing some new set, or off on a shore excursion with your girlfriends."

There was that tiny hesitation again, before Misty batted her lashes at him. "Okay, but just one drink. I need to rest my voice."

"Deal," Rob shot back, snaking an arm around her waist.

"I'll happily do all the talking just as long as I get to look at you."

They said goodnight to the other musicians and made their way down to the crew bar on the back deck, selecting a seat on the teak-planked open-air patio.

"The usual?" Rob asked.

Misty ran her fingertips delicately over her sweeping blonde tresses. "Actually, I'll have a Daiquiri."

Rob frowned. "Since when did you start drinking Daiquiris?"

Misty shrugged her bare shoulders, sending a delicious tingling down his spine. "It's good to change things up now and again, don't you agree?" She peered up at him from beneath her perfectly arched brows in a way that usually made Rob go weak at the knees. But, tonight, he couldn't help thinking she was trying to tell him something that he didn't want to hear.

His mood soured as he waited at the bar for their drinks. Maybe it wasn't such a good idea to confront her about their relationship after a long shift when she was already tired. He was beginning to regret not waiting until they could spend a few hours together at some intimate Caribbean café, far from the souvenir-toting cruise ship passengers pouring out of air-conditioned buses, and the natives flogging everything from hair-braiding services to beach towels.

"How about I take tomorrow afternoon off?" Rob suggested, placing their drinks on the table before sitting down opposite Misty. He reached across for her hand and pressed it to his lips. "We can find ourselves a secluded spot on a quiet beach and have a picnic—just the two of us."

Misty stifled a delicate yawn as she twirled the stem of her glass between her fingers. "I don't know. I promised the guys I'd go over the new set with them again tomorrow. We still need to work out a few bugs."

Rob sipped on his gin and tonic. "I'm not buying it. You don't need another practice session. To be honest, I get the impression you've been steering clear of me in the past few days."

Misty twirled a lock of hair, avoiding meeting his eyes. "Maybe I have. I need some time to think, Rob. I've been mulling over my future lately, and I don't want to do this cruise gig forever. Maybe we both want different things."

Rob let out a frustrated breath. "What makes you think I want to work on a cruise ship forever?"

Misty cocked her head to one side. "What else would you do? Security's not exactly a lucrative career path. Not when you have rent, utilities, and groceries to contend with."

Rob leaned back in his chair. "I could apply to the Academy. I've been considering becoming a police officer. Or maybe setting up my own security firm."

Misty took a sip of her Daiquiri, studying him over the rim. "You don't know what you want either. Which is why I think we could both benefit from some time apart. So we can work out where we want to go from here."

"We don't need to be apart to do that. We can do it together." Rob straightened up and leaned across the table once more. "You know how I feel about you, Misty. I can't imagine my life without you."

She tightened her lips and shook her head. "I'm not there yet. I don't want to feel trapped. I think we should give each other some space."

Rob frowned, jutting out his chin. "Are you breaking up with me?"

"We've had fun together," Misty said. "But it's not as if either of us was seriously entertaining a long-term relationship off the ship."

A gnawing desperation formed in the pit of Rob's stomach. "We might not have talked about it much, but it's always been on my mind. You know I'm crazy about you, Misty. It's not like I made a secret of it. I thought you felt the same way."

She patted his hand like a teacher trying to bolster the spirits of a dejected student. "I like you, Rob. I really do. But I've got my whole life ahead of me. I'm not ready to commit to anyone before I even know what I want to do."

"Why not? I'll support you, whatever you decide," Rob replied, vaguely aware that his voice was growing testy. "I won't stand in your way."

Misty exhaled a long breath and reached for her purse. "I'm tired. We can talk about this again some other time." Before Rob could stop her, she glided out of the crew bar leaving him with his jaw hanging open. Had Misty just dumped him? The shock hit him like a punch to the gut. *How dare she!* After all he'd done for her. It was him who'd landed her the job on *Diamond of the Waves* in the first place—secured the audition when she'd missed the deadline to apply. She hadn't had a dime to her name when he met her—money ran through her fingers like water. How did she think she was going to manage without him? Rob knocked back the rest of his drink and stood abruptly.

He strode back to his office, his anger mounting with every step. How dare she dump him like a piece of trash—in the crew bar of all places. He threw himself into his swivel chair and stared morosely at the computer screen. His thoughts ricocheted back and forth inside his head like a tennis ball. Had Misty grown tired of him, or was there someone else? A haunting sense that he was losing control of the thing that mattered most to him took hold. Before he could talk himself out of it, he logged into the security cameras and pulled up the CCTV footage from earlier that evening in the hallway outside Misty's room. The least she could do was have the decency to tell him if she was cavorting with someone else on board the ship.

He rested his elbows on the desk, curling his hands into fists as he studied the screen. He wasn't sure yet what he would do if he saw another man coming out of her cabin. He didn't trust himself. He flinched when Misty's cabin door opened at 8:17 p.m. Seconds later, she emerged, dressed as a cabin steward. Rob blinked in confusion. What was she doing? Was she in costume? Was this part of some show she was in? When she disappeared out of the frame, he frantically clicked around the keyboard, dialing in additional cameras in a desperate bid to figure out where she was headed. At last, he located her getting into the staff elevator. It took him another twenty minutes to work out which floor she exited on.

He watched in disbelief as she ducked her head, crossed the hallway to room 10664, and waved a key card to open the door.

7

ALLISON

Allison woke the following morning with a pounding headache. Her first thought was that she had a hangover, but she hadn't consumed that much alcohol —a couple of glasses of wine. For several minutes, she lay in bed trying to recollect what was gnawing at the back of her brain. In an instant, it came rushing back. *Her missing necklace!* She groaned as she sat up in bed, rubbing her temples. Doug was already out on the balcony, enjoying the view of the open water, looking as if he hadn't a care in the world. A lazy start to their sea day en route to the first Caribbean port of call, Labadee, Haiti. It would have been the perfect morning if it hadn't been for what had happened last night.

Allison smoothed her hair back from her face and swung her legs over the side of the bed. Fingers crossed, the security officer would call soon with a favorable update and put an end to her misery so she could enjoy the rest of the day. Kabul had to be the culprit—what other explanation was there? She padded over to the miniature coffee maker and popped in a pod. After indulging in a long, satisfying sip of coffee, she opened the slider door and joined Doug on the balcony.

He turned and gave her a lopsided grin, searching her face to gauge her mood while trying to pretend he wasn't. "Hey, baby! Sleep good?"

"Great," she lied, averting her gaze as she took a hasty sip of coffee, scorching her lips in the process.

"Beautiful out here, isn't it?" Doug commented, resting his arms on the wooden railing.

"It's spectacular," Allison agreed, not wanting to put a damper on things by bringing up the missing jewelry right away. The fact that the sapphire-and-diamond necklace had likely cost more than the cruise itself bothered her frugal nature almost as much as the thought that someone had been rifling through their personal possessions.

"What's on the agenda today?" she asked. "Any of the activities catch your eye?"

"I thought I might try the FlowRider after breakfast," Doug said, ruffling a hand through his wind-tousled hair. "I'm itching to put my surfing skills to the test, but I want to get there early and beat the crowd. Wanna give it a go?"

Allison laughed. "I'm not that adventurous. I'll shoot the video and rate your Kelly Slater poses."

"First, I need sustenance." Doug rubbed his non-existent belly in an exaggerated fashion. "Where do you want to go for breakfast?"

"I like the sound of the Cabana Bistro—breakfast with a view from the front of the ship," Allison said. "The reviews are great. I'll call and see if we need a reservation." She opened the slider door and went back inside the cabin. After snagging a table for 9:45 a.m., she texted Sophia and arranged to meet up with her and Cody that afternoon on the pool deck.

The Cabana Bistro did not disappoint. While Allison

munched on a smoked salmon bagel and a side of papaya, Doug tucked away a Cajun omelet and toast washed down with fresh squeezed orange juice.

"I could go for seconds," he raved. "But I don't want to risk regurgitating my food on the FlowRider."

Allison drained her cappuccino and set down her cup. "I'm surprised we haven't heard anything from the security officer yet—you know, about the theft."

Doug wiped his lips on his napkin, his jaw tensing slightly. "I'm sure he'll be in touch as soon as he has any news. Ready to get out of here?"

Allison nodded, sensing he didn't want to revisit the topic when there was nothing more they could do about it for now. She would go to the FlowRider with him and fake having fun in the meantime—he'd had enough of her moping around.

After changing into their swimwear, they made their way up to deck sixteen where the FlowRider was located. Doug handed her his towel, grinning from ear-to-ear like a kid hyped up for Christmas. As soon as he joined the line that had already formed, Allison slipped behind the railing and discreetly dug out her phone and Officer Benson's business card. She'd waited long enough for his promised call back.

"Hi Rob, it's Allison Robinson from room 10664. I was wondering if you'd had a chance to pull up the key card report on our room."

There was a brief silence on the other end of the line before he answered. "Uh, not yet, unfortunately. We're having some … technical difficulties with the system. I'll get back with you as soon as it's up and running—hopefully by the end of the day."

Allison chewed on her lip and cast a quick glance in Doug's direction. He was deep in conversation with the man standing next to him in line, oblivious to the fact that she was no longer in sight. "What about the maintenance worker who reset the lock on our safe? Did you search his room?"

"Yes. As expected, we didn't find anything. Kabul has an impeccable record. He's worked for Bella Oceania for almost five years."

"I see," Allison said. "Well, that's good, at least." She was sensing a brusqueness in Officer Benson's tone that hadn't been there the previous evening. He'd struck her as extremely helpful and courteous when he'd shown up in their cabin. But this morning, he seemed overly eager to end their conversation—his tone verging on curt. Did he think she had made it all up or something? Had he picked up on Doug's skepticism? She inhaled a calming breath of salty ocean air. Her insecurities were afoot again.

Maybe she was being too harsh. Officer Benson was probably exhausted after a long night shift. It was possible he hadn't even clocked off yet. She thanked him for his efforts and hung up in time to see Doug waving at her as he moved onto the FlowRider platform holding the attendant's hand. She waved enthusiastically back, and then positioned her phone to start videoing him, chuckling at his unsteady attempts to ride the wave. Doug wasn't a surfer by any stretch of the imagination, but he was giving it all he had—like he always did.

When he got back in line for a second turn, Allison took the opportunity to scroll through her Facebook feed, frowning when she saw that Sophia had posted a new photo of her wearing the necklace in The Chophouse Grille. Underneath it she'd written: *This is how you know your husband loves you! #TenYearsTogether #TrueLove #SpoiledRotten.* Allison couldn't help begrudging the liberty she'd taken, but she supposed Sophia had meant well. And in this case, it could prove useful. In a few deft clicks, she forwarded the picture to Officer Benson. At least now he would know that the necklace existed.

"That was an absolute blast!" Doug jabbered in her ear, shaking water droplets out of his hair when he joined her a few minutes later.

"You didn't do too badly compared to some of the folks out there." Allison gestured to an overweight, bald-headed man who was attempting to knee board, jerking every which way in a desperate bid to balance on the wave, before falling flat on his face and being sucked back up to the wall of shame where he was helped to his feet by a staff member.

"Why don't we take a stroll along the esplanade before we go up to the swim deck," Allison suggested. "We've got plenty of time before we meet up with Sophia and Cody."

"I'm game," Doug said agreeably. "I need to walk off some of my energy after that adrenaline rush anyway."

They whiled away the next couple of hours strolling along the esplanade with its strategically placed landscape lighting, admiring the opulent plant life that somehow flourished aboard the ship, and meandering in and out of stores.

After a late lunch, they headed up to deck fifteen to meet up with Sophia and Cody at the sixteen-and-older pool and jacuzzi area.

"Over here!" Sophia yelled, waving a hand dramatically overhead to get their attention.

Allison grinned and waved back as she and Doug picked their way across the crowded deck. Sophia and Cody were sprawled out on adjacent lounge chairs near to a viewing deck overhang where people were checking out the view with binoculars.

"Happy Anniversary!" Allison said, setting down her beach bag.

"Thank you! Isn't this view fabulous?" Sophia gushed. She patted the empty sun lounger next to her, while Doug wandered over to talk to Cody. "We saved you a couple of spots. Thank goodness Cody ordered breakfast in our room. I crashed when we got back last night and only woke up a couple of hours ago. How about you?"

Allison spread her towel out on the lounger and sank down on it. "Actually, we had a bit of a fiasco last night after we got back from the show, so we didn't get to bed right away."

Sophia balanced herself on one elbow and peered over her sunglasses at Allison, arching a brow. "Oh? Lover's spat?"

Allison winced. What had happened had led to a spat, but she wasn't about to admit to that. "No, nothing like that. My necklace was stolen out of my room."

"What?" Sophia gasped. "Did someone break in? When did it happen?"

"When we were at the show. There was no sign of a break in so they must have used a key card. Our safe wasn't working properly and we had to call maintenance to reset the lock. I hid the necklace under a hoodie at the bottom of my case. Someone must have gone through our stuff."

Sophia gaped at her as she adjusted her towel beneath her. "Did you call security?"

"Yes. A security officer came up to the room and took our statement. He said he'd pull a key card report to see who had entered our room while we were out. I called him a little while ago to check up on the status, but I think he was busy —he seemed distracted. Supposedly, their system's down. He said they searched the maintenance worker's cabin, but the necklace wasn't there."

"That's awful." Sophia shook her head. "I can't believe a maintenance worker would steal jewelry from a guest's cabin. But who else could it have been?"

"Ladies! Your attention, please!" Doug called to them. "I'm taking cocktail orders. What will it be?"

Sophia widened her eyes at Allison. "Piña colada's all around?"

Allison shrugged. "Sure, works for me."

Doug returned from the bar a few minutes later, balancing a tray of fruity drinks festooned with umbrellas and fruit. They clinked their glasses together and Sophia snapped her customary picture. "Here's to *#FindingYour-Necklace!*"

For the next hour or so, they chatted and laughed while enjoying their cocktails and getting a kick out of watching the video of Doug's escapades on the FlowRider.

"I think I'm going to take some pictures on the overhang for my Facebook feed," Sophia said, rolling off her sun lounger and stretching her arms above her head.

Allison watched as Sophia joined the other passengers on the overhang and posed against the railing, snapping selfies that rivaled the Titanic in terms of dramatic tension. Allison wasn't a fan of heights, and Sophia's carefree antics made her stomach drop.

"You should check out the view," Sophia said, when she returned after a few minutes. "It's pretty spectacular."

Doug looked at Allison expectantly. "Want to? I could do with stretching my legs."

Quashing her reservations, Allison walked tentatively out onto the glass overhang with Doug and took a turn viewing the horizon through the binoculars. Her stomach flipped at the vast expanse of sky and ocean stretching out as far as her eye could see. She didn't dare look down for fear she would pass out—breathing out a sigh of relief when Doug announced he'd had his fill of the panoramic view.

"I'm going to find a restroom," she said as they exited the overhang. Doug mumbled something to her, but she didn't catch it as he turned to head back over to their lounge chairs. Allison smiled to herself as she walked off in search of the closest restroom. She was proud of herself for conquering her fear and accompanying Doug out onto the overhang—a small victory, but every step in the right direction was significant. Despite the unfortunate theft of her necklace, this was shaping up to be a great trip. Sophia and Cody were fun to hang out with. Exactly what she and Doug needed.

When she returned a few minutes later, there was no sign of the others. Allison glanced around the adult pool area in confusion wondering if she'd come back to the wrong spot. She peered out at the overhang, but the only people out there were a group of middle-aged women jabbering away in another language. Befuddled, she made a beeline for the bar to see if the others had popped in to refresh their drinks.

Growing increasingly frustrated, she pulled out her phone to check if there was a message from Doug. She was tempted to text him, but she didn't want to come across as a complete idiot if they'd simply switched loungers for some reason, and were a few feet away, giggling at her inability to spot them. She resolved to walk the entire pool area first and see if she could find them. Trying not to look like a complete loser, Allison searched the area where they'd been sitting once more, and then sauntered over to the opposite side of the deck.

Casting a glance up and down the rows of lounge chairs, she finally caught sight of Doug's head in the hot tub. Relief and frustration melded as one inside her. Why on earth had they moved all the way around to the other side of the deck without letting her know? Wiping the irritation off her face, she made her way over to them. "What are you guys doing over here?"

Sophia threw an uncertain look Doug's way.

"Baby!" he protested with a halting laugh, "don't you remember I said we'd meet you in the hot tub? We were in the shade on the other side. It's a little warmer over here."

Allison shook her head, a tight smile on her lips. "No, you didn't mention anything about moving spots."

Doug playfully splashed some water on her. "I knew you weren't listening to me, *again*! Come on, jump in. It's the perfect temperature. Your stuff's over there on the chair next to mine. We got you another piña colada."

Sophia raised her glass with a flourish as if to confirm they were all in on a second round of drinks. Allison detected a flicker of pity on her face. Evidently, she'd bought into Doug's explanation of things. The truth was, he *had* muttered something to her—maybe he'd assumed she'd heard him. Masking her annoyance, Allison slipped off her swim coverup, grabbed her drink, and joined the others in the jacuzzi. Her icy mood soon began to thaw under Sophia's good-natured humor, and the rest of the afternoon went off without a hitch.

When they eventually found their way back to their cabin that evening after a steak dinner to celebrate Cody's and Sophia's wedding anniversary, Doug grabbed Allison's hand and pressed her fingers to his lips. "Let's watch the sunset together on the balcony tonight."

"Sounds good," she said, smiling up at him. This might be a good opportunity to talk about their marriage and bring up the things that were niggling at her.

Doug opened the slider door and ushered her onto the balcony. As they huddled together next to the railing watching the coral-tinged horizon slowly saturate with color, Allison shivered in the evening breeze. "I'm going to pop back inside and grab a robe," she said. "It's chilly out here in bare shoulders."

She stepped back inside the cabin to fetch one of the soft white robes she'd seen hanging in the closet. Pulling it on, she tightened the belt around her waist, frowning when her fingers brushed against something hard. She slid her hand into the left pocket, sucking in a sharp breath when her fingers closed around a rectangular box. She yanked it out and stared at it in disbelief. *No!* It wasn't possible. With trembling fingers, she lifted off the lid and examined the contents.

There was no mistaking the diamond-and-sapphire necklace glittering up at her from the soft folds of crushed velvet.

8

ROB

It was after dinner the following day before Rob had a chance to sit down and go back through the footage and re-watch everything from the beginning to make sure he hadn't misinterpreted what he'd seen. He realized he hadn't actually caught a glimpse of Misty's face. Maybe the woman exiting the elevator on deck ten wasn't her at all. For all he knew, it might have been Brezina Novak, head down, engrossed in her phone.

He clicked on the CCTV camera outside the Robinsons' state room and opened the file in question. This time through, he froze the image of the woman stepping out of the elevator and enlarged it, studying the blonde head of hair tied up in a ponytail. Rob unscrewed the cap on his water bottle and took a hearty swig as he scrutinized the image. It appeared to be straighter than Misty's hair, but then again, he wasn't much of an expert when it came to the finer points of women's hairstyles. Whoever the woman was, she appeared to be deliberately angling her face so she wouldn't be seen.

He rolled the tape again and observed her making her

way across the corridor to cabin 10664. His heart slugged against his chest when she waved a key card in front of the door with an all-too-familiar flick of her wrist. Still desperately trying to deny what he didn't want to believe, Rob pulled Brezina Novak's personnel file back up on the screen and compared the two images side-by-side. As best he could tell, Brezina's hair was a shade lighter. But that could be attributed to the poor lighting in the corridor at night. If he was being honest with himself, the most compelling part of the footage was the woman's gait and that familiar snap of her wrist. Rob had spent enough time watching Misty Murano to know exactly how she moved.

Groaning, he buried his face in his hands. Now what? He'd been taken off guard when Allison Robinson had called earlier to get an update on the investigation. He'd had to lie about the key card report. He needed more time to think about how he was going to handle this. And to figure out what was going on with Misty. Was she in some kind of financial trouble? Was that why she'd distanced herself from him of late? It was certainly possible she was living beyond her means. She liked to shop in the tax-free stores—designer purses and shoes mainly—but she had an eye for an exquisite watch or piece of jewelry too. Rob had fed her addiction himself a time or two. She'd never been good with money and she had extravagant taste—the kind that would appreciate the value of a sapphire-and-diamond necklace. But how had she known the necklace was in the room?

Rob closed up the multiple windows on his computer screen and got to his feet. Misty might have eaten at The Chophouse Grille last night and witnessed Doug presenting the necklace to his wife. With her appetite for the finer things in life, Misty didn't make a habit of eating in the staff mess hall.

He scratched at the back of his neck as he paced back-

and-forth across his office, mulling over what to do. With the evidence at hand, he could haul Misty into the office and dismiss her on the spot—simply entering a guest's cabin without a legitimate reason was grounds for dismissal—but that was a last resort as far as he was concerned. He'd prefer to handle this quietly, in a way that wouldn't expose her.

To some degree, it was almost a relief to know that the competition for her attention wasn't another man after all, but rather a vice. It wasn't ideal, but this was something he could fix. If Misty was in financial trouble, he could loan her the money to bail her out. First things first. He needed to retrieve that necklace. And there was no better time than now when Misty would be busy entertaining guests in the Slow Vibes piano bar.

Granted, it was a risk entering her cabin, but, even if he was spotted, no one would question a security officer, especially not one she was dating. The staff didn't know that she'd broken things off with him last night—maybe they would never need to know if he played his cards right. If he could fix this, be the hero for Misty, he could win her back. All that talk about needing space had been a bunch of hot air. No doubt she was embarrassed at the trouble she'd gotten herself into, and the last person she wanted to tell was a security officer who could have her arrested and handed off to the port authorities in half a heartbeat. It was all beginning to make sense now.

Rob exited his office with a new spring in his step. He made his way down to the deck where Misty's cabin was located and strolled along the corridor, nodding in passing to the occasional crew member heading out to start a shift or returning from one. He made a point of striding past Misty's cabin when a group of wait staff came walking toward him. As soon as they disappeared into the stairwell, he made an abrupt U-turn, switched off his radio, and waved his master pass key to open Misty's door.

Once inside, he wasted no time getting to work combing through the space. He'd searched enough cabins to know how to do it without making it look like anything had been disturbed. Misty wasn't the most organized person at the best of times, which irked his inclination for order, but worked in his favor now. Ten minutes later, he still hadn't found the necklace, but he'd come across a cabin steward uniform hanging at the back of her closet. Rob scowled, twisting the material in his fist. The fact that it was still in her cabin seemed to suggest the theft of the necklace wasn't a one-off incident—that she was planning to use the uniform again. He'd wager she'd stolen it from the laundry. Had she stolen Brezina Novak's key card too?

He rubbed his jaw, wondering if Misty had managed to sell the necklace already—there could be some kind of ring operating on the ship. Or perhaps she had some place onboard where she'd stashed it until they docked. It made sense that she wouldn't want to keep stolen property in her cabin. He would have to review all the footage of her movements and see if he could find out where she was hiding her wares, or who she was handing them off to. He pulled his brows together, contemplating another possibility. Perhaps she was being blackmailed by someone she'd borrowed money from. Misty might very well have secrets she hadn't shared with him.

His phone buzzed, making him jump. He pulled it out of his pocket and glanced at the screen, taking a moment to clear his head before answering the call. "Hey, what's up?"

"I've been trying to reach you," Dave grumbled. "Got your radio off, or what?"

"Yeah, I forgot to turn it on after I charged it."

"That couple that reported the missing jewelry in 10664 —the husband just called. They found it."

"Wh—what?" Rob sank down on the edge of the bed, frowning as he tried to make sense of what Dave was telling him. "Are we talking about the same couple—the stolen necklace from last night?"

"Yeah, that's the one. The wife thought Kabul from maintenance had helped himself to it." Dave let out a hearty chuckle on the other end of the line. "Guy's as honest as the day's long. Wouldn't lift a packet of ketchup from the mess hall."

"Where ... did they find the necklace?" Rob asked, still scarcely able to take it in.

"The husband said it was in the wife's pocket—in her robe or coat or something. I don't remember what exactly. Evidently she didn't either." Dave let out an amused snort. "We can chalk it up to one drink too many on the first night if you ask me."

"I'll head up to their cabin right away and take another statement," Rob said before ending the call. He pocketed his phone and blew out a flustered breath. It didn't make any sense. Had Misty had a change of heart and returned the necklace? Or had she gone to the cabin for some other reason entirely?

He sat staring down at the floor for another minute or two, before he collected himself enough to make his way up to the Robinsons' state room on deck ten.

Doug opened the door to him almost immediately, his expression a blend of apologetic and abashed. "I can't tell you how sorry I am for the inconvenience," he blurted out as he ushered him inside.

Allison was sitting in one of the club chairs, her arm resting on the adjacent table next to a rectangular velvet box.

Rob gave her a tentative nod, trying to gauge her mood. Her eyes conveyed both relief and confusion. But there was something else there too, something he couldn't put his finger on. "No need to apologize," Rob assured them. "It's all part of my job. It's not the first time things have gone missing and shown up later. I'm just happy you recovered your anniversary gift. Do you mind if I take a look at it—just to confirm for the record that it matches the photo you sent me?"

Allison reached for the box and opened it, holding it out for Rob to see. She flashed him an absent smile.

He whistled softly as he pulled out his phone. "The picture doesn't do it justice. That's a real beauty. I'm not surprised you were upset about losing it. Can I ask where you found it?"

"It was in the pocket of one of the robes hanging in the closet." Allison darted an apprehensive look in Doug's direction before adding, "I didn't put it there."

Rob stared at her briefly, and then averted his gaze. He was half afraid she might be able to read in his eyes that he believed her, even if her husband didn't. Not that he had any intention of admitting to it. To protect Misty, he had no choice but to take Doug's side and pretend that he too supposed Allison had simply forgotten where she'd put the necklace. No theft, meant no investigation. At all costs, he would do whatever it took to keep Misty out of trouble. "When did you discover your necklace was in the room, after all?"

Allison snapped the lid shut on the jewelry box and set it on the table next to her. "I discovered it had been *returned* when we got back from dinner, about thirty minutes ago."

Rob opted not to challenge her. The last thing he wanted was for this to get dragged out any further. He made a show of jotting down a few things in his notebook and then glanced at Doug. "Did either of you use the robe before tonight?"

Doug stroked his jaw. "Not that I remember. We went out on the balcony to watch the sunset after we came back to the cabin. Allison was cold so she went inside to find something to—"

"Is the key card report working now?" Allison cut in.

Rob wet his lips. "I'll ... have to check with my colleague. I haven't been in the office much in the last twenty-four hours."

"Perhaps someone came back into our room and returned it while we were out today," Allison suggested, pinning a penetrating gaze on him.

Rob coughed discreetly as he put away his notebook. He shot a loaded look at Doug who gave a barely perceptible shrug of his shoulders as if to say he knew it was unreasonable, but his hands were tied.

"I'll look into that report as soon as I get back to the office," Rob assured her, shooting her an assertive smile. "Unless you have any other questions, I'm going to close this case out now—thankfully, with a happy outcome."

Doug thanked him again and shook his hand before showing him to the door. Once outside, Rob exhaled a weighty breath and strode back to the elevator. He urgently wanted to find Misty and have it out with her, but being impetuous hadn't worked out so well for him last night. He needed to think it over before he decided how best to raise the topic with her. Perhaps he should interview Brezina Novak first and see what she had to say about her missing key card. On a whim, he decided to go by The Chophouse Grille and talk to the hostess to see if she remembered anything useful.

He pulled out his notebook again as he entered the restaurant. "Hi, Rob Benson from security," he said, displaying his ID for the hostess. "Do you happen to remember a party of four celebrating a wedding anniversary last night? The husband presented the wife with a necklace over dinner."

A glimmer of recognition flickered in the hostess's eyes. "Oh, yes! We were all making excuses to walk by the table and get a look see."

"Is there any chance they might have inadvertently left the necklace behind?" Rob inquired.

The hostess's lips formed a silent "O" as she digested the implication. "I ... don't think so. I mean, I can check with their waiter, but nothing was turned in."

"Yeah, I figured as much. Just wanted to make sure." Rob snapped his notebook shut and slipped it into his back pocket. He turned to go and then hesitated. "By the way, did Misty Murano eat here last night?"

The hostess gave an enthusiastic nod. "Yes! She and the band were in their usual spot in the corner booth. Misty couldn't take her eyes off that guy when he got down on one knee. She said it was the most romantic gesture she'd ever witnessed."

9

ALLISON

Allison adjusted the brim of her sun hat for the umpteenth time as she and Doug waited at the guest services deck for Sophia and Cody to join them for their first excursion off the ship. *Diamond of the Waves* had docked at Labadee, Haiti, shortly before eight that morning, and a steady stream of passengers were already disembarking, eager to begin exploring their surroundings.

Doug had made a zipline reservation for the four of them with Sky High Flight Line, which he was eagerly anticipating. But Allison was beginning to regret agreeing to it. Not being a fan of heights to begin with, she'd offered to meet them at the bottom and take their pictures, but Doug had pleaded with her to make the effort to join in with the group's plans.

"I don't want to leave you out," he implored. "We're here to make memories together. Besides, it's only an hour long. After that you can shop your heart out at the market and relax on the beach. The rest of the day is all yours, I promise."

Still baffled by the sudden reappearance of her necklace—which Doug had written off as forgetfulness on her part—

and unwilling to add to his frustration with her, Allison had caved on the ziplining. After the mix-up at the pool yesterday, she also felt a need to prove herself to Cody and Sophia, not wanting to come across as the lame duck in the party, yet again. She still cringed when she thought about the look on Sophia's face when Allison had finally found them in the hot tub. She must have looked like a lost puppy sniffing around the pool deck looking for its pack. It irked her that Doug had somehow managed to make her look stupid while ostensibly playing it down. She'd given him the benefit of the doubt to save face, pretending to believe that he hadn't meant anything by it, but she wasn't entirely convinced.

When she caught sight of Sophia and Cody winding their way toward them, she fixed a smile on her face and forced herself to put everything that had happened behind her. Today was a new day. Doug had gone to a lot of trouble to book this cruise and take the time off work. The least she could do was reciprocate. She would focus on having fun—something that seemed to come so naturally to Sophia.

"I can't wait for our first adventure off the ship," Sophia chirped, tucking her arm into Allison's as they strolled down the gangway to the pier in the port town of Labadee. "I'm so glad you decided to join us on the zipline after all. Doug said you haven't done anything adventurous since the miscarriage. Not that he holds it against you or anything. He seems very understanding. But you know guys, they can only handle so many frayed emotions before their brains glaze over."

The Gigi Burris sun hat slipped over Allison's eyes again and she swiftly removed it and tossed it into her beach bag with an irritated grunt.

Sophia peered at her curiously. "Don't you like it? It looks pretty sexy on you."

"It's too big," Allison responded testily. "Doug bought it

for me for the trip. It was expensive so I thought I'd wear it, at least one day. I should have just left it in the cabin."

Sophia giggled. "Get yourself a new one at the market. He'll never know the difference."

"Most men wouldn't," Allison replied. "But you don't know my husband. He loves his designer brands."

Sophia let out a sudden squeal, pointing at a colorful wooden *Welcome to Labadee* sign up ahead. "We need to take our picture right here while we still look good. We'll be a hot, wet, sandy mess on the way back." She motioned over her shoulder to Doug and Cody, shepherding everyone into position before pulling out her selfie stick and holding up her iPhone for the perfect shot. "Okay, my lovelies. Strike a pose."

They all obliged, trying to tune out the commiserative looks of the other passengers walking by. When she was done, Sophia promptly posted the cheesy shot to Facebook, along with the hashtags, *#LabadeeFunInTheSun #ParadiseWith-NewFriends.*

With the requisite photo op behind them, they wandered along the sandy trail to the zip line check-in booth where they signed a waiver releasing the company of any liability for injuries sustained. Allison took a quick calming breath as she set down the pen, reminding herself that Sky High Flight Line had an excellent record. After being strapped up and given their safety and flight instructions, they were driven up to the launching platform. Allison glanced around at the spectacular view, her insides churning. Out on the crisp, blue water, their snow-white ship floated like a giant pristine duck. Below them, sandy beaches curved around the coast-line as far as the eye could see. Gritting her teeth, she waited for the inevitable descent to begin. Doug reached over and squeezed her hand. "I'm proud of you, baby. See you at the bottom. I'll be right behind you."

Allison gave an uneasy nod and then she was off. She had anticipated a sudden stomach drop, or a sense of falling, but it was more like a gentle swing away from the platform, and then a sensation of flying. After the initial shock, she settled back to enjoy the panorama as she descended from the hill-side over the water to the landing zone. Before she knew it, the ride was over, and two employees were helping her onto a stepstool and undoing her harness. Her skin tingled from head to toe—she'd done it. She hadn't passed out and made a fool of herself, and she hadn't emerged from her harness a blubbering wreck either.

Waving excitedly, she watched as Doug, Sophia, and Cody landed in quick succession, looking equally as exhilarated as she felt inside.

"You're smiling," Doug said, planting a kiss on her fore-head. He turned to Cody and Sophia. "Told you she wasn't really scared of heights. What do you guys want to do next? I know Allison wants to browse the artisan market, don't you, Ally?"

She gave a stiff nod by way of response, annoyed that Doug had lied about her fear of heights instead of acknowl-edging that she'd mustered up the courage to conquer it.

"I like the sound of that. I'm always up for a little shop-ping," Sophia said.

"So long as we get to hit the beach afterward and sample the Labadoozie," Cody added.

Sophia threw him a perplexed look. "What's a Labadoozie?"

"Only the island's number one drink. According to the activity guide, it's a mouthwatering concoction of mixed fruits with rum."

A look of relief spread across Sophia's face. "You had me nervous there for a minute. It sounded like a dog breed. I was hoping it wasn't a hot dog or something."

They took a leisurely stroll over to the artisan village, a colony of wooden huts snaking along the road, draped in psychedelic cotton t-shirts and handmade wares painted every color of the rainbow.

"Brace yourselves," Cody said. "These guys are ready to haggle."

"I like those statues over there." Allison pointed to a stall replete with colorful carved figures in a variety of poses. "Hey, Doug! Come take a look at these! Aren't they cute?"

He wandered over and studied them. "Where would we put it?"

"I don't know. We can figure that out later. But we need a souvenir from our ten-year anniversary trip. Which one do you like best?"

Doug ran his fingers through his hair. "I don't know. Get whatever one you want."

"He just wants to get this over with so he can get to the beach," Allison muttered to Sophia.

Sophia cast a quick glance at Cody who was frowning at his phone. "At least Doug's living in the moment. Cody's still tied to his work. The only thing he's expressed an interest in so far is a Labadoozie."

In the end, Allison decided against a carved figurine and selected a painted gecko instead.

"I like that a lot better than those creepy statues," Doug said, when she showed it to him. "Are we done here?"

"I'm all set," Sophia announced, sweeping into their midst, laden down with shopping bags.

Cody eyed the bags in her hands with a look of trepidation. "What do you have there?"

"Just some wooden toys for the boys and a few T-shirts. And I got us a set of souvenir shot glasses with a map of Haiti on them. Oh, and a couple of lace tops, and a baseball cap with the Haitian flag on it for Dad."

Judging by the disgruntled look on Cody's face, Allison suspected that Sophia's spending habits were a point of contention between them. Apparently, Cody wasn't the only one with an addiction.

After a quick BBQ lunch at a local stand, they made their way across the soft, white sand to a group of unoccupied chaises next to a mango tree a few feet from the turquoise water.

"It doesn't get any more idyllic than this," Sophia gushed, sinking down on her chaise with a sigh of satisfaction. She tucked her bags beneath it and lay back, closing her eyes. "Now this is what I'm talking about."

"Speaking of Labadoozies," Doug said, "I think they might be coming our way." He gestured to a waiter carrying a tray of frozen, fruit drinks in oversized souvenir sports bottles.

Doug waved him over. "We'll take four," he said, pulling out his wallet and handing the beaming man some cash.

Cody raised his drink in the air. "Thanks man, cheers everyone!"

They all joined in, and Sophia captured the toast and uploaded it to Facebook. "Check your feed!" she called across to Allison. "It's my favorite photo of us so far."

"Well the Labadoozie certainly lives up to its reputation," Cody said with a contented sigh. "They're generous with the rum."

Allison took a sip of her drink and then checked her Facebook. Sophia had managed to capture a snippet of the turquoise water backdrop, as well as the white sand and the four of them holding their souvenir sports bottles aloft. Beneath the photo she'd added, *#LoveMeALabadoozie.*

"It's a great shot," Allison agreed, putting her phone away and adjusting the back rest on her chaise so she could enjoy her drink while taking in all the activity around her. Before long, her eyes grew heavy. Lack of sleep was beginning to catch up with her. She sat up and slid her legs over the edge of the chaise. The last thing she wanted to do was fall asleep and get sunburned.

She drained the rest of her drink and got to her feet, feeling groggy. "I'm going to take a dip. Anyone want to go in with me?"

"I will," Sophia said, rolling off her lounger. "I need to cool off."

They peeled off their sundresses, kicked their flip-flops under their chaises and strolled down to the water.

"Oh! It's the perfect temperature," Sophia cried, falling back into the water with her arms outstretched. Allison waded out a little farther and then turned and floated on her back, squinting up at the sun. She felt disoriented—she was probably dehydrated from the alcohol. Cody was right. They'd been overly generous with the rum.

Suddenly, she felt herself begin to drift into unconsciousness. Panicking, she thrashed the water around her, her stomach heaving as she struggled to get to her feet.

The last thing she remembered was Sophia's terrified cry. "Help! She's drowning!"

10

ALLISON

When Allison regained consciousness, she was lying in the sand next to their loungers staring up at the blinding sun. On her right, a paramedic was reaching into a medical supply kit. Allison rolled her eyes to the left, barely able to make out the fuzzy outline of Doug's face peering down at her from among the herd of spectators pressing in around them. Her mind grappled with a vague memory of splashing around in the water. How had she ended up back on the beach? She blinked to clear her vision. Everywhere she looked, strangers skewered her with stares of morbid fascination. A few of them actually had their phones out and were filming her lying motionless and helpless. She gritted her teeth in frustration. No doubt she'd already been uploaded to Facebook with a few befitting hashtags. *#TooMuchFunInTheSun #OneTooManyLabadoozies.*

As if reading her mind, Cody began shooing people away. "Everyone, back up, please. Give her some space."

Sophia leaned anxiously over her. "Allison, can you hear me? You're going to be all right."

The paramedic adjusted an ice pack behind her neck. "Feeling better?"

Allison wet her parched lips and croaked, "What ... what happened?"

"You passed out in the water. It was likely heat stroke," the paramedic replied. "Do you want to try and sit up now?"

Allison nodded, and the paramedic grabbed one arm while Doug gripped the other.

"I'll get you some water, baby," Doug said, his voice gravelly with concern.

"Are you her husband?" the paramedic inquired.

Doug nodded. "Yes."

"Is your wife on any medication?"

"She has a prescription for an antidepressant."

"Do you happen to know what it's called?" the paramedic asked. "Just so I can make a note of it on my report."

Doug reached behind him for Allison's purse and rummaged around inside it for a minute. He pulled out the prescription bottle and then hesitated, his forehead trenched.

Allison watched him, her anxiety mounting with every passing second. "What is it? What's wrong?"

"Nothing. It's just that—" He broke off and fixed a crestfallen gaze on Allison. "I thought you said you weren't taking them."

"I'm not."

Wordlessly, Doug handed the bottle to the paramedic who noted the name and dosage on his incident sheet before giving it a shake. "It's about a quarter full. Did you take any today?"

"No!" Dread tightened in Allison's chest as an all-too-familiar fog of confusion took hold. Had she taken a dose? "I ... I want to go back to the ship now."

"That's probably a good idea," the paramedic responded,

removing the ice pack from her neck. "Are you able to walk or would you like me to arrange for a wheelchair?"

Allison brushed him aside and struggled to her feet with Doug's help. "I'm fine. I can walk. Please, I just want to get out of the sun and away from all these people."

The paramedic handed the prescription bottle back to Doug who quickly gathered up their towels and the rest of their gear. Sophia helped Allison hobble over to her lounger and put her flip-flops and sundress back on. Doug pulled her sun hat out of her bag, but she shook her head. "No. I don't want it."

Under the curious stares of the straggling gawkers, they made their way slowly back up the beach and along the path to the dock. The careless gaiety that had marked their mood all day had evaporated. Their brief exchanges were stilted.

"Are you sure you're okay?" Sophia asked.

"I can get you a wheelchair if you want," Doug offered.

"I'm sure it was the Labadoozie," Cody said, more to himself than anyone.

Allison said nothing. After a promising start to the day, she had ended up a spectacle for the other passengers. No doubt she'd be the topic of conversation over dinner tonight —they'd all assume she'd Labadoozied herself into a drunken haze and was lucky to be alive.

Allison bit back a whimper, trying to tune out the accusatory voices in her head. She wanted nothing more than to get back to the cocooning space of her cabin and stand under the shower until every last grain of sand that was stuck to her skin had circled down the drain. She always did her best thinking under a hot shower—she'd sift through everything then and try to figure out what had happened. Cody was most likely right. The vendor on the beach had been a little heavy handed with the rum. But it was her own fault for not hydrating more before she'd gone in the water.

Even so, that didn't explain why most of the antidepressants were missing from her prescription bottle. The lid had been screwed on tight when Doug knocked her purse to the ground in The Chophouse Grille. The only way the pills could have gotten out of the bottle is if someone had removed them. But she hadn't taken any out, had she?

She frowned as she tried to think back over the past couple of days. Was she becoming forgetful again in unfamiliar surroundings? Was it possible she'd got up during the night and taken them? Maybe Kabul had pilfered them, or the cabin steward. Her head began to pound as she considered a third possibility. Perhaps Doug, for some unknown reason, had removed the pills. But he'd seemed genuinely shocked on the beach when he'd noticed how many were missing. She couldn't make any sense of it.

When they were safely back on board *Diamond of the Waves,* Allison turned to Sophia. "Thanks for helping me get out of the water. I don't know what I would have done if you hadn't been there."

Sophia enveloped her in a warm hug. "I screamed so loudly half the beach came running to help. You scared the living daylights out of me—gagging and passing out like that. I'm glad you're all right. Text me later and let me know how you're doing. If you're up for it, maybe we can meet for dinner."

Allison gave her a tepid smile. "I'll probably skip dinner tonight. I still feel a bit nauseous. If I'm hungry later, I'll order room service."

"Get some rest," Cody said, giving her shoulder an awkward squeeze. "You don't want to miss out on all the fun in Jamaica tomorrow."

They parted ways and Doug and Allison headed for the elevator. Inside, she leaned her head against the cool glass and closed her eyes.

"Baby, are you okay?" Doug asked, his voice creeping up an octave. "You're not going to pass out again, are you?"

Allison shook her head. She didn't want to get into it with him here in the elevator. "I'm fine. Just resting my eyes. Everything's still a bit blurry."

When they arrived back at their cabin, Doug carried Allison's beach bag inside and set it down on one of the club chairs. "You should drink some more water," he said as she slipped off her flip-flops and lay down on top of the bed.

"I will. I just want to rest for a few minutes first."

"Okay, I'll be out on the balcony if you need me," he said, setting a bottle of water on her nightstand.

Allison opened one eye and observed him as he opened the slider door and sank down in one of the deck chairs on the balcony, casually stretching out his legs and crossing his ankles in front of him.

She exhaled a shallow breath, wrestling with the myriad thoughts that had been plaguing her ever since she'd left the beach. No one other than she and Doug had access to her prescription. So where had the pills gone? Had she taken them and forgotten about it—was she really that far gone? She pressed her fingertips to her aching temples and rubbed them gently in a circular motion. She'd felt oddly disoriented after drinking that Labadoozie. Was it possible Doug had slipped the antidepressants into her drink? It didn't make sense. Why would he do that? He had booked this cruise to celebrate their anniversary, and to work on their marriage in an environment other than a therapist's sterile office. And yet, he had pestered her to refill her prescription and bring it with her.

Moaning softly, she forced herself into a sitting position and got to her feet. She still felt dizzy, but considerably better than before. Resolved to have it out with Doug, she joined him on the balcony.

He grinned as he reached across and squeezed her hand. "Your color's back. Feeling better?"

She pulled her hand away from his under the pretense of sweeping her hair out of her face. "A little."

Doug pressed his lips together. "I blame myself. I should never have bought those drinks on the beach from that vendor. We had no idea what was in them. We should have gone to the bar." He let out a sigh. "And of course mixing alcohol with antidepressants is dangerous."

Steeling herself, Allison turned to face him. "I'm not taking the pills. Which begs the question, where is the rest of my prescription?"

Doug blinked at her, a flush creeping up over his jaw line. "What are you getting at?"

"Let's think about this for a minute, shall we? There are only two of us in this cabin, and only the two of us had access to my purse where my prescription was. I still don't know how the pills ended up in there to begin with, and now most of them are missing. I didn't take them. Did you?"

Doug gripped the armrests of his deck chair, his countenance darkening. "Are you seriously suggesting that I took your prescription? Why would I do that?"

"I don't know, you tell me. Did you add the pills to my drink?"

"Baby, listen to yourself! You're not making any sense. How would I even do that on a crowded beach?"

"It's not that hard. We all had the same drinks. And we were dozing on and off. No one would have noticed."

Doug stood abruptly. "I can't believe I'm hearing this. I really thought we were making progress, Allison. I had high hopes for this trip, but you've been lying to me, and now you're trying to manipulate me. You've been forgetful, misplacing things, mixing things up, and now this crazy incident today where you almost drowned. Are you trying to kill yourself again? Is that what this is about? A cry for attention. You know what, I don't think you gave up the antidepressants at all. I think you've been deceiving me all along. And I'm sick of it. I'm the one making all the effort here, accommodating you at every turn, constantly reassuring you that I'm not looking at other women, even buying you an extravagant gift for our anniversary to prove to you that I want to spend the next ten years with you too. And what do I get in return? A crazy accusation like this."

He turned on his heel and yanked the slider door open.

"Wait! Where are you going?" Allison called after him.

"Out. Maybe I'll meet up with Cody and Sophia for dinner."

He disappeared into the bathroom and emerged a short time later, showered up and changed. When Allison glanced back over her shoulder a few minutes after that, the cabin was empty. She let out a long shuddering breath before getting to her feet. What was happening to them? They were supposed to be celebrating ten years together, but everything was falling apart. Or maybe she was falling apart. Doug had made it clear their relationship was at a tipping point. And he blamed it on her hysteria. But his outrage and denials struck a hollow note with her. She had to make sure he wasn't lying.

After showering up, she dressed in white capri pants and a cerise off-the-shoulder top, before grabbing her laptop and making her way to one of the wired internet stations aboard the ship. She slid into a booth and fired up her laptop. As she waited for the screen to load, she peered around the partition at the other guests seated along the narrow corridor. She hurriedly retreated back inside her booth after spotting Cody at the far end. Sophia hadn't been kidding. The guy seemed incapable of setting his work aside for more than a few hours at a time.

Her screen finally loaded. She launched her browser and

logged-in to the Bella Oceania Wi-Fi. She didn't bother reading the charges. It didn't matter. The information would be worth whatever it cost her. She held her breath as she typed *symptoms of antidepressant overdose* into the search bar and waited for the results. She clicked on the first article that appeared and began to read the list of symptoms: dilated pupils, confusion, headache, drowsiness, dry mouth, blurred vision, nausea.

With shaking fingers, she snapped the lid on her laptop shut. She'd read enough to know her drink had been spiked. Either she'd overdosed this afternoon on the beach and didn't remember doing it, or her husband had tried to kill her.

11

ROB

Rob Benson lay stretched out on the bunk in his cabin, hands folded behind his head, staring morosely at the ceiling as he mulled over the hostess's words: *Misty couldn't take her eyes off that guy.* No doubt she'd taken a second, or even a third look at the strikingly handsome Doug Robinson. But what the hostess didn't know was that it was the sapphire-and-diamond necklace that had really caught Misty's eye.

He was still trying to wrap his head around the idea that Misty had brazenly stolen the necklace and then returned it later on that evening. Either she'd lost her nerve afterward, or she'd had difficulty unloading the expensive piece of jewelry to whomever she'd tried to sell it to. What other explanation was there?

He grimaced when he remembered how insistent Allison Robinson was that her necklace hadn't been in her state room all along. He'd finally called her back and informed her that the key card report indicated no one had entered the cabin after Kabul had reset the safe. A blatant lie, of course, but given the fact that Allison's necklace had been returned, he could live with a little deception if it spared Misty from prosecution. He wasn't about to let that happen and watch her slip from his grasp in the process.

He'd spent some time during the course of the day going through prior weeks' CCTV footage in an effort to try and figure out what Misty was up to. He hadn't been able to spot her acting suspiciously on any other occasion—neither dressed in a cabin steward uniform, nor loitering on any of the guest cabin decks. He'd gone so far as to check the corresponding ship logs and there hadn't been any record of cabin break-ins—just the usual slew of misplaced sunglasses and lost phones, a missing set of false teeth, even an unaccounted for kid who'd thankfully shown up in the arcade later.

Rob glanced at his watch. Almost time for Misty to clock off—and for him to have a little chat with her. He'd delayed confronting her for an entire day while debating what to do about it, knowing he would have to come up with some plausible explanation as to how he'd discovered the footage. In the end, he decided to keep it simple and say there had been an incident on deck 10. While reviewing the CCTV footage, he'd seen her entering 10664 dressed as a cabin steward. He wouldn't bring up the necklace, at least not yet. He wanted to see what she had to say for herself first.

He made his way down to *Slow Vibes* where Misty and her band were performing and watched from the sidelines while they wrapped up their final number. Misty gave him a decidedly icy look when she spotted him walking toward her, but he didn't let it deter him.

"You look as ravishing as ever," he said, presenting her with a smile. He didn't make any attempt to kiss her this time. He didn't want to give her an excuse to run him off before he'd had a chance to talk to her.

She pulled a gold tube from her clutch and stretched her

lips taut before applying a slick layer of peach gloss. "What do you want, Rob?"

"I need to talk to you."

She let out a dramatic sigh. "I already told you, I need some time to figure things out."

Rob stuffed his hands into his pockets. "This isn't about us. It's about something else."

Misty arched a curious brow. "Oh? What's that?"

Rob glanced at the other band members. Dimitri was watching them like a hawk from beneath his shaggy brows while ostensibly helping load equipment onto a cart.

"We can't talk here," Rob muttered.

Misty put a hand on her hip and struck a coquettish pose. "This better not be some disingenuous attempt to get me to change my mind."

Rob shook his head. "It's a security issue. We can talk in my office."

A twitch of unease crossed Misty's flawless cheekbones before she quickly schooled her face to neutral. "Now, you've got me curious. Am I in some kind of trouble, *Officer*?" She batted her eyelashes at him, her tone switching to flirtatious.

Rob pressed his lips together tightly, resisting the sudden urge to take her in his arms and crush her to his chest. "I … just need you to clear something up for me."

Misty shrugged and turned to the other band members. "You boys good to wrap this up without me?"

"We've got it," one of them called back to her. "Enjoy a nightcap with lover boy. See you at the show tomorrow."

"You're singing in *Hairspray*?" Rob asked.

Misty gave a curt nod. "I'm standing in for someone who's sick. Please don't come. You've seen it a thousand times before."

"If that's how you feel about it," he replied stiffly. He wasn't used to Misty dismissing him, and he resented it. But she'd soon change her tune once she saw the footage he had of her breaking and entering.

They made their way to the elevator and rode down a level, an awkward silence wedged between them.

Inside the security office, Rob pulled out a chair and gestured to Misty to take a seat. "Can I get you some water? Or coffee?"

She settled into the chair and crossed one leg seductively over the other, the slit in her gown sliding up her leg. "We both know this isn't a social visit. What can I help you *clear up*, as you put it? Let me guess, one of my band members has been smoking pot in the cabin again."

Rob rested his elbows on the desk and interlaced his fingers, his default pose when he was about to discipline a crew member. It was important that Misty understood he was in control—she wasn't the one pulling the strings anymore. "We had an incident on one of the guest decks, an argument between passengers." He cleared his throat before continuing, "I was reviewing the footage to write up my report and I noticed something curious."

Misty raised a flattened palm in a gesture of helplessness, elbow bent—that peculiar little gesture that had become so familiar to him. "Where is this going, Rob? I'm beginning to feel like you lured me here under false pretenses."

Wordlessly, he turned to his computer and pulled up the CCTV footage. He angled the monitor so they could both view it.

As the clip began to roll, he took stock of Misty's expression. Surprisingly, she didn't seem bothered by it, in fact, she seemed to visibly relax as the video continued to play.

Rob let it run all the way through to the moment she emerged from the Robinsons' cabin and then switched it off. He pasted a sympathetic smile on his lips. "As you very well know, we have a zero-tolerance policy when it comes to crew entering guest quarters, other than to carry out their duties. What were you doing in there, Misty? If you're in some kind of trouble, you need to tell me. Maybe I can help."

Rob was well aware that he wasn't handling the situation the way he'd handle any other disciplinary action, and he certainly wasn't adhering to company policy. But his goal wasn't to drive Misty away—it was to draw her in. To let her know that, even when her world was about to come crumbling down around her, he was here for her, her knight in shining armor who had the power to make this all go away.

Misty tilted her head to one side and tinkled a laugh. "I have to give it to you, Robbie, you caught me red-handed playing The Good Samaritan."

Rob gave her a blank look. "What are you talking about?"

Misty slid forward on her seat. "I was doing another crew member a favor—Brezina Novak. She needed me to cover the end of her shift so she could, you know … meet someone."

"Meet someone?" Rob echoed, suddenly unsure of where this was heading.

"Her fiancé," Misty said in a conspiratorial tone. "He works on the ship—in engineering. He's a plumber. They haven't had any time off together since she came on board. His boss gave him the evening off, so she asked me to help her out, turn down the last couple of cabins so she could take off early. She loaned me her key and borrowed a uniform for me."

"That's strictly against policy," Rob blurted out, scrambling to keep his composure, his carefully rehearsed speech failing him. He'd anticipated several different explanations, but nothing this innocuous. He'd imagined Misty breaking down in tears, begging him not to fire her, disclosing that she'd got herself into financial trouble, or that she was being blackmailed by someone she owed money to—all scenarios Rob had been prepared to handle.

"Seriously?" Misty said in a mocking tone. "If we're talking policy, you haven't exactly been doing everything on the up-and-up yourself, have you, Officer Benson?"

Heat rose inside Rob's collar as he met Misty's derisive stare. He'd started out this meeting with the upper hand, but Misty had completely turned the tables on him and now he was wrestling with how to proceed. It was possible she was telling him the truth. In which case, he had lost all leverage to win her back. He felt like a fool and he didn't like it. A hard cord twitched in his neck. No matter what, he wasn't going to let Misty Murano walk out of his office, or his life.

"Don't worry, Officer," Misty went on in a coy tone. "I promise not to violate a sacred state room again."

Rob drummed his fingers on the desk, building up to the point of no return. "The thing is, Misty. Something very valuable has gone missing from cabin 10664."

12

SOPHIA

Sophia woke early the next morning and went out onto the balcony to watch the sunrise, leaving Cody to sleep. He'd been up until all hours trying to get some *critical work* done, as he dubbed it. It frustrated her that several days into their cruise he was still as tethered to the business as ever. It wasn't as if he had to be—he *chose* to be. They had good managers in place now. He needed to let them get on with it.

She leaned over the balcony and peered down at the cabin below, wondering how Allison was doing this morning. She'd heard her and Doug arguing last night. It hadn't been loud enough to make out everything, but she'd heard them mention Labadee, and she suspected it had something to do with the incident on the beach.

Sophia and Cody had discussed it over dinner and concluded that Allison had either got a little too much sun, or the Labadoozie hadn't agreed with her—or some combination of the two. Cody felt awful for insisting they all partake of the island's signature drink, but Sophia had assured him it wasn't his fault. It wasn't anyone's fault. She picked at the skin on her finger, second-guessing herself in the light of day. The thought had crossed her mind that Allison might have a prescription drug problem. She got very defensive any time the subject of her antidepressants came up, and she'd gone to great lengths to let everyone know she wasn't taking them, despite the fact that the bottle was as good as empty yesterday. A case of the lady protesting too much, perhaps? Doug seemed genuinely concerned about her. He'd alluded to her struggle with severe postpartum depression, and the forgetfulness and confusion she often exhibited.

Sophia turned her head at the sound of the slider door opening. Cody yawned as he threw himself into the deck chair next to her. "You should have woken me."

"You were in such a deep sleep I figured you must have taken a sleeping pill," Sophia said. "What time did you finally come to bed?"

Cody shrugged, not meeting her eyes. "Late. What do you want to do for breakfast?"

"Let's skip the buffet and grab a latte and pastry at Cafe Esplanade," Sophia suggested. "I can't keep eating huge meals three times a day or I'll have to be wheeled off this ship when we get back to Florida."

Cody let out a snort of laughter.

Sophia grinned at him. "It's good to hear you laugh. You don't laugh much anymore."

His face instantly clouded over and he got to his feet. "I'm going to hit the shower."

"I'll text Allison and Doug and see if they want to grab a latte with us," Sophia called after him. She turned her attention back to the ocean view and stared distractedly at the horizon. Maybe Cody was depressed, like Allison. She'd never considered the possibility before, but it was an avenue she should explore once the cruise ended.

. . .

FORTY-FIVE MINUTES LATER, the two couples convened at the bustling Cafe Esplanade. They snagged a table outside and settled into the comfy club chairs with their coffees and pastries.

Almost immediately, Sophia noticed that Allison had been crying. She had tried to cover it up with makeup—done a decent job of it, too—but a perceptive woman could tell.

"How are you feeling this morning?" Sophia asked.

Allison reached for her apple pecan muffin. "Better, thanks."

Sophia sipped her latte, catching Doug's eye in the process. He tilted his brows a fraction and then dropped his gaze. She wasn't sure if he was simply trying to convey a feeling of helplessness, or something more.

"I'm really looking forward to *Hairspray* tonight," Sophia said, opting to change the subject and keep things upbeat. "The music and dance routines are supposed to be out of this world."

"How long does the show last?" Allison asked, slicing her muffin in two.

Sophia dotted her lips with her napkin. "Ninety minutes. We'll make sure to get back to the ship in plenty of time so you can take a nap before dinner. You should take it easy after yesterday."

"Speaking of getting off the ship," Doug interjected, "we haven't decided yet what we want to do on Jamaica. My vote's for the Falmouth Swamp Safari."

Allison grimaced. "Not sure I want to spend my time viewing crocodiles in a smelly swamp. I thought the Green Grotto Caves looked interesting."

Sophia couldn't help but notice that Allison hadn't looked directly at Doug since they'd sat down. Evidently, they hadn't resolved their argument yet. She hoped that whatever was going on between them wouldn't make for an awkward day out. "How about we do both?" she suggested. "I wouldn't mind a crocodile photo op. The swamp's only five minutes from the port, and the Green Grotto Cave tour only lasts an hour."

"Sounds like a deal," Doug said. "Something for everyone."

"Then let's go explore Jamaica," Cody said slapping a palm on the table and getting to his feet.

AT THE GREEN GROTTO CAVES, they donned the requisite helmets and followed their guide, a young Haitian man dressed in shorts and a Hawaiian shirt, to the entrance. He proceeded to lead them through a labyrinth of caves, regaling them with tales of pirates, runaway slaves, and rum storage during World War II.

"I should also mention that there are an estimated ten million bats living in these caves," he announced at one point, flashing a gap-toothed smile when Sophia let out a horrified gasp.

"Another fun fact," he continued, as they exited the cave and made their way to the green grotto, "is that James Bond made a movie here."

The group followed him down sixty-five steps to a breathtaking underground lake with an eerie green reflection. "This is where Roger Moore and Jane Seymour were lowered into the shark tank," he disclosed, beaming around at the suitably impressed expressions on everyone's faces.

"Picture time!" Sophia chirped, leaning her head in next to Allison's. "One, two, three … "

She studied the shot on her phone. "Perfect! Now, what's a good hashtag?"

"*#LiveAndLetDieTheRemake*," Allison said with a chuckle.

"Oooh! Cheesy and ominous," Sophia replied. "Works for me."

After finishing up at the grotto, and purchasing some souvenirs, they headed to the Falmouth Swamp Safari.

"Brace yourselves, ladies," Cody joked. "Supposedly, they have over eighty crocodiles here—snakes and iguanas too."

"Snakes!" Sophia pulled up short and fixed an accusatory gaze on her husband. "I hate snakes! Why didn't you tell me?"

Cody gave an apologetic shrug. "You can stick to the crocodiles."

Sophia rolled her eyes at Allison. "Me and my big mouth. I should never have suggested visiting both places."

They spent the next hour strolling around the compound, taking turns holding a baby crocodile, and watching with morbid fascination as the keepers moved around inside the enclosures with buckets of meat and sticks, intermittently tossing a treat, and taunting the reptiles to snap by tapping their noses with the stick.

"I can't believe they walk around in bare feet and shorts," Sophia exclaimed, reviewing the video she'd taken. "I'd be terrified one of those crocs would snap my leg off."

"Okay, I'm ready to hold a snake next," Cody said. "That'll be another good photo opportunity, Sophia."

She held up the palm of her hand and turned her face away. "Nuh-uh. I have my limits. I'm staying right here by this enclosure with these cute little monkeys until you come back for me."

"I'll pass too," Allison chimed in. "You boys go get your fill of draping snakes around your neck."

She let out a heavy sigh and sat down on a nearby bench, as Cody and Doug strode off in the direction of the reptile house.

Sophia shot her a concerned look. "Are you feeling all right?"

"I'm fine, just hot," Allison replied, fanning herself.

Sophia joined her on the bench. "You didn't look so good this morning. I could tell you'd been crying."

Allison twisted her lips. "I had an argument with Doug last night. It was stupid."

"I heard you on the balcony," Sophia admitted. "I couldn't make out what you were saying, but it was obvious you were arguing."

Allison slipped her fingertips behind her sunglasses and rubbed her eyes. "It was about the antidepressants."

Sophia laid a hand on Allison's shoulder. "Look, I know you're embarrassed about the pills. But it's nothing to be ashamed of. Cody takes prescription sleeping pills. It's the only way he can get to sleep these days. We all need help in different ways. After what you went through, losing the baby and all, it's understandable."

"That's just it," Allison said. "I stopped taking the antidepressants over a month ago." She furrowed her brow, staring down at the dirt path. "When Doug surprised me with this cruise, he made me refill my prescription and bring it along, in case I needed it. The thing is, I don't remember taking any of the pills in the past few days, and yet somehow the bottle's almost empty."

"I'm sure there's a perfectly reasonable explanation," Sophia soothed, wondering, even as the words fell from her lips, what it could be. She supposed it was possible the cabin steward had stolen some pills. The more likely explanation was that Allison was confused about it.

"I can't help worrying about it," Allison went on, pulling on her lip. "Doug thinks I'm losing it." She traced the toe of her sandal in the dirt. "I suppose I must be, because the only other alternative is that Doug took those pills out of the bottle. And why would he do that and then lie about it?"

Sophia frowned. "He wouldn't. It's obvious he cares about you deeply."

Allison turned to her, a frenzied look in her luminous eyes. "What if he doesn't? What if he's trying to kill me?" she said, so softly that Sophia almost didn't catch it.

"Don't say that," she chided. "You're upset. Doug loves you. He has no reason to harm you."

"I wish that were true."

Sophia pulled at a lock of her hair nervously. "You're scaring me now. What are you talking about?"

Allison covered her face with her hands and shook her head slowly. "I can't ... I promised Doug."

"Promised him what?" Sophia gritted her teeth, quashing down the wild conjectures coming to mind. "Does he have some kind of hold over you? Allison, please talk to me."

She looked directly at Sophia, her eyes filled with a defeated air. "Promise you won't let slip that I told you. You can't say anything to Cody either."

"No, of course not." Sophia hesitated and then prompted, "You can trust me."

"I didn't have a miscarriage." Allison's voice trailed off into a despairing sob. "I killed our daughter."

13

SOPHIA

Sophia clapped a hand over her mouth, reeling from Allison's dramatic confession. For a long moment, she stared at her, wondering if she'd misheard her over the noise of the chattering monkeys. Sophia was never at a loss for words, but this had taken her breath away. Had Allison actually killed her own child? Or was she confused, mentally ill? Maybe she was blaming herself for the miscarriage. Sophia opened and shut her mouth but came up short on an appropriate response.

Allison, for her part, didn't seem to notice. She continued talking, almost as though she was having a conversation with herself. "The thing is, I didn't mean to. It was—"

She broke off abruptly at the sound of the men's voices drifting their way.

"That was radical!" Doug said, striding up to them with Cody grinning at his side. "You girls missed out."

Sophia furnished them with a feeble smile. "You'd better have the pictures to prove it. Otherwise it never happened."

Cody pulled out his phone and tapped on the screen,

before handing it to Sophia. "Here you go. In living color. We got to hold a few different types of snakes."

She shrank back from the screen and passed the phone off to Allison. "Ugh! I'm going to have nightmares about those slimy reptiles crawling all over me."

"They're actually not slimy at all," Cody said. "It felt kind of like handling a garden hose, smooth and dry."

"Stop!" Sophia protested. "You're not making this any better for me."

Doug peered down at Allison. "You look pale, baby. Are you all right?"

"I think I've had enough sun for one day."

"You should have your hat on," Doug chided, reaching for her bag. "Let's get you back to the ship."

"What are you planning on wearing to the show tonight?" Sophia asked Allison, as they made their way back to the port area.

"I'm not sure. I only brought one dress with me."

"Why don't we stroll around the onboard stores, just the two of us," Sophia proposed. "Maybe we'll find something fun to wear. The guys can entertain themselves for an hour or so."

Allison wet her lips, a look in her eyes that reminded Sophia of an animal tempted by food in a human's outstretched hand, but afraid it might be a trap.

"Look, I'm not going to pressure you to talk about what you told me earlier if that's what you're afraid of," Sophia assured her. "You should know by now I'm a straight shooter. If you want to talk, I'm here for you. Otherwise, we can just have some girl time. I don't know about you, but I'd rather run my hand over a Chanel purse than a snakeskin any day."

Allison threw a furtive glance behind her at Doug who was deep in conversation with Cody. "Okay, I guess."

Back on board the ship, Sophia and Allison handed their bags off to the men and headed up to deck five where most of the retail stores were located. Their first stop was a beauty product store and parfumerie from which they emerged a short time later with a new Chanel lipstick each.

"Eek! There's Kate Spade!" Sophia cried out, gesturing to a store front. "We have to at least take a look. I've been wanting a new summer purse."

"I hope I don't regret this," Sophia confided to Allison as she paid for the floral tote she'd settled on after checking out all her options. "It's perfect for a vacation, but I'm not sure I'll get much use out of it at home. I'm almost tempted to go back in and get the dome satchel in tutu pink as well."

"Why don't you think about it for a while first?" Allison suggested.

Sophia pouted her lips. "That's code for quit spending money, isn't it? You sound just like my husband."

Allison laughed. "You can always go back and get it later."

"You're right. Let's focus on finding something to wear to the show tonight."

"To be honest, I'm not in the mood to try on clothes."

Sophia slowed her pace, picking up on a wistful note in Allison's voice. "Do you want to grab a coffee and talk instead?"

Allison gave a grateful nod. "Sure."

They found a quiet corner on the esplanade and sat down with macchiatos in hand.

"I need to explain what I said earlier," Allison began.

Sophia held her coffee cup to her lips and waited impatiently for Allison to continue. She had a bad habit of rushing to fill any length of silence with throwaway words, but she sensed Allison was the type of person who needed time to formulate her thoughts before she would share what was really on her heart.

"We had a daughter," Allison carried on. "Her name was Ava. I had a hard time after the birth. I struggled to breast feed and I suffered from postpartum depression. There were days I could barely get out of bed. When I did, I kept bursting into tears over the stupidest things. I had panic attacks when I had to leave the house. Doug tried to help, but he was busy with work, traveling for days on end. I had always wanted to be a stay-at-home mom, but I envisioned it differently." She traced her finger distractedly around the plastic lid on her coffee, falling silent.

Sophia held her breath, wondering what was coming next. Her heartbeat thrummed in her chest. She wasn't sure how she would react to what Allison was about to admit to. Would she feel sympathy for her, or outrage? Depression or not, it was incomprehensible to Sophia that a mother could kill her own child. She really hoped Allison didn't pull out a photo of Ava to show her. It was hard not to feel sickened at the thought that Allison might carry around a picture of the daughter she had murdered.

When Allison started up again, Sophia took a hasty gulp of coffee, reminding herself to reserve judgement. "Ava was a fussy baby. I was exhausted all the time. Between the nonstop feedings, and diaper changes, and lack of sleep, I hardly knew if it was day or night at times." Allison stared intently at the paper cup in her hands, her voice cracking. "I woke up one morning and she was lying in bed next to me, cold as a stone figurine."

Sophia tensed, her fingers gripping her paper cup so tightly she dented it. "I'm … so sorry. I can't comprehend going through something that awful," she whispered.

Allison's eyes glistened with fresh tears, but she plowed on, staring down at her untouched macchiato. "Her bassinet was next to the bed. I was too scared to co-sleep, terrified one of us might accidentally smother her." She closed her eyes briefly before continuing, "I must have fallen asleep after I nursed her. I don't remember." She cast a pitiful look Sophia's way. "Afterward, I wanted to die too. I felt like the worst mother in the world. I tried to end my life—took a bunch of pills. Not enough to kill me, as it turned out. I don't even recall taking them, to be honest. The days were one long blur of existence back then."

"I'm so sorry, Allison," Sophia said softly. Inwardly, her thoughts were crashing in rapid succession like surf on rocks. Had Allison tried to commit suicide on the beach at Labadee too? Sophia took another sip of her drink. She urgently needed to talk to Doug and find out what was going on. She hated the thought of breaking Allison's confidence, but it was irresponsible to keep quiet if her life was at risk.

"I can't even imagine how devastating that must have been for you," Sophia said. "I can hear in your voice how much you loved Ava. But you didn't kill her. What you described was an accident. Surely you can see that?"

Allison wiped the tears from her lower lids with her fingertips, sniffing as she reached for a napkin to wipe her face with. "That's just it," she blubbered. "The police suspected me of deliberately killing her. There was an autopsy. The coroner said it looked as if Ava had been suffocated. The investigation dragged on for months before they dropped it. It was horrible."

"Even if she did suffocate," Sophia interjected, "it was an accident. You can't blame yourself. Nobody blames you."

Allison twisted her lips, waiting a beat before whispering, "Doug does."

Sophia stared at her, aghast. "No! I don't believe that for a minute. What makes you say that?"

Allison shook her head, a distant look in her eyes. "I was a mess back then, with the antidepressants and all. The truth is, I might have done something awful and not remembered it. Doug never accused me directly, but sometimes I think he suspects as much. That's when we began to drift apart. I even wondered if he was having an affair—I went through all his receipts. Paranoid, I know, but when you see the amount of attention he gets from other women." Her voice faded away, her face crumpling.

Sophia fidgeted with the cardboard sleeve on her coffee cup, weighing what Allison had told her with what she'd observed herself since the beginning of the cruise—the missing pills, the incident on the beach, the argument on the balcony. Allison had wondered aloud if Doug might be trying to kill her. Sophia had dismissed it as wild conjecture at the time—the ramblings of a possible addict. But what if it was true? What if Doug did blame Allison for their baby's death? Sweat dampened her palms. *No!* It couldn't be true. Allison's paranoia was beginning to rub off on her. Doug had been nothing but attentive and loving every time they'd been together. He genuinely seemed to be doing his best to keep her happy. Besides, he could file for divorce if he didn't want to be with her. The more likely explanation was that Allison was still taking the antidepressants and had overdosed. Whether she'd genuinely forgotten she'd taken them, or was intentionally lying about it, was another matter entirely. The important thing was to assure her that her husband wasn't trying to harm her. The drugs were feeding her paranoia.

"I'm sure Doug doesn't blame you in the least for what happened," Sophia said firmly. "He brought you on this cruise to celebrate your ten-year anniversary. What does that tell you? And what about that fabulous necklace he gave you? He's doing everything he can to reassure you that he still loves you."

Allison blew her nose. "Do you really think so?"

"I'm sure of it," Sophia rejoined. "I wish Cody was half as attentive to me as Doug is to you. Don't push him away by doubting him. You've both been through something traumatic, you need to be supportive of each other."

Allison smiled wanly at her. "That's what my therapist says. Thanks for listening, Sophia. It's hard to think through the fog in my brain some days. It's easy to read situations all wrong."

Sophia got to her feet and tossed their cups in the trash receptacle. "Let's get out of here. It's afternoon nap time."

LATER THAT EVENING, they sank into their plush front row seats in the theater at the *Hairspray* musical.

"I can't believe we scored such good seats," Sophia said.

"It pays to get here early," Doug replied. "There's nothing worse than being stuck in the back of the theater."

They fell silent as the lights dimmed and the music began. Sophia was lost in the show when she became aware of Allison nudging her.

"I'm going to head back up to the cabin," Allison whispered.

"What?" Sophia sat up in her seat. "Is Doug going with you?"

Allison shook her head. "I told him to stay and finish watching the show."

"Are you feeling all right? Do you want me to go with you?"

"Shh!" A voice in the row behind them hissed.

"I'm fine, just tired," Allison answered, clutching her purse to her chest as she sidestepped past Sophia.

Sophia watched her anxiously for a few minutes as she made her way to the nearest exit. A security officer standing in the shadows at the exit exchanged a few words with her before she disappeared out the door.

After a moment or two, Sophia turned her attention back to the musical, and was soon riveted once more by the phenomenal set and talented cast. If she wasn't mistaken, the woman playing Penny Pingleton looked like the blonde, Misty, who'd conducted their muster drill on the first day.

"That was absolutely incredible," Sophia said, when the show finally ended with a standing ovation. "I wish Allison could have seen the whole thing."

"Me too," Doug agreed, as they filed out of the theater. "She's still feeling a bit wiped out after yesterday."

"Do you guys want to get a nightcap?" Cody asked, looking from Sophia to Doug.

Doug hesitated, his eyes crinkling with concern. "Let me text Allison first. She might want me to go back up to the cabin."

He typed out a quick message and, a moment later, his phone dinged with a response. "She's resting—watching TV. She told me to grab a drink with you and have one for her too."

"I'm glad she's all right," Sophia said. "I was worried about her."

"Do you want to try the Robo Bar?" Cody asked. "Supposedly the bartenders are two robotic arms."

"I was reading up on that place," Doug responded. "Sounds intriguing."

After making their way to the bar and placing an order, they watched in rapt fascination as two robotic arms proceeded to measure out the drinks from bottles hanging upside down from the ceiling.

"Would you look at that!" Sophia exclaimed. "They're even shaking up our cocktails."

Cody swiped his key card and, seconds later, their drinks slid along grooves in the bar toward them.

"This cracks me up," Sophia said. "I've never seen anything like it before."

They took their drinks over to a seating area and sat down. Sophia tossed her purse onto the chair next to her and cast a curious glance around at the other guests. "Hey! There's that woman who played Penny Pingleton," she said, tilting her head. "She led our muster drill the first day too. I looked her up in the program. Her full name's Misty Murano. Beautiful, isn't she?"

Doug and Cody peered discreetly over to the other side of the room where a blonde woman was sitting with a uniformed officer.

"You're out of luck, boys." Sophia chuckled. "I bet that's her boyfriend. I saw him hanging out by one of the exits watching the show earlier." She lowered her voice. "Although, I have to say they don't look like they're having a very good time."

Cody stirred his drink. "She's a looker, I'll give her that."

"She can sing too," Doug added, before taking a swig of his gin and tonic.

After enjoying their round of drinks, and making some tentative plans for the following day, they decided to call it a night.

"I'm going to look for a restroom," Doug said as they exited the bar. "You guys go on ahead. See you at breakfast." He waved goodbye and strode off.

"I've got some work I need to take care of when we get back to the room, so don't get mad at me," Cody said, as he and Sophia waited for the elevator doors to open.

"Are you serious? Can't you leave it alone for one night?" Sophia moaned, rummaging around in her purse. "Shoot! My

Chanel lipstick must have fallen out. It's brand new. I'm going to run back and look for it. Go ahead on up."

She retraced her steps to the Robo Bar and wound her way over to the lounge area. To her relief, she spotted her lipstick lying partway under the chair she'd been sitting on.

As she turned to leave, she caught sight of Misty Murano at the bar. Sophia's blood ran cold. The officer Misty had been talking to earlier was nowhere in sight. The man whispering in her ear was Doug Robinson.

14

SOPHIA

Sophia quietly retreated out of the bar and stood in the hallway with her back against the wall, seething with rage and shock. Her heart screamed at her to march back inside and rip Doug apart in front of everyone, but she forced herself to take a moment and compose herself first. The unsettling tête-à-tête between Doug and Misty played in her mind, as she tried to come up with a plausible explanation for what she'd witnessed. Doug might have decided to have another drink and, quite innocently, got into conversation with Misty Murano—she could have made a play for him. Admittedly, he was the kind of man who attracted unprovoked attention wherever he went. But if he was innocent, why was he even entertaining Misty's advances?

Sophia breathed slowly in and out, debating the possibilities. Had Doug lied to them about going back to his cabin, all the while intending to make a move on Misty? Everything Allison had confided to Sophia swirled in a blur of misgiving in her brain. If Doug was serious about celebrating his ten-year anniversary with a fresh start, he had a funny way of going about it.

Anger simmered in the pit of Sophia's stomach. It wasn't right, not after everything Allison had been through. She was up in her cabin, still recovering from her ordeal at the beach —oblivious to the fact that her husband was making a move on the hottest woman on the ship.

Sophia clamped her lips together tasting her rose-scented Chanel lipstick. She had to do something. What choice did she have? She would be a poor friend if she let this slide after Allison had divulged her fears and suspicions to her. Her mind made up, she eased her way back inside and marched straight up to the bar.

"Doug!" she exclaimed, letting the note of surprise in her voice hang in the air for an extended moment. "I ... didn't expect to see you back at the bar."

His eyes widened momentarily before he quickly rearranged his expression. "Sophia! What are you doing here?"

"I came back to look for my lipstick. It must have fallen out of my purse," she replied, planting a cold gaze on Misty, perched on a bar stool, sipping on a Daiquiri.

"You might have dropped it where we were sitting earlier," Doug said. "I'll help you look for it. Sophia, this is Misty Murano. She played Penny Pingleton in *Hairspray* tonight. I noticed in the activities guide that she's singing in the *Slow Vibes* piano bar tomorrow night so I thought I'd request a song for Allison—it might lift her spirits a bit." He hesitated and tweaked a bashful smile. "*At last,* by Etta James. It was our ... wedding song."

He choked on the words and Sophia blinked, suddenly unsure of herself. Had she totally misinterpreted what she'd witnessed? Jumped to a conclusion too swiftly. Something Cody was always accusing her of.

"It's a great song choice. One of the band's favorites," Misty said in a sultry voice. "Now, if you two will excuse me, it's time for me to get some rest. Lovely to meet you, Sophia. Enjoy the rest of your evening, folks."

She picked up her purse and glided across the room, stopping briefly to talk to a group of admirers on the way out.

"Let's hunt down that lipstick," Doug said, offering Sophia an impish grin. "I know how you girls are. Allison was raving about hers earlier."

Sophia gave a disconcerted nod. She trailed Doug over to the seating area and pretended to help him look, hoping he wouldn't suggest she check her purse on the off chance that she'd overlooked the lipstick.

"Well, that's a bummer," Doug said getting to his feet after crawling around on his hands and knees for several minutes.

"Not to worry," Sophia said. "Maybe I left it in the cabin after all."

Doug leveled his eyes at her. "I'd appreciate it if you would keep the song request a surprise. I feel bad that Allison missed half the show tonight. I wanted to do something special for her to make up for it." He cleared his throat before continuing. "To be honest, she's struggling a bit. She's in denial about her depression, you know, taking the pills and all. She doesn't want anyone to know. It's the first time she's been away from the house since we lost the baby."

"Of … course," Sophia stammered. "That's sweet of you to arrange something so thoughtful for her. I know she'll appreciate the gesture. Good night, Doug."

She turned and made a beeline for the exit before he could engage her in any further conversation. As she rode the elevator up to her state room, her thoughts gravitated to the couple in the cabin below. Their stories weren't converging in a way that made sense. Who was the real villain here? Was Allison abusing prescription medication? Were her suspicions about Doug legitimate, or the product of her paranoia?

When she opened the door to her cabin, Cody was tapping furiously on his keyboard. A half empty bottle of whiskey sat on the table next to him, along with one of the shot glasses she'd purchased in Haiti.

"Find your sunglasses?" he asked, not even looking up from his screen.

"Lipstick," Sophia snapped back. "And yes, I did find it."

Cody's head whipped in her direction. "You sound testy. What's wrong?"

"You mean, apart from the fact that you're completely preoccupied with work, and only half living in the moment," she said, throwing herself into the club chair next to him.

Cody scowled. "I don't want to start an argument with you."

"What's really bothering me is that I just saw Doug Robinson talking to Misty Murano in the Robo Bar," Sophia said.

Cody raised an eyebrow. "And?"

"Don't you think that's a little odd? We'd already called it a night. He said he was going back to his cabin."

"After he used the restroom," Cody pointed out. "Maybe he decided to have one more for the road. Trust me, if that blonde had been at the bar earlier, I'd have tried talking to her too. It's not a crime to talk." He broke off and rubbed the back of his neck. "Unless, it was more than that?"

"No." Sophia furrowed her brow. "But they looked pretty cozy."

"Did Doug see you?"

Sophia let out a snort. "You know me. I walked straight up to the bar and made my presence known. It didn't bother him in the least. He introduced me to Misty and said he was putting in a song request for Allison—the one they danced to at their wedding. I have to admit, he acted pretty choked up about it."

"There you have it," Cody responded. "He's just a guy trying to do his best to celebrate his ten-year wedding anniversary. Give him a break, Soph. He's making more of an effort than she is, if you ask me."

"That's unfair. Allison's been through a difficult time."

"So has he. It was his kid too."

Sophia fell silent. She'd promised Allison she wouldn't divulge the truth about Ava's death to Cody. She couldn't risk letting it slip out now. She walked over to her nightstand and took a swig from her water bottle before switching gears. "Don't you find it odd that Doug booked a cruise to celebrate their ten-year anniversary knowing how depressed Allison was?"

Cody pulled at his ear, staring at her uncomprehendingly. "Why's that odd?"

"She was suicidal at one point. A cruise ship isn't exactly the safest place in the world if you're mentally unstable. People throw themselves off bridges and stuff."

"Stuff? You mean like cruise ships?" Cody's tone was skeptical.

"I know, I know," Sophia said with a defeated groan. "I'm probably being paranoid, but I feel like she's fragile. And if she even suspects that Doug's flirting with other women, it might be enough to put her over the edge."

"You're not being fair to him," Cody said. "He's very patient with her if you ask me, walking around on eggshells all the time." He reached for the whiskey bottle and poured himself another shot.

"How many of those have you had?" Sophia asked, picking at the label on her water bottle.

He flicked a warning gaze her way. "Don't mother me, Soph."

"I wouldn't have to if you'd be more responsible. You've been drinking far too much lately, especially on this cruise."

He lifted the shot glass and threw the contents back, slamming it down on the table before glaring at her again. "I'm trying to keep up with your shopping habits."

Sophia flinched, spilling water onto the bedcover. "What's that supposed to mean?"

Cody's lips flattened. "It means you're more interested in spending our money than in how I earn it."

Sophia loosed an aggrieved breath. "Don't you dare start! I work equally as hard as you, raising our two boys and keeping our house clean and stocked. I haven't had a proper vacation in years. I've been looking forward to this trip for ages. And if I feel like shopping, I will. It's not as if we can't afford it."

Cody averted his gaze. A moment later, he resumed his tapping on the keyboard.

Quashing her frustration that he'd shut down the conversation, Sophia walked over and peered over his shoulder, "What are you working on anyway that's so important?"

Cody shrugged and snapped his laptop closed. "Just finishing up some emails and stuff."

"What kind of stuff?" Sophia pressed.

A flicker of irritation crossed Cody's forehead. "Since when did you become interested in the mechanics of the company?"

"Why are you so defensive?" Sophia frowned. "Is there something you're not telling me? You're always sneaking off to the business office so I can't see what you're working on. Why did you close up your laptop just now?"

Cody made an incoherent sound and poured himself another shot.

"Like that's going to help," Sophia yelled, placing her hands on her hips.

Ignoring her outburst, Cody knocked the shot back, staring morosely at the wall in front of him.

"Is it the business, or something else?" Sophia demanded. "I have a right to know. Are you in some kind of trouble?"

Cody rubbed a hand over his jaw and turned to face her.

Goosebumps pricked their way down Sophia's arms. The look in her husband's eyes was little short of desperate.

"Your name's on the paperwork too," he choked out. "We're both in trouble."

15

ALLISON

Allison stood ruminating in the hot shower until Doug banged on the bathroom door. "Baby! Are you almost done in there? We're meeting Cody and Sophia for breakfast, remember?"

She hurriedly turned off the water and stepped out of the tub. "Two minutes, just drying off." After wrapping the white cotton towel around her shoulders, she rubbed the steamed-up surface of the mirror and stared at her hollow-eyed, catatonic reflection, her expression halfway between trance and terror. It was an accurate portrayal of what was going on inside her.

She hadn't decided yet what she was going to do about what she'd discovered in their room last night, but she had to do something. She hadn't left the *Hairspray* musical early because she'd been tired—it had simply been an opportunity to go through Doug's things while he was out of their cabin. She'd been searching for the antidepressants, which in retrospect was stupid because if he had taken them, he would most likely have flushed any remaining pills down the toilet to get rid of the evidence.

In the end, it hadn't mattered—she'd forgotten all about the missing pills. What she'd discovered instead was equally disturbing. And it had left her with more questions than ever. Apparently, her husband of ten years was leading a double life. After all, burner phones were synonymous with a need for anonymity. Logic told her you didn't hide a phone in your clothes if you were using it for legitimate purposes.

After staring dumbstruck at the phone stuffed inside Doug's socks for several minutes, she had pulled it out and exhausted all possible combinations that she could think of to unlock it. She'd even Googled how to crack a password on a burner phone. There were options to unlock the device using your Google account, but according to the article she'd read, there was a good chance anyone with something to hide had a second Gmail account. In the end, she'd abandoned all attempts to unlock it, and put it back where she'd found it until she could figure out what to do about it.

She squirted a dab of toothpaste onto her toothbrush and turned on the water. She'd tossed and turned all night, vacillating between perfectly reasonable explanations for the burner phone's existence—a backup phone for work perhaps—and the wildest possible scenarios—Doug was an undercover agent for the FBI, or a drug dealer. Her heart shivered at the thought. If he was conducting some kind of illicit business activity, she might be implicated. She stopped scrubbing her teeth and frowned, her thoughts returning to the missing pills. Did they have something to do with the phone? Her head throbbed as she tossed around one explanation after the other, each crazier than the last. The most likely explanation was the simplest—that Doug was cheating on her. And that was the hardest one to accept.

Allison dabbed her mouth on a towel and quickly tugged a comb through her hair before exiting the bathroom. "It's all yours," she said brightly.

Doug grinned at her. "You sound like you're feeling better this morning."

"Like a million dollars," she lied, wrestling with the somewhat maniacal thought that Doug might have a million dollars of drug money stashed at home, for all she knew.

While Doug showered up, Allison went out onto the balcony to get some fresh air and devise a plan. She could confront him outright, but it might accomplish nothing—it wasn't as though she could force him to tell her the truth about what he was using the phone for. How would she know if he was lying? If she could catch him using it on the sly, she might be able to listen in and find out what he was up to. But that would be difficult, next to impossible. It wasn't as if he was stupid enough to use it while she was in the cabin.

Another option was to take the phone, toss it into the ocean, and deny any knowledge of it if Doug brought it up—which he'd be unlikely to do. She could stage a break-in to cover her tracks, call security and have that officer, Rob somebody-or-other come up and inspect the room again. She grimaced, remembering the skeptical look he'd exchanged with Doug when her necklace had shown up. She'd rather not go that route. Rob would likely take one look at her and know she had staged the whole thing. She wasn't a good liar and her aptitude for criminality was sorely lacking.

She was leaning on the railing, staring down at the ocean, when, all of a sudden, two dolphins jumped out of the water right in front of her. A small child on a nearby balcony let out a delighted squeal. Without warning, Allison's eyes pricked with the tang of tears. Ava would have been almost eight months old by now, if she had lived. She would have been in Allison's arms, her bright eyes fixed on the dolphins' graceful movements.

Allison swallowed the lump in her throat. Sophia had

been so easy to talk to when she'd finally broken down and told her the truth about Ava. Maybe she should tell her about the burner phone too. Sophia would know what to do. She was that type of person—capable, decisive, always on top of things.

"I'll have to hit the treadmill after this," Doug joked, as he sat down with a plate piled high with bacon, eggs, fried potatoes, papaya, and a blueberry muffin the size of his fist.

"Let's do it. I wouldn't mind checking out the fitness center," Cody said, pouring a liberal helping of syrup over his stack of strawberry pancakes.

Sensing an opportunity, Allison turned to Sophia. "Fancy going to the spa this morning? We could get massages or facials, or the works."

Sophia shot a worried look in Cody's direction. "Uh—"

"My treat," Allison added, desperate to secure some time alone with Sophia. "We deserve a little pampering putting up with those workaholic husbands of ours."

"Can't argue with that," Sophia answered, her smile more strained than usual.

Allison picked up her coffee and sipped it thoughtfully. Sophia wasn't her usual bubbly self this morning. Perhaps she shouldn't have told her the truth about what happened to Ava. She wondered if Sophia viewed her differently now. Maybe it wasn't such a good idea to bring up the burner phone, after all.

Allison slid a glance at Doug bent over his plate. She'd been struggling to look him in the eye ever since she'd found the phone. Evidently, he hadn't noticed—at any rate, he hadn't commented on it. He'd probably chalked it up to the fact that she was still recovering from passing out at the beach.

After finishing up their breakfast, they wandered up to deck fifteen and played a round of mini golf on their way to the fitness center and spa. Doug and Cody headed straight for the weight room while Allison and Sophia made their way to the spa lobby and sat down to study the menu of services.

"Right now, I could really go for a massage," Sophia said.

"Massages it is," Allison said, getting to her feet. "And pedicures, too, if we have time. The beach took a toll on my toenails."

After a couple of hours of being pummeled, kneaded, lotioned, and painted, Allison and Sophia stretched out on a pair of teak lounge chairs next to a gently trickling wall fountain with cucumber-infused waters in hand.

"Ahhh, I needed that," Sophia said with a satisfied sigh. "Thanks for springing for a spa morning."

"You're very welcome." Allison threw Sophia a quizzical look. "You seemed a little deflated at breakfast. Is everything all right?"

Sophia rubbed her fingertips over her eyelids. "Ugh! I'm not doing a real good job of hiding it, am I?"

"You listened to me yesterday, so I'm here for you now if you want to talk about it."

Sophia smiled gratefully at her. "I don't know where to begin. I'm still reeling from shock. Thinking back, I should have known something was wrong. Cody's been working round the clock for weeks on end now, always stressed out, drinking more than he should."

"Is it ... your marriage?" Allison asked in a delicate tone.

"No. That's not it." Sophia straightened up in her chair and poked at the floating cucumber in her water. "We're in trouble with the IRS. Turns out Cody hasn't been paying our taxes."

A small gasp escaped Allison's lips. An unpleasant tingling

traversed her spine as her shock turned inward. Was Doug in some kind of trouble with his business too? That angle hadn't even occurred to her last night. But how did the burner phone fit? Had he borrowed money from some shady operation? She shook her head free of the thought and turned her attention back to what Sophia was saying.

"Cody's always handled our finances. He has more of a head for numbers. But if I'd thought for one minute that he wasn't paying our taxes, I'd have jumped right back in. We worked together to build the business in the early years. I quit when I got pregnant with the twins. Anyway, all I've heard from him in the past two years is how well the business is doing. He tells all our friends we're killing it. Even his parents think we're raking in the money. And we are—we just haven't been paying taxes on it, apparently." She pressed her palms to her cheeks and groaned. "And I've been throwing money around like crazy on this trip—never suspecting for one minute that we couldn't afford it."

Allison was quiet for a moment. "That's why you hesitated when I asked if you wanted to go to the spa this morning."

Sophia nodded morosely. "I'm not sure how bad the situation is. But, judging by the amount of time Cody is spending on his laptop on this trip, I'm guessing things are falling apart."

"I'm so sorry. It must be a terrible shock to find out about it like this, in the middle of your vacation."

"It sucks, but enough about me," Sophia said with a sigh. "How are you doing?"

Allison rumpled her forehead. "Not great, to be honest."

Sophia set down her glass and gave Allison her full attention. "What's wrong?"

"I didn't leave the musical early because I was tired," Allison confessed. "The thing is, I wanted to search through Doug's things when he wasn't around."

Sophia lifted her brows. "What for?"

Allison gave an embarrassed laugh. "I know it sounds stupid, but I was looking for my missing pills."

Sophia rubbed her arms, looking increasingly uncomfortable.

"I know what you're thinking," Allison hastened to add. "That I just don't remember taking them."

"I ... don't know what to think," Sophia replied. After a minute, she added, "Did you ... find them?"

Allison shook her head. "No, but I found something else—a burner phone hidden in Doug's clothes."

The look in Sophia's eyes switched from guarded to one of alarm.

"It was password protected. I tried all sorts of combinations, but I couldn't crack it." Allison drew her knees up to her chest and hugged them. "I have no idea if Doug's doing drugs, or evading taxes, or having an affair, or something else entirely."

Sophia sucked in a breath, her face taut with apprehension. "Allison, there's something I need to tell you."

16

ALLISON

"I hate to have to tell you this, but my guess is that Doug's having an affair," Sophia said quietly.

Allison's jaw went slack. "How ... I mean ... did he say something to you and Cody?"

Sophia shook her head. "No. But last night, after the musical ended, we all went up to the Robo Bar for a nightcap. After we finished a round of drinks, we decided to call it a night. Doug went off to look for a restroom, while Cody and I headed for the elevator. I realized I'd dropped my new Chanel lipstick, so I went back to look for it." Her voice trailed off and she gave an apologetic shrug. "There's no easy way to tell you this. Doug was at the bar chatting with that blonde woman from the show, Misty Murano."

Allison's heart cranked up a beat in her chest. "Just chatting?"

"Yes, but it seemed a little too intimate, if you know what I mean."

"I ... think so," Allison stammered. "Did Doug see you?"

"Oh yeah," Sophia retorted. "I made sure of that. I walked right up to him, so he'd know he'd been busted."

Allison tightened the soft spa robe around her. "What did he say when he saw you? Did he explain himself?"

Sophia furrowed her brow. "Well, he did have an explanation, but … it's supposed to be a secret."

"A secret!" Allison choked out. "I don't understand. Please, just tell me what's going on!"

Sophia clenched her jaw. "If I do, you can't tell Doug I told you."

Allison wrung her hands. "Okay, I won't."

"He asked Misty Murano to dedicate a song to you in the Slow Vibes piano bar tonight—the song you danced to at your wedding." Sophia set down her water on the table between them. "Frankly, it looked to me like they were flirting. I may have misinterpreted everything, but based on the fact that you found that burner phone, my gut tells me Doug's a player."

Allison's eyelids twitched as she considered Sophia's words. She wasn't sure if she was on the verge of bursting into tears or a fit of rage. Aware that there were other guests within earshot, she fought to keep her voice under control. "I suspected him of having an affair months ago—all that traveling for work he was doing all of a sudden. But even then, I couldn't get mad at him. I didn't think I deserved him anymore. I was struggling with so much guilt over what happened to Ava."

"Maybe I shouldn't have said any—" Sophia began, but Allison cut her off.

"No, I'm glad you told me. If Doug is flirting with women behind my back on board the ship, then there's a good chance he is having an affair back home—probably with someone from work. I just have to figure out who it is. It's time for me to stop living in denial."

Sophia adjusted her position on the lounger. "Seems

neither of us knew our husbands as well as we thought we did."

"What are you going to do now?" Allison asked.

Sophia cocked her head to one side contemplatively. "Hard to say, when I don't know how bad things are. I could kill Cody for being this stupid. Right now, I can hardly look at him without wanting to choke him. He's risked everything—our livelihood, our future, our kids' futures. But I still love him—we were high school sweethearts. I don't want a divorce. And the boys need their father." She turned to Allison. "What about you? What's your next step?"

"I'm not sure. That's why I wanted to talk to you. You always seem to know what to do."

Sophia let out a mirthless laugh. "I always have an opinion on everyone else's problems. I just don't know what to do about my own."

"Do you think I should confront Doug?" Allison prodded.

Sophia gave an adamant shake of her head. "No—not yet, at least." She drummed her fingers on the arm of her lounger, a calculating look in her eyes. "I think we should give him enough rope to hang himself. The next time he sneaks off on his own to use the phone, one of us needs to follow him and try to listen in—maybe he'll say a name that you recognize."

They were silent for a moment and then Allison said, "You probably think I'm crazy for wondering if Doug was trying to kill me."

Sophia mumbled a grunt of acknowledgement. "I admit I did think you might have forgotten that you took the antidepressants. You seemed a little confused once or twice—you know, when you couldn't find us on the pool deck, for instance."

Allison stared down at the light reflecting off her freshly painted toenails. "Honestly, I'm not sure if Doug told me you were going to move to the other side, or not. He did mumble something to me before I went off to look for a restroom, but I didn't catch it—maybe that was his intention."

"So, you suspect he deliberately tried to make you look stupid," Sophia mused.

"I'm not sure," Allison conceded.

"What would be his end goal?"

"I have no idea. That's the part that baffles me."

"He acts as if he really cares about you."

"*Acts* being the operative word." Allison said. "Until I find out what he's hiding from me, I can't believe anything he says."

"Here's how we're going to get to the bottom of it," Sophia replied, the words flying from her lips as she became more animated. "From now on, don't give him an opportunity to be alone in the cabin without you. If he goes back to the room, you go with him. Force him to take the phone elsewhere if he wants to use it. That way one of us can follow him and try and listen in."

Allison pressed her chin to her knees in thought. "What if he goes into a restroom?"

Sophia let out a humph. "Good point. We're going to have to bring Cody in on this."

"Do you think he'll help us?"

"Absolutely! He doesn't have a choice, not with the kind of leverage I have on him now," Sophia shot back.

Allison's phone pinged with an incoming text, and she picked it up and read it. "It's Doug. They're done at the gym. They want us to meet them in the juice bar next door."

Sophia grabbed Allison's arm. "Remember, act normal. You can't let him know that you're on to him. Not until we know for sure what he's playing at."

Allison gave a dutiful nod and got to her feet.

Ten minutes later, they strolled into the Boost Juice Café.

"How was the spa?" Doug asked, kissing Allison on the cheek.

"Great!" she answered, trying not to flinch. "I had a super relaxing massage."

"Just what the doctor ordered," Sophia piped up, wriggling her shoulders appreciatively.

The barista smiled across the counter at them. "Can I help you, folks?"

"I think I'll try the Island Apple," Sophia answered, beaming back at her.

"And I'll have the Berry Oasis, please," Allison said.

"I'm going to go for a power smoothie and one of your homemade granola bars," Cody added.

Doug gave an approving nod. "Make that two."

When their drinks were ready, they carried them over to a corner table.

"I have a feeling I'm about to drink all the calories I just burned," Cody remarked, eying his power smoothie.

"Yikes!" Sophia exclaimed, pulling away from her straw. "This is sour!"

"Mine's good," Allison said.

"What do we want to do this afternoon?" Sophia asked, looking around at everyone.

Doug and Cody exchanged knowing grins.

"We were hoping we could talk you girls into a round of laser tag," Doug said sheepishly.

"You're kidding, right?" Sophia responded in a tone of mock outrage. "It's only going to be a bunch of kids in there."

Doug rumbled a laugh. "They let big kids in too."

"Let me check it out." Sophia pulled up the Bella Oceania app on her phone and opened the activities tab. "Hmm. It says here they don't allow open-toed shoes. I don't want to mess up my new pedicure."

"Your nails are bound to be dry by now," Cody said. "I'll run back up to the cabin and grab your tennis shoes."

"You're awfully quiet," Doug said, slipping an arm around Allison's shoulder. "Come on, it'll be fun—we came here to have fun, remember?" Without waiting for a response, he leaned over and kissed her softly on the lips.

A quiver of fear ran through her. She was taken aback by the unexpected show of affection, unable to reconcile it with the burner phone she'd found stashed in his socks.

"Are you in, Sophia?" Cody asked. "Guys against girls. Losers have to belly flop into the pool."

"In that case, we accept the challenge," Sophia responded with a mischievous grin, as she stirred the dregs of her juice. "So long as I get to post the video on Facebook."

EQUIPPED with sensor vests and laser guns, the two couples huddled with the other guests in the command center, a dark rectangular room with neon display units built into the walls. An attendant welcomed them and went over the rules. "No running, no jumping, no sliding. Keep both hands on your laser gun at all times. Now, please pay attention to our planetary portal for an important message."

All eyes turned to the screen as a disembodied head appeared. "Martians, Earthlings, welcome to the galaxy. You are here on a mission of great consequence that will change the course of our future. You have been provided with all appropriate inter-galactic equipment for your mission. Good luck and thank you for your service."

The screen faded to black and the attendant resumed his instructions, "Backs against the walls, recruits! If your vest has orange lasers, you are a Martian. Please move to the left. If your vest has blue lasers, you are an Earthling, step to the right."

"See you ladies on the battlefield," Cody said with a wink, as he and Doug joined the other Earthlings.

"Guess we're Martians," Allison said, glancing down at her vest.

The speaker overhead crackled to life and a voice boomed, "Ten, nine, eight—"

"Let's hope our pedicures hold up!" Sophia muttered to Allison.

"... two, one, commence battle!"

A door slid open and, all at once, they were released into a shadowy maze of tunnels, corners, obstacles, and windows. Allison instinctively took off running, before she caught herself. Slipping into an alcove, she hunkered down and took stock of her surroundings. All around her, pencil-thin beams of light were flashing in every direction. An Earthling ran by and she belatedly aimed her gun and shot at the retreating figure, missing the target on the blue vest entirely.

Suddenly, Allison spotted Sophia edging her way along the tunnel.

"Over here!" Allison yelled, waving frantically at her.

Sophia dashed over and took shelter beneath the window Allison was shooting through. "I need to catch my breath," she gasped. "This is more work than I thought it would be."

An electronic voice echoed through the arena, "Attention! Earthlings have taken the lead. I repeat, Earthlings have taken the lead."

Allison prodded Sophia with her foot. "Did you hear that? Get up! We've got work to do."

Sophia got to her feet with a groan. Side-by-side, they inched forward shooting at every blue vest that came within range.

"Before long, they spotted Cody in hot pursuit of a Martian. They trained their weapons on him, firing relentlessly until he fled around a corner.

"Have you seen Doug yet?" Allison asked.

"Don't think so," Sophia panted. "Hard to say. I'm too busy firing to be sure who I'm hitting in the dark."

"Congratulations Martians," the electronic voice echoed overhead, as the pulsing music began to fade. "The battle has now ended, and the intergalactic federation recognizes your victory."

"We won!" Sophia let out a jubilant shout, high-fiving Allison.

Out of nowhere, the attendant reappeared to lead them back to the command center. "Don't forget to check your scores on the way out."

Allison removed her vest and turned in her laser gun, before scanning the screen for her name.

"How'd you do?" Sophia asked.

"I sucked. 2960 points. You did all right. You clocked up 3490."

Allison scanned through the rest of the scores on the board. Cody had excelled scoring 3900 points in total. She frowned as her gaze settled on Doug's name at the very bottom of the scoreboard. How was it possible that he'd only scored a measly 100 points?

17

ALLISON

"You girls ready to get out of here?"

Allison swung around, startled, at the sound of Doug's voice as he walked across the laser tag command center toward her and Sophia. Her pulse fluttered with a strange sense of foreboding. "What ... what happened to you?"

He followed her gaze to the scoreboard. "Oh yeah, it sucks. Just my luck I got a defective vest. The attendant was very apologetic. Told me to come back any time and he'd let me go straight to the front of the line."

"I'd be up for another round," Cody said, joining them. "Turns out I love blasting Martians. That was the most fun I've had in ages."

Doug let out an appreciative guffaw as he reached for Allison's hand. "I thought we could go for an early dinner. I'm hungry after working out and skipping lunch."

Cody gave an approving grunt. "Works for me."

Allison caught Sophia throwing a quizzical look Doug's way. She had to be thinking the same thing as her—that Doug was lying about his vest being defective. The real reason he'd only clocked up 100 points, was that he hadn't been in the laser tag arena the entire time. Neither she nor Sophia had spotted him once during the battle. She desperately wanted to ask Cody if he'd seen Doug at all. But she'd have to get him alone first. Where had Doug gone, and why? Had he slipped out to use his burner phone? Or to meet someone?

"Let me see if I can get us an early dinner reservation at Wonderland," Cody said, pulling out his phone. "It's that place with the weird imaginative menu. Sophia's been ranting about wanting to try it."

"Oooh, yes! Let's do it!" she cried, eyes sparkling. "I watched a few reviews of it on YouTube. That place is insane. Smoke and explosions coming out of the food."

After Cody set them up with a five o'clock reservation, they returned to their cabins to shower up and change.

"You go first," Allison told Doug, throwing herself down on the bed. "I'm just going to rest for a few minutes."

"All right. Won't be long," Doug muttered, disappearing into the bathroom. Moments later, Allison heard the sound of water running.

She whipped out her phone and promptly messaged Sophia. *Pretty sure Doug was lying about the defective vest. He might have left to use the burner.*

A moment later, her phone pinged with a response. *Is it still in the drawer?*

Allison got up off the bed and quietly padded across the room. Slowly, she slid out the drawer containing Doug's socks and felt around them, even flattening them with her palms. She slid the drawer closed again and returned to the bed to text Sophia. *It's gone!*

Yikes! Guess you were right. Talk later. Cody's out of the shower.

Allison stared absently at the drawer, an uncomfortable

nagging at the back of her mind. She hadn't imagined the burner phone, had she? *No!* She'd held it in her hands. And it was definitely a phone and not some other gadget. Doug must have taken it with him when they left the cabin this morning. It had to be in the pocket of the shorts he was wearing. She glanced at the bathroom door. She could slip in under the pretext of grabbing her make up bag, and check Doug's shorts while he was in the shower.

Willing herself into action, she got to her feet and picked her way across the floor to the bathroom. Silently, she twisted the doorknob and pushed against the door, but it didn't budge. Gritting her teeth in frustration, she gently released the handle. Evidently, Doug wasn't taking any chances. The shower turned off abruptly, and she hurriedly retreated to the bed. She heard the sound of Doug whistling as he toweled off. Moments later, he emerged from the bathroom dressed for dinner.

"I have a surprise for my darling wife tonight," he said in a mysterious tone.

Allison forced her lips into a mildly curious smile, her insides churning. "Oh? What kind of a surprise?"

"Just a little something to celebrate our ten-year wedding anniversary," he answered, his smile deepening the hollows of his freshly shaved cheeks.

Allison arched a reproving brow. "You already gave me an expensive necklace."

Doug took her hand and pulled her to her feet. "This is different. It's more of a memory than a gift. Tonight is going to be a night you'll never forget." He brushed his lips against her forehead. "Now, go get cleaned up and wear something sexy."

. . .

WONDERLAND PROVED to be every bit the insane experience Sophia had predicted. From the mismatched chairs to the whimsical decor, and neon lighting, everything hinted at a trip through the looking glass.

"Check this menu out," Cody said when they sat down. "It's blank!"

"You have to paint it first and then the text appears," Sophia said, lifting the brush next to her menu and dipping it in a tiny container of water to demonstrate. "See? It's divided into elements; sun, fire, sea, earth—"

"Look at that!" Allison grabbed Sophia's arm and gestured to the next table.

A waiter lifted the dome off a dish and smoke wafted up from the nest-like creation resting on it.

"This place is unbelievable," Doug said. "It's like an edible chemistry lab."

"The cocktails look interesting too," Cody added, perusing the menu. "I could go for *Down a Rabbit Hole.*"

"The *Cheshire Cat Cosmo's* calling my name!" Sophia said.

"Here comes our waiter." Allison chuckled softly. "In full costume!"

They all turned and stared, jaws agape, at the elegantly attired Mad Hatter approaching their table. "Ladies, Gentlemen," he said, with an elaborate bow. "Welcome to Wonderland."

For the next few minutes, he patiently answered their questions and recommended some intriguing appetizers. When they arrived, artfully arranged in test tubes, and on jiggling spoons, Sophia let out a delighted gasp and immediately pulled out her phone and started snapping pictures. "These shots should generate some buzz," she raved. "*#QueenOfHeartsEatYourHeartOut.*"

Their waiter dutifully posed for a picture at Sophia's request, and then took their orders for the main course.

Sophia licked her spoon as they ended their meal with a white chocolate and pistachio mousse magical mushroom dessert. "Divine! I could eat like this every day for the rest of my life."

Doug leaned back in his chair and stretched his arms overhead. "Are you guys ready to get out of here? They have live music in Slow Vibes tonight if you're interested."

Sophia shot a knowing look Allison's way. "Sure, why not? Maybe I can talk Cody into slow dancing with me."

They made their way up to the piano bar and ordered a round of drinks before settling into a sunken leather seating area near to where the band was setting up. It wasn't long before Misty Murano appeared, dressed in a full-length sapphire gown, her blonde hair gleaming under the lights, diamanté hairpins glittering throughout.

Allison took a gulp of her Lemon Drop Martini, trying not to stare. The woman was breathtakingly beautiful. It wasn't just her flawless features; it was the air of vitality that radiated off her. The minute she started singing, the murmuring voices in the lounge stilled. Her rich, velvety tones drifted toward them like beckoning tendrils, a siren luring sailors to an unknown fate. She sang several sets to her captivated audience before grabbing the mic from the stand. "How's everyone doing this evening?"

A smattering of applause and appreciative whistles filled the air.

"Thank you, thank you, you're too kind—all of you," Misty said. "Now, I have a very special request tonight for a very special couple. They're here on *Diamond of the Waves* celebrating their ten-year wedding anniversary. How about that, folks?"

Sophia led the applause, stamping her feet, hooting and hollering.

Allison's cheeks simmered.

When the noise died down, Misty continued, "There's nothing I love more than a man who's a true romantic at heart. And, folks, we have one here tonight, Mr. Doug Robinson. He's requested that we perform *At last*, by Etta James—the song he danced to at his wedding with his beautiful bride, Allison. Ladies and gentlemen, give it up for Doug and Allison."

Allison shrank down in her seat, as thunderous applause filled the space. She felt her face flush even hotter as all eyes turned to look at her. Her stomach knotted, the alcohol swirling in her gut. It was the same insecurity that always reared its head when people stared too long, a feeling that they were weighing her and finding her wanting at her husband's side.

She was thankful when Misty finally began crooning, and the crowd fell silent, turning their attention back to the star in their midst.

All at once, Allison felt Doug's fingers squeezing her hand. "Let's dance," he whispered.

She froze. "No! Not here in front of everyone. I can't!"

"Of course you can." He leaned over and whispered in her ear. "I want everyone to see my beautiful Jackie O."

He tugged her gently to her feet. Several people around them clapped as they stepped out on the floor in front of the band and began to sway to the music.

"Try to relax," Doug said. "Pretend it's our wedding day all over again."

She managed a wan smile, letting him lead as Misty's sultry voice washed over them. *The night I looked at you.* Words that brought back so many memories. Allison's eyes misted over. In some ways, this wedding anniversary trip was everything she'd hoped it would be. If only she'd never stumbled on the stupid burner phone. She wished she could erase it from her mind, along with all of her suspicions and doubts about her husband. But she couldn't unsee what she'd seen. And he couldn't undo what he'd done—whatever that turned out to be.

When the song came to a close, Doug twirled her around and then swept her back and kissed her to the delight of the crowd. They clapped and oohed and aahed while the band made the most of the moment by belting out a few accompanying chords.

"Ladies and gentlemen, please give it up one more time for Doug and Allison," Misty crooned into the mic.

Allison's heart pounded as she and Doug made their way back to their seats.

"You two make such a stunning couple," Sophia gushed. "I was sobbing when you were dancing. It was so romantic, wasn't it, Cody?"

"Yes, it was," he said setting down his empty glass. "I'll get us some refills." He returned from the bar a few minutes later with another round of drinks.

Misty Murano sang a final song, and then thanked the band members before bidding everyone a good night and walking off the stage.

Doug grinned sheepishly at Allison. "Hope I didn't embarrass you too much."

"I was mortified. But it was a very romantic gesture. Thank you, honey."

"I propose a toast to another ten years," Doug said, raising his glass.

Allison reached for her drink with shaking fingers, accidentally knocking the glass into her lap. "Oh no!" she cried, jumping to her feet. "I'm such a klutz."

Doug grabbed a handful of napkins and attempted to blot the stain on her dress.

"I'm going to run up to the cabin and change," she said. "I don't want to sit in wet clothes all night."

"Want me to come with you?" Doug offered.

"No, you can get me another martini. I won't be long."

Safely ensconced in the elevator, Allison examined the unsightly stain on the only dress she'd brought for the trip. Maybe she could get it cleaned tomorrow. She'd have to call housekeeping and ask if they could pick it up.

As soon as the elevator doors opened, she dashed out and across the hallway to her cabin. She waved her key card at the lock, stepped inside, and let out a sigh of relief. The sooner she got out of her wet dress, the better.

"Hello Allison," a sultry voice behind her said.

18

ROB

Rob Benson arrived back at his office after making his rounds and sank into the creaky swivel chair in front of his computer desk. His fingers itched to log into the security camera in the corridor outside Misty's cabin and track her movements like he'd been doing obsessively for the past few weeks—on and off for months if he was being honest with himself. He knew it wasn't ethical, but it was becoming harder and harder to resist the pull. It was like she had the power to hijack his brain until she was all he could think of.

He was still struggling to interpret the look that had come over Misty's face when he'd told her a valuable necklace was missing from cabin 10664. It wasn't the fear he'd expected to see, which surprised him. Rather, her expression had teetered between shock and disbelief. Of course she'd denied stealing the necklace—denied even seeing it in the room. She wasn't fooling Rob though. He was certain she'd taken it, and then, for some inexplicable reason, returned it. The only question was why. He was eager to interview Brezina Novak to hear if her story matched Misty's, but, inconveniently for him, she'd come down with the flu and was confined to her cabin.

With an exasperated breath, he pulled the keyboard toward him and logged into the security system. He couldn't stand it any longer. It was eating him alive. He needed the rush of relief that came with knowing exactly what Misty had been up to over the last few hours. His fingers flew over the keys as he pulled up the CCTV footage and scanned through the images of various crew members walking up and down the corridor past her cabin earlier that evening. He fast-forwarded through the footage until he spotted Misty leaving her room, blonde hair trailing over her shoulders, contrasting with the deep sapphire of her evening dress. He hit pause, studying her exquisite profile, drinking her in like a man who'd been deprived of water for days on end. She had the power to knock the breath from his lungs every time he set eyes on her. She was a vision he yearned to wake up to every day of his life.

Rob rubbed his jaw in contemplation. He would never give up on that dream. He and Misty belonged together. He took a quick screen shot of her and added it to the hundreds of others he'd amassed in a private folder on his computer, before restarting the video. He switched cameras and watched her perform in the Slow Vibes lounge, quickly losing all track of time. Even without sound, she was mesmerizing. James Taylor had said it best—*Something in the way she moves.* She was a disruptive force that he craved more than any drug. He glanced at the clock on the wall. He didn't have all night. Dave would be back soon. He needed to find out if she'd met up with anyone later on this evening.

He skipped through the footage of the remainder of the performance and watched as she exchanged a few words with Dimitri before leaving the stage. After checking the timestamp, Rob switched his screen over to the camera in the corridor outside Misty's cabin. It was one of his favorite times to observe her. It felt so intimate watching her return to her cabin each night. The only thing better would be if he could be there to greet her. But, for now, she was holding him at bay. He tapped impatiently on his desk as he waited for her image to appear on the screen.

"Hurry up, Misty! It's just you and me now," he whispered to the empty hallway. He frowned to himself as he fast-forwarded through the footage looking for any sign of her returning to her cabin. Biting back his frustration, he panned to the camera in the lounge area once more. Maybe she'd stopped off somewhere else after she'd left Slow Vibes. Surely, she wouldn't have gone to the crew bar. Unless she was meeting someone there. His heart begin to pound as a sense of urgency washed over him—a burning need to find out if Misty had betrayed him.

Frantically, he scanned through the images again until he came upon the clip of her saying good night to Dimitri. After that, he tracked her to the elevator. Beads of sweat pricked at his hairline. It was impossible to know which deck she would get out at. He began at the bottom and worked his way up. A chill passed over him when she exited the elevator on deck ten. Was she planning on stealing Allison Robinson's necklace again? What was she thinking?

Gritting his teeth, Rob made full use of the three-hundred-and-sixty-degree camera in the hallway to keep tabs on Misty's movements. She walked slowly down it in one direction and then turned and came back the same way. For some reason, she kept peering at the elevator, but made no attempt to approach any of the guest cabins. An elderly couple walked by, and she ducked her head, pretending to be engrossed in something on her phone. As soon as they disappeared around the corner, she resumed her sentry duties.

Rob shook his head in bewilderment. *What are you up to,*

Misty? Are you waiting on someone? And then a disturbing thought struck him. Was it possible she was having a fling with a passenger? He let out an infuriated snarl, fisting his hands on the desk in front of him. Had she lost her mind? If she were caught, even he couldn't dig her out of that mess. A feeling of helplessness gripped him like a vise. It was a worse scenario than the idea that she was cavorting with another crew member. He could easily find a way to take revenge on a Bella Oceania employee, and ultimately get them thrown off the ship. But a passenger was another issue entirely. Guests had full immunity.

All at once, the elevator doors opened. Rob glanced briefly at the woman who exited, and then took a second look. His mouth fell open. *Allison Robinson.* She hurried over to her cabin, waved her key pass at the door, and stepped inside. Quick as a whip, Misty slipped in after her and closed the door behind them.

Rob stared mutely at the screen in shock. What had he just witnessed? Blistering fear rippled over his skin. This might have been his doing. He had lied to Misty and told her the necklace was still missing. What if she intended to confront Allison about it? This could turn ugly. With shaking fingers, he rewound the footage to see if he could pick up anything in Misty's body language that hinted at her intentions. The only thing that was apparent was that she was bound and determined to get inside that state room before the door closed.

Rob squeezed his jaw, his chaotic thoughts tumbling around in his brain. Watching Misty on the CCTV over the past few months had been a soothing indulgence, one that allowed him to feel in control of the woman he loved. But now it felt as though she was slipping through his fingers. Keeping secrets from him, pushing him away, lying to him. Rob advanced the footage again until he caught a glimpse of her exiting the Robinsons' cabin. She peered up and down the corridor, before quietly closing the door behind her, a somber expression on her face. Rob frowned at the screen, his mind going back to his earlier suspicion. Had she come back for the necklace? She didn't look like she'd been in a scuffle with Allison—she certainly wasn't disheveled in any way. Maybe Allison had given the necklace to her. Was it possible Misty was involved in some kind of scam—scheming with the Robinsons to rip off the insurance company?

Rob tapped his fingers restlessly on the desk in front of him. He zoomed in on Misty's flawless features until her face filled the screen. *What are you playing at, my love? Whatever it is, you need to let me help you.* He got up and paced back and forth, hands on his head, almost jumping out of his skin when Dave burst through the door.

"You're never gonna believe what happened—"

Dave broke off, staring at the enlarged image of Misty on Rob's screen. He shook his head in disgust. "You've got to be kidding me. How long have you been ogling her this time?"

Rob quickly logged out of the security program before settling back down in his chair. "It's none of your business."

Dave perched on the edge of the desk with a humph. "It's my business when it affects security on the ship. You've crossed so many ethical boundaries, I should have turned you in a long time ago. Look man, I'm only trying to get you to see sense here—you need to get your act together. What you're doing is illegal. You don't need me to tell you that. More to the point, it's downright creepy." He motioned to Rob's monitor. "Does Misty know you watch her all the time?"

"I don't watch her all the time," Rob snapped back. "I was checking a security issue at Slow Vibes and I happened to come across her performing."

"Oh yeah?" Dave threw him a skeptical look. "What kind of security issue?"

Rob gave a dismissive wave of his hand. "Just an unruly passenger."

Dave scratched his scalp. When he spoke again, his voice softened. "There's no easy way to tell you this, Rob, but Misty's been trying to let you down gently for weeks. You're simply not getting the hint. She's done with you, man. Get over it. What did you expect? A woman like that's not gonna settle down with a guy like you or me."

Rob skewered him with a glare, anger roiling up from his gut. He had a sudden impulse to lift his monitor and smash it over Dave's head. The man was spitting on his dreams, ripping up the script of the life he'd written for himself and Misty. "Don't come in here and unload your jealousy on me!" Rob growled. "You're just like every other red-blooded male on this ship. You're jealous because Misty picked me. You can't stand the thought of that because you want her for yourself and—"

"Stop it, Rob! Listen to yourself. You're falling apart. You've got to let this go. Move on. She's not the only woman out there."

"She's the only woman for me."

Dave made an incoherent sound before getting to his feet. "You're gonna leave me no choice. If you don't knock this off, I'm reporting you. It's for your own good. If you can't help yourself, then you need an intervention."

Seething inwardly, Rob took a step toward Dave and scowled in his face. "If you cause any trouble for me, I won't hesitate to return the favor."

Dave narrowed his eyes at him. "What are you talking about?"

"That little fling you had with a passenger last year, or have you forgotten about it?"

Dave let out a snort. "She didn't file a complaint."

"She doesn't have to," Rob replied, calmly. "All it would take is for me to produce the footage of you two tumbling into her cabin with your lips locked on hers."

Dave opened his mouth, an uncertain look flickering across his face. "You don't … you didn't …"

A contemptuous smile curled across Rob's lips. "Yes, I kept a copy of the tape."

19

ROB

"You're lying!" Dave yelled. He lunged at Rob, but he sprang to his feet and dodged him.

"I knew the day might come when I'd need some dirt on you," Rob hissed. "I won't let you or anyone else come between me and Misty."

Before Dave could respond, their radios crackled to life and the patrol security guard came on the line. "Patrol to base, do you copy?"

Rob unclipped his radio and depressed the talk button. "This is Charlie one, go ahead."

"We have a code alpha on the esplanade."

"Roger that. On our way."

Rob met Dave's brooding glare. "Our conversation here is over. As in it never happened."

Dave clamped his jaw shut before following him out of the office.

DOWN ON THE ESPLANADE, Rob and Dave worked to set up a cordon and clear the area of onlookers while the doctor and nurse on call stabilized a passenger who'd collapsed and removed him below deck to the infirmary. Rob wasn't optimistic about the man's chances. His pallor suggested a possible heart attack. The doctor had already dosed him with nitroglycerin, but there was nothing much else they could do, other than hook him up to an IV and monitor his oxygen, until they reached Mexico in a few more hours.

Rob threw a furtive glance after Dave as he strode off to respond to another call on the pool deck. He was confident Dave would keep his mouth shut—he needed this job too much to risk jeopardizing it. Two years earlier, his ex-wife had walked away with everything, including their two kids.

Once Dave was safely out of sight, Rob made his way to Misty's cabin. It was late and there was a chance she would be asleep, but he would use his master key to gain entry if he had to. This couldn't wait any longer. It was eating him up inside. He needed to know what business Misty had with Allison Robinson.

Outside Misty's cabin, Rob removed his cap and smoothed a hand over his hair. His heart constricted in his chest—the way it always did right before he set eyes on her. That hypnotic rush of anticipation that he was powerless to control. He dragged in a deep breath, then raised his hand and rapped on the door four times, waited a moment, and then rapped again four more times. Misty had been the one to come up with their special signal.

Four quarter beats to a bar. Common time. Methodical and steady. That's how I'll know it's you—get it?

He hadn't got it until she'd explained it to him—Rob knew nothing about music. At first, he'd been worried she was laughing at him. But she'd assured him it was a compliment—that she considered him to be her rock, dependable and steady, her loyal knight.

But that was then. There was no guarantee she would

open the door to him tonight. After everything that had transpired between them over the course of the last few days, no amount of quarter note knocking on her door was likely to sway her. He was fishing his key card out of his pocket when the door suddenly swung open. Misty arranged herself artfully in the door frame, still dressed in her sapphire gown, her eyes traveling unabashedly over him. "Officer Benson, I was just about to call security about the racket, but it looks like security has come to call on me. To what do I owe the pleasure of this late-night welfare check? Or am I in trouble again?" Her lips parted in an impish grin, and Rob's stomach flipped. She was back to the Misty he loved, bantering with him in a way that drove him wild.

He cleared his throat. "Can we talk?"

Her perfectly penciled brows rose a fraction. "I thought that's what we were doing. Color me dumb, but your lips are moving, Officer."

Rob gestured over her shoulder. "Can we do this inside?"

Misty gave an indifferent shrug, her skirts rustling as she spun around. Rob followed her into the cabin and closed the door behind him. Misty perched on the edge of her bed, gesturing to the desk chair opposite her.

"You seem tense. You're not still mad at me for wanting a little space, are you?" she asked, batting her heavily-coated lashes at him.

Rob blinked, momentarily losing his train of thought. "No. Actually, yes—but that's not what I'm here about."

"Well, that clears everything up." Misty chuckled softly. "Is this an official visit? Please tell me it's not the case of the missing necklace again. I told you I didn't take it."

Rob interlaced his fingers in front of him and tried to imagine he was sitting at his desk conducting a formal interview. He needed Misty to come clean with him, and if he wasn't able to cajole her into it, he would have to resort to other tactics—namely, shock and awe. "Why did you follow Allison Robinson into her cabin this evening?"

A flash of fear lit up Misty's eyes, but she quickly extinguished it. "Are you tracking my movements now? I'm not sure whether to be flattered or insulted."

"I know you took that necklace. It's time you told me what's going on."

Misty let out a gasp of mock outrage. "Are you accusing me of stealing from our guests?" She pulled her lips into a playful pout. "You know what your problem is, you've been at sea too long. I'm not Jack Dawson chasing after the Heart of the Ocean."

"Don't play games with me, Misty," Rob replied, a familiar heat creeping up the back of his neck. He was never entirely sure when she was laughing at him, and when she was trying to seduce him. It was a line she crossed so smoothly it left him spinning. Tonight, he needed to assert control. "You know I could turn you over to the port authorities in Mexico," he added in a somber tone. "I want to help you, but first you need to explain to me what you were doing in cabin 10664."

Misty kicked off her high heels and leaned back on the bed on her elbows, eying him with a hint of amusement. "I wanted to talk with Allison Robinson, woman-to-woman, to explain why I stepped in as cabin steward the evening her necklace went missing. I knew she would be understanding when I told her about Brezina and her fiancé. As for her necklace, I told her exactly what I told you—I never set eyes on it."

Misty sat up and dangled her long legs over the edge of the bed. "The funny thing is, she told me her necklace had shown back up." Misty's molten gaze bored into Rob. "But you already know that, don't you? Is that what you really came here to tell me?"

Rob blinked rapidly, his brain unable to string together a coherent thought. "I, uh …"

"You know, I've been thinking." Misty traced a finger slowly over her bottom lip. "Brezina could have set me up. She might have stolen the necklace and then asked me to clean the room to cover her tracks."

"But you just said it showed back up," Rob replied.

"Perhaps she was scared of getting caught with something so valuable and decided to return it." Misty smiled mischievously at Rob. "I guess we'll never know for sure. But I've learned my lesson. I won't be covering for a crew member ever again." She tilted her head at him in that maddeningly seductive way of hers and held out her wrists. "If you're going to arrest me, please be gentle. Or we could always kiss and make up."

Swallowing back the last of his pride, Rob reached for her and pulled her into his lap, kissing her hungrily. His brain was blaring a warning that there was something wrong with this picture. Why was she kissing him so readily after telling him she needed her space? He let the question slide into oblivion. He didn't care anymore if she was manipulating him. It was better than losing her—anything was better than losing Misty. The only thing that mattered was that she was back in his arms. And this time he wouldn't let her go.

20

SOPHIA

Sophia yawned as she reached for her phone. 7:15 a.m. The ship was probably already docked at Cozumel. They hadn't yet made any arrangements to meet up with Doug and Allison after their late night in *Slow Vibes*. After going back up to her cabin to change out of her wet clothes, Allison had texted Doug to say she was tired and had decided to turn in after all. The rest of them had enjoyed another round of drinks before calling it a night.

Deep down, Sophia wasn't sure what to make of Allison. Had she really been too tired to come back down to the bar last night, or had she wanted to search through Doug's things again? She came across as coherent and intelligent most of the time, but then she turned around and did some pretty absent-minded things, which seemed to suggest she might be abusing her prescription medication.

The whole thing about the burner phone was peculiar, but then again, did it even exist? Allison had insisted it was there one minute and gone the next—just like the necklace. Was she simply looking for attention? She had admitted to attempting suicide once before. Maybe she'd tried it again at Labadee.

Sophia's mind flitted back to the conversation she'd had with Allison about her baby. Suffering a miscarriage was one thing, but accidentally suffocating your child would be an awful thing to have to live with—*if*, that was, in fact, what had happened.

Maybe Allison had fabricated the whole story because it garnered more attention than a miscarriage. Sophia rubbed her eyelids and stretched. She wasn't going to be able to resolve any of this in the final forty-eight hours of their cruise. She had her own problems to go home to as it turned out.

She prodded Cody gently with her elbow. "Do you want to jump in the shower? We should make the most of our last shore excursion."

"You go first," he mumbled. "I need a few more minutes."

As Sophia stood beneath the steaming water, her thoughts drifted away from Cozumel, Mexico, and back to Fort Lauderdale, Florida, where they would soon return to reality with a crash landing. Not the reality they had left—one in which she and Cody had been successful business owners, able to afford the kind of vacations their parents could only ever have dreamed of. Their new reality involved a lot of uncertainty, and would necessitate a whole lot of paring back, and a heavy dose of reassessing their priorities. She tried to quash the unsettling thought that they might even have to sell their house. They'd only just finished remodeling the kitchen—the dream kitchen she'd waited a decade for. Sophia grimaced as she turned off the water and stepped out of the shower. Bankruptcy wasn't out of the question, either. She had no idea how much they owed the IRS, and she'd been too afraid to ask. Cody hadn't thrown out any numbers—maybe he didn't know for sure himself.

Dread curled in her stomach when she pictured the boys' reactions. She couldn't tell them what was really going on. They wouldn't understand anyway, and she didn't want them repeating anything to their friends who would only turn around and ask their parents what the IRS was—instantly igniting the gossip chain. But, beyond that, she didn't want to throw Cody under the bus. Gavin and Will worshipped their father, and he adored them too. She wasn't willing to let anything tarnish that relationship. She would have to come up with some other reason for why their business had taken a sudden downturn, and they could no longer afford everything the boys set their hearts on.

She pinched the bridge of her nose, forcing herself to refocus on the day ahead. Nothing could be done about the situation until they got home and started crunching numbers in earnest with their lawyer and accountant. Today was already paid for. She might as well enjoy it. She'd always been an optimist. They would get through this, somehow or other. It was just another problem to be tackled and resolved, and she was good at getting her arms around problems. She'd always gone about things with gusto, and it had served her well in life so far. Her biggest mistake had been taking a back seat from the business after the twins were born. She shouldn't have handed the reins over to Cody entirely, never questioning anything as long as the money kept flowing. She dried off and hung her towel on the rack, before peering at her lightly tanned reflection in the mirror. She resolved not to waste the day beating up on Cody. The remonstrations could wait.

After combing her hair, and dressing in denim shorts and a white ribbed tank top, Sophia exited the bathroom. "Your turn!" she called to Cody. "Let's get moving. You can laze about tomorrow while we're cruising back to Fort Lauderdale."

Cody groaned as he rolled out of bed. "Did I ever tell you you're way too cheerful in the mornings?"

Sophia cupped her chin in her hands and pretended to think about it. "Not since yesterday."

He shook his head as he yawned and tripped his way into the bathroom.

After grabbing a water bottle, Sophia wandered out to the balcony to let her hair dry in the morning sun. She sat down in a deck chair and sucked in a lungful of fresh air, watching the activity on the International Pier where they had docked. Supposedly, they were only a five-minute taxi ride from downtown San Miguel where all the good shopping was. Sophia smoothed a hand over her damp hair. Not a good idea in light of their current situation. Her designer shopping days were over. They would have to stick to something more budget friendly. In fact, she should probably return the Kate Spade bag she'd bought earlier in the week. She pulled out her phone and sent off a quick text to Allison.

Want to meet for lattes and make some plans for the day?

Several minutes went by before Allison responded. Sophia hoped she hadn't woken her up after their late night.

Doug and I are going to spend the day by ourselves. Need a chance to talk. Let's hang out again tomorrow.

Sophia quickly tapped out a response. *Catch you then. Have fun!*

She hit send and then re-read the message, wishing she'd thought to ask Allison if she'd confronted Doug about the burner phone. She thought about sending a follow-up message but decided against it. It could wait until tomorrow. Maybe by then Allison would have some answers.

Sophia sank back in the deck chair and closed her eyes. All things considered, it was a good thing that she and Cody would get to spend some time alone too. He needed to know that she wasn't going anywhere, no matter how dire their situation turned out to be. Mad as she was at him for what he'd done, or hadn't done as it turned out, she still loved him. They'd been together ever since they'd met at a football game on her sixteenth birthday, and she wasn't about to give up on the memories they'd built, and those they had yet to make.

When Cody emerged from the shower a few minutes later, she surprised him by wrapping him up in her arms and squeezing him tightly. "We're going to have the most fantastic day ever. Doug and Allison are off doing their own thing today. So we get to pick whatever we want to do. How about we start with coffee and a breakfast bagel. Then we can sit and talk about our options for our day on Cozumel."

"Sleeping on the beach is about my speed," Cody said.

Sophia jabbed his arm playfully. "You just need some caffeine in your system. Let's get out of here. I'm starving."

After standing in line at the Park Café, and whittling down their selections to bagels and cappuccinos, they took their order over to an empty table in the patio area.

Sophia bit into her apricot cream cheese bagel and let out a satisfied sigh. "How come I never knew about the existence of apricot cream cheese before this cruise?"

Cody gave a hollow laugh. "Don't get too used to it. It will be a pared down version of life as we knew it once we get back home. No more eating out."

Sophia swallowed a mouthful of bagel and washed it down with a sip of coffee before asking, "How bad is it? Do you know how much we owe the IRS?"

"Shush!" Cody darted a discomfited look around them. "Keep your voice down."

Sophia reached for her napkin. "Nobody knows us here."

"It's embarrassing, that's all."

"So why did you let it get to this point?"

Cody gave a helpless shrug. "It was like a runaway train. I didn't know how to stop it. The kitchen remodel was almost double what we planned. You wanted the boys to go to private school. The credit card bills kept mounting each month."

Sophia threw him a look of reproach. "You should have told me. If I'd known, I would have cut up the credit cards and thrown them away."

Cody dropped his gaze. "I felt like a failure. I didn't want you to know. I wanted you to keep enjoying the life we had. You deserve it, Soph. You built that business up with me."

She reached across the table and squeezed his hand. "All the more reason for you to share with me what was going on. That's why you've been drinking so much lately, isn't it? You've been trying to carry the burden of it all on your own."

He blinked, looking across at her with glistening eyes.

"Let's not talk about it anymore today," Sophia said resolutely. "Today is all about relaxing and having fun. In a budget-conscious way, of course."

Cody picked up his cup and drained the last of his cappuccino. "Do you need to go back to the cabin for anything?"

"No. I brought my beach bag with me," she replied.

Hand-in-hand, they strolled to the elevator and headed downstairs to line up with the other passengers disembarking for the day.

"Look! There's Doug and Allison up ahead," Sophia said pointing to the front of the line.

"Where?" Cody asked, scouring the crowd.

"Behind the couple in the matching Hawaiian shirts. Doug's in a blue short-sleeved polo shirt and Allison's next to him in the wide-brimmed hat and Jackie O sunglasses."

"Allison!" she yelled, waving exuberantly.

Doug spun around at the sound of her voice, searching through the sea of faces until he spotted her. He gave a tight smile and waved back before nudging Allison. She muttered something to him and then turned and gave a perfunctory wave as Doug scanned their key cards at the check-out booth.

"If we hurry, we can catch up with them," Cody said, as the line moved forward.

Sophia shook her head, watching Doug and Allison disappear down the pier. "No. They didn't seem overly excited to see us. We shouldn't impose. They wanted a day to themselves, so let's give it to them."

21

SOPHIA

"So, what do you fancy doing?" Sophia asked as she and Cody strolled past the stores and restaurants in the Bella Oceania section of the International Pier at Cozumel. "We could go exploring, visit some Mayan ruins."

"You hate history," Cody said, throwing her a sidelong grin. "I can't picture you picking your way through crumbling ruins listening to a guide jabbering on about Mayan culture for hours on end."

Sophia pulled a face. "True. Not really my thing. *#OhLook-AnotherRock*."

Cody let out a bark of laughter. "That's what I love about you. Even on the worst days, you always make me smile."

"And we're going to keep smiling." She tugged on his hand, gesturing to some colorful signs advertising snorkel boat tours. "How about we go snorkeling today? I brought the GoPro. That way we can still get some beach time in afterward."

"I could go for that," Cody answered. "Let's check it out."

After browsing through the tours on offer, they settled on

an economical two-hour coral reef snorkeling trip in a glass bottom boat.

"All your equipment, chilled beers, sodas, and waters are included," the woman processing their credit card payment rambled off. "We depart in thirty minutes from dock six. Next in line, please."

Cody and Sophia found a bench in the shade where they sat down to wait for their tour to begin.

"I wonder what Doug and Allison are up to today," Sophia mused.

"It would be funny if we bumped into them snorkeling at one of the reefs," Cody said.

"I'm still trying to figure out what's going on with those two."

"They wanted a day to themselves—that's all. No harm in that."

Sophia picked at her fingers. She was itching to get Cody's take on what Allison had revealed about how her baby died, but she restrained herself, settling instead for the burner phone. "Allison told me she found a second phone hidden beneath Doug's clothes in the cabin."

Cody frowned. "Did she ask him what it was for?"

Sophia shook her head. "She thinks he might be having an affair—someone at work. Apparently, he's been working away from home a lot. He seems very attentive to Allison, but maybe that's all for show. He could be a player. Let's face it, he's easy on the eyes. I could have sworn he was flirting with Misty the other night in the Robo Bar, but then when I saw how loving he was toward Allison in front of Misty while she was singing their song, I started second-guessing myself. I began to think maybe Allison was the one with the problems. You know, spacing out, losing her necklace, the missing pills, passing out on the beach—that was odd, and scary."

Cody scratched the back of his neck. "Now that you mention it, she asked me for some of my sleeping pills yesterday. She said she was having trouble falling asleep because it was the first time she hadn't slept in her own bed since the miscarriage."

Sophia stifled a gasp. "Please tell me you didn't give her any."

Cody spread his hands in a gesture of helplessness. "Of course I did. What was I supposed to do?"

"Use your head, for starters! She might be an addict in denial. How many did you give her?"

"A handful. I didn't count them."

Sophia pressed her fingertips to her scalp. "I can't believe you did that after what happened on the beach the other day. If she tries to drown herself again, you could be held responsible."

Cody widened his eyes. "You don't seriously think she tried to kill herself, do you?"

"I don't know." Sophia groaned. "Now I'm going to be worrying about her all day instead of enjoying myself with you."

Cody put an arm round her and squeezed her shoulder. "I'm sure she'll be fine, Soph. Doug's with her. He won't let anything happen to her."

Sophia pulled her lips into a grimace. What if Allison was right and Doug was trying to kill her? Her heart began to thump in her chest. Had it been his idea for them to spend the day alone? She should have texted Allison and made sure she was really okay instead of responding with a flippant text telling her to have fun.

"Back to the burner phone," Cody said, interrupting her thoughts. "It could simply be a backup Doug has for work or something."

"So why hide it from Allison?"

Cody shrugged. "I don't know. You've only her word for it that he was trying to hide it from her. Like you say, she's been a bit scatty at times. Maybe he mentioned it to her, and she forgot."

Sophia gave a vague nod. "Regardless, I promised her I'd help her get to the bottom of it. We can't do anything about it today, but we have a plan for tomorrow. We're going to follow Doug if he takes off on his own again." She locked eyes with Cody. "We'll need your help if he goes into a restroom."

Cody raised his hands in protest. "No! I'm not getting involved in surveilling Doug. If Allison wants to know what he's doing with a burner phone, all she has to do is ask him."

"The problem is, it's disappeared. It's not in the drawer anymore. He could just deny it exists."

"Right. Here we go again," Cody said in a skeptical tone. "Now you see it, now you don't. Look, Soph, I like Allison and all, but some women get a little crazy after they lose a baby. Maybe you shouldn't take everything she says at face value."

"There's a chance she might just be looking for attention," Sophia admitted. "But my gut tells me there's more to it than that. I don't think she made up the burner phone—she seemed genuinely cut up about finding it. And who has a burner phone for their business? Maybe an illicit business—like drugs or something."

"So Allison's an addict and Doug's hawking drugs. We really know how to pick them." Cody glanced at his phone. "Time for us to head over to the dock. Let's drop this for now. The plan was to forget our problems and focus on having fun together today."

After connecting with the rest of their tour group and listening to the safety speech, they removed their shoes and climbed aboard the glass bottom boat.

A shiver of excitement passed over Sophia's shoulders as

they settled into their seats. She gripped Cody's knee and beamed at him. "I've always wanted to go snorkeling."

Out on the water, Cody and Sophia kicked back with ice cold beers. En route to the reef, their guide handed out optional float packs to put around their waists, as well as snorkels, masks, and flippers, and patiently explained how the equipment worked.

"I hope I see a giant sea turtle," Sophia said to Cody, as she slathered on more sunscreen.

"What if you see a shark?"

"Yikes! That would be an Instagrammable moment."

"I thought you posted on Facebook," Cody said.

Sophia quirked a grin at him. "I do, but a Facebookable moment doesn't sound right."

At the reef, a crew member helped Sophia down the ladder into the clear turquoise water, and she swam off into an unknown world of exotic colors and shapes she had never even imagined could exist, everything from starfish to stingrays, reef sharks, and more than one giant turtle. She snapped one picture after another with her GoPro, as shoals of exotic fish streamed past from every direction, some tiny gray specks, others puffy-lipped giant clowns of color.

"That was the best thing we've done this entire cruise," Sophia declared, when they finally resurfaced and climbed back into the boat. She snapped a quick picture of Cody with his mask on. "That's a good one. *#MyMaskedMan #Snorkeling-InParadise.*"

"The boys would love this," Cody said, taking off his float vest. "I wish we could take them. I've screwed everything up."

"We will take them, one day." Sophia flashed him an encouraging smile. "That will be our goal. We'll commit to digging ourselves out of this hole and building the business back up, stronger than ever. I'll get back on board with the day-to-day operations and throw my weight behind it too."

She leaned over and gave Cody a salty kiss. "Don't worry, we can pull the emergency brake on this runaway train. We can fix it."

"I'm a lucky guy to have you, Soph," Cody said. "Spending time alone with you today was a good reminder of how much you mean to me, and how much fun you are. I hope Doug and Allison are having half as good a time as we are."

Sophia gazed out over the ocean, that niggling feeling of unease at the back of her brain returning with a vengeance. She wasn't sure a fun day on Cozumel was what Doug and Allison had in mind at all.

22

SOPHIA

Sunkissed and bone weary after their day on Cozumel, Sophia and Cody wound their way back to the International Pier where *Diamond of the Waves* was docked.

"What do you want to do for dinner tonight?" Cody asked. "We haven't tried Trattoria del Mare yet—it's right opposite that place we ate breakfast. I'm in the mood for some good pasta."

"Sounds good to me." Sophia hesitated, and then added, "There's a cover charge though. We could just go to the main dining hall instead."

"No. This is our last chance to dine alone. We'll likely end up eating dinner with Doug and Allison again tomorrow. Let's make it special tonight. Besides, the cover charge isn't going to move the needle one way or another."

"All right," Sophia agreed. "I'll text Allison when we get back to the cabin and find out how their day went. You never know, they might want to join us."

"Are you sure that's a good idea?" Cody countered. "Like you said, they weren't too thrilled to see us this morning."

Sophia flapped a hand dismissively at him. "They were probably afraid we were going to attach ourselves to them for the day. Now that they've had some time alone, they might like to get together and regale us with their adventures on Cozumel. No harm in asking."

Cody looked unconvinced as they waved their key passes at the check-in booth and boarded the ship. "Don't push it if they turn you down. There's always tomorrow."

"Are you suggesting I'm pushy?" Sophia laughed, poking him playfully in the ribs. "Don't worry, I'll keep it casual."

While Cody was in the shower rinsing off the salt and sand from their day in the sun, Sophia scrolled through the pictures she'd taken on Cozumel. She smiled to herself when she came to a picture their guide had taken of her and Cody kissing in their snorkeling get-up. Sophia loved everything about the photo—the luminous turquoise water in the background, the brightly-colored masks, the pristine white boat, the pastel blue sky, but mostly the goofy grins on their faces. It reminded her of their carefree high school years when every day was a grand adventure, unencumbered by obligations or responsibilities of any significance. Sophia selected the photo and uploaded it to Facebook, adding the hashtags, *#DorksSnorkelToo #BestDayEver.* On a whim, she pulled up Allison's Facebook page to see if she had uploaded any pictures of their day on Cozumel, but there were no new posts.

Sophia chewed on her lip, pondering whether or not to text her. Maybe Cody was right, and she shouldn't press them to join them for dinner. It was simply her nature to want to connect. Besides, it was more fun going to dinner as a group. It wouldn't hurt to shoot Allison a quick text and ask about her day. She would decide what to do about dinner after that, based on Allison's response.

How was your day? We went snorkeling. I think I missed my calling. I was born for eighty-degree water!

She waited a few minutes but there was no response. Cody came out of the bathroom, rubbing his hair with a towel. "I'm all done. Your turn."

Freshly showered and dressed for dinner, Sophia and Cody took the elevator down to deck eight where Trattoria del Mare was located.

"Do you want to eat inside or outside?" Cody asked.

Sophia cast an eye over the outdoor seating area, an assortment of wooden tables with industrial-style metal chairs. "Inside. The seating out here doesn't look all that comfortable."

As soon as they stepped into the restaurant, Sophia knew she'd made the right choice. The appointments were upscale, and recessed lighting added to the romantic ambience. Nestled in leather club chairs at a table for two, they nibbled on buttermilk buns with garlic butter while they waited for their main course to arrive.

"These are to die for!" Sophia raved. "They melt in your mouth."

"They're too good. Get them away from me," Cody said, pushing the bread bowl out of reach. "I'm going to be full before our food gets here."

"Those alcoves with the murals are spectacular," Sophia said. "And look at all those cheeses hanging around the chalkboard. I feel like I'm in some Italian matriarch's kitchen waiting on some good old-fashioned home cooking."

"Stop!" Cody protested. "You're making my mouth water."

Sophia reached for her wine glass while glancing at her phone on the table.

"Now you're the one who's obsessed. Can't you put that thing away for an hour?" Cody said. "I haven't gone near mine all day, in case you hadn't noticed."

"I was just checking to see if there were any messages."

"From the boys?"

Sophia shrugged.

Cody directed a knowing look at her. "From Allison? I take it she hasn't got back with you yet?"

Sophia shook her head. "I hope she's not ticked off at me for texting. I didn't mention dinner. I only asked how their day went." Sophia took a sip of her wine. She didn't add that she was hoping nothing had happened to Allison. Cody would tell her she was being paranoid—and she probably was.

"She'll get back with you when she's ready," Cody assured her. "Take the hint and leave them alone until then."

The waitress approached their table balancing a plate of prawn linguine for Cody and prosciutto and shaved pear salad for Sophia. She set down the plates with a flourish. "Is there anything else I can get for you?"

"I think we're good, thanks," Sophia responded with a smile. "This looks delicious."

"Buon Appetito," the waitress said with a bow before flouncing off to the next table.

Cody drained his wine glass and raised a hand to get the waitress's attention. Sophia reached for his arm and pulled it back down. "You've had two already. You don't need another one."

Cody tightened his lips. "You're right," he said, reaching for his water glass instead. "I don't even want it. It's just force of habit."

Sophia's phone pinged with an incoming message. She set down her fork and read the text. "It's from Allison."

Went on a jeep tour of the island. Great day but wiped out. Grabbing dinner in our room and sleeping in tomorrow.

A wave of relief washed over Sophia. She'd worked herself up into a state for nothing, as it turned out.

"Are they joining us?" Cody asked.

"No. They're eating dinner in their room. They went on a jeep tour and they're all tuckered out."

"I told you Allison would be fine," Cody said.

Sophia shot him a sheepish grin as she texted Allison back.

Glad you had a good day. Did you get a chance to talk to Doug?

She chewed on a forkful of salad, waiting for Allison's response.

Yes, all good.

Sophia swallowed her food, wondering if she should leave it at that. Curiosity was eating her alive.

What did he say about the burner phone?

After a few minutes, Allison responded. *Let's talk tomorrow. Want to meet up for the ice show matinee at two? We can make dinner plans then.*

Sophia texted her a thumbs-up emoji. She set down her phone and looked across at Cody. "They want to sleep in and meet us at the ice show in the afternoon."

"Sounds like a perfect sea day to me. I especially like the part about sleeping in. Let's order breakfast in our cabin again."

"Right now, I'm not thinking about breakfast," Sophia said. "I'm wondering what's on the dessert menu."

"How does the coconut cheesecake sound?"

"Not very Italian," Sophia responded with a yawn. "I think I'll go with the tiramisu. After that, I'm heading up to bed on my fullest stomach of the cruise yet."

SOPHIA WOKE with a start a little after ten o'clock the following morning. Cody was snoring gently next to her, oblivious to the knocking on their door. Her brain kicked into gear. *Room service.* She jumped out of bed and reached for the Bella Oceania robe she'd left crumpled on the floor. With it firmly belted around her waist, she dashed over to the door and yanked it open. The tantalizing smell of bacon and scrambled eggs greeted her.

After tipping the waiter, Sophia poured herself a cup of coffee and woke Cody. "Breakfast's here. You should eat while it's warm."

Cody sat up on one elbow and rubbed his eyes. "Let's take it out on the balcony. Might as well make the most of the view on our last day."

After a lazy breakfast, they read and dozed in the sun for the remainder of the morning, before showering up and heading down to deck five where the ice rink was located.

"There's Doug standing over there!" Sophia said, nudging Cody. "I don't see Allison anywhere. She must be in the restroom or something." She lowered her voice. "Which reminds me, you need to follow Doug if he goes to the restroom."

Cody threw her an irritated look. He opened his mouth to respond just as Doug came striding over, grinning broadly. "Don't you two look all tanned and relaxed!"

"Where's Allison?" Sophia asked.

A tiny furrow appeared between Doug's brows. "She's not feeling well. Didn't she text you?"

A tremor of fear spidered its way across Sophia's shoulders. She fished out her phone and stared at it. Sure enough, a message from Allison had come through a couple of minutes earlier.

Sorry, not feeling up to the show. Dreading going home tomorrow. I don't want to go back to the house where Ava died.

23

SOPHIA

Sophia's jaw went slack. She reread the text aloud in a halting voice and then looked at Doug in alarm. "Should you even be here? She sounds really down."

"Allison insisted I come—she wants to take a nap." Doug gave a rueful grin. "She enjoyed this vacation a lot more than she thought she would. It's hard for her to imagine going back home tomorrow. We spent a lot of time talking about it yesterday on our jeep tour. We're probably going to put our house on the market and move out of the area after this. It's a good time to sell, and Allison's ready for a fresh start in a new neighborhood—we both are."

Cody gave an approving nod. "We might end up putting our house on the market too."

Sophia forwarded him a warning look. She didn't know how much Allison had shared with Doug about their financial predicament, but she wasn't interested in airing their dirty laundry in the crowded foyer at the ice rink.

"Maybe I should run up and check on Allison," Sophia suggested. "If you want to give me your key card, I can have a quick chat with her, woman-to-woman—just to make sure she's all right."

Doug gave her an ingratiating smile. "That's very thoughtful of you, Sophia, but I don't think she'd want to be disturbed when she's trying to take a nap. I'll check on her as soon as the show's over."

Sophia pulled her brows together. "You don't think she'd ... you know, harm herself or anything, do you? It's just that ... after what happened at Labadee ..."

A somber look flitted across Doug's face. He reached a hand into his pocket and pulled out a prescription bottle. "I took this out of her purse, to be on the safe side."

"That was smart." Sophia swallowed hard. "There's something I need to tell you. Cody gave Allison some of his sleeping pills the other day."

Cody shuffled his feet apologetically. "I never imagined it would be a problem. She said she was having trouble sleeping."

"She's struggled with insomnia on and off since the miscarriage," Doug said, a hitch in his voice. "She forgot to bring her sleeping pills with her. I appreciate your concern, but Allison's going to be fine—she just needs a good nap. We've come a long way as a couple on this trip. It will be a big change for us selling up and moving on, but we're excited for the next phase of our lives."

Sophia gave a hesitant nod. Her insides were in turmoil, the contents of her stomach swirling almost as much as the thoughts in her brain. Doug sounded so convincing. She had to get a grip and let it go. It wasn't as if she could force her way into their cabin. Allison would be fine for the duration of the show. There was no reason to think otherwise.

They took their seats just as the lights dimmed and the music started to play. A voice with a polished British accent began to narrate. "Ladies and gentlemen, I invite you to join our time-traveling heroine Octavia on a new adventure in 2031, as she sets out to recover her Emperor's Energy Stones from the mysterious and cunning galactic thief known as Dark Darius..."

His voice faded as Sophia's thoughts drifted back to Allison curled up asleep in her cabin. At least Doug had had the sense to remove the prescription drugs from her purse, but Sophia was only half reassured. She couldn't help entertaining the macabre thought that Allison might have procured the sleeping pills from Cody for an ulterior purpose.

"Are you even paying attention to this?" Cody muttered, prodding her. "Don't ask me halfway through what the plot is."

Sophia slid him an apologetic smile and fixed her gaze forward, pretending to focus on the British voice echoing over the rink.

"... in a galaxy that is swirling with rumors that Dark Darius has been spotted. The hunt begins as we take you to the planet Sagaton ..."

Sophia frowned, squirming in her seat as her mind began to wander again—this time coming to rest on the burner phone. Did it exist? If so, where was it? And why had Doug hidden it?

An engine throttled up, the sound reverberating around the rink, and, seconds later, revolving floating lights lit up the 3-D rink, which was now rippling like water before their eyes. The music began to pump, and a skater in a space suit appeared out of nowhere. After showcasing his agility in a stunning opening sequence, he was joined by a regiment of the emperor's Galactic Guards outfitted in full-dress uniform, skating over the ice in an impressive choreographed march.

Sophia tried to lose herself in the production, but her

attention kept wandering, and before long, the plot became a disjointed blur of leaps and spins. She found herself counting the minutes until it ended and Doug could return to his cabin and reassure them that Allison was okay. Unable to stand it any longer, she lifted her purse into her lap and opened it partway, fumbling around inside for her phone. She typed out a quick text to Allison—loathe for either Cody or Doug to notice what she was up to.

Just checking up on you. Do you need anything?

Cody stole a glance in her direction, a questioning look on his face.

She made a show of pulling out a tissue and wiping her nose.

As soon as he looked away, she glanced inside her purse again to see if Allison had responded, but the screen was blank. Reluctantly, she slid her purse back down to the floor, leaving it open in the event her phone lit up with a message.

All of a sudden, she became aware of rustling on Cody's left. Her eyes widened when Doug got out of his seat. She prodded Cody with her elbow.

He leaned over and whispered in her ear, "He says he's going to the bathroom."

"Follow him!" she hissed through gritted teeth. "Remember what we talked about?"

"What if he sees me?"

"He won't if you keep your distance. It's too dark. Get me a bottle of water or something in the foyer. That can be your cover story if he spots you."

Cody cast a glance over his shoulder in the direction Doug had disappeared, and then hesitantly got to his feet and shuffled out into the aisle.

Sophia shifted impatiently in her seat, not even pretending to pay attention to the show anymore. Every thirty seconds or so, she peered behind her to see if there was any sign of the men returning. An irritated patron in the row behind tutted her disapproval. Sophia stared coldly back at the woman until she looked away. Sophia checked her phone again but there were no new messages. She considered leaving her seat and heading out to the foyer, but it would do no good if Doug and Cody were in the restroom. Reluctantly, she resigned herself to the fact that there was nothing she could do other than wait.

Doug was the first to arrive back. He slipped into his seat and leaned over to her. "Where's Cody?"

"He went to get me a drink," she whispered back.

Moments later, Cody reappeared clutching a water bottle, much to Sophia's relief. He sank back into his seat and held it out to her. Smiling her thanks, she made a point of taking a long swig.

When the music crescendoed a few minutes later, Sophia leaned over and whispered to Cody, "Did he make a phone call?"

Cody gave a slight tip of his head.

"Could you hear anything?"

"Bits and pieces. Right before he hung up, I heard him say, *I can't believe I did it.*"

24

SOPHIA

Sophia mulled over Cody's words, her heart hammering out a panicked beat beneath her ribs. She angled her head slightly and tossed a sidelong glance in Doug's direction. Face aglow, he appeared to be caught up in the gripping performance. But the ominous words Cody had overheard kept swimming around inside her head.

I can't believe I did it.

What exactly had Doug done? It didn't sound like he was having an intimate conversation with a woman—more like he was talking business. An illicit transaction? Or was he simply excited about landing a new account or something? Whatever the case, he looked pretty pleased with himself right now.

A sliver of fear pulsed its way across Sophia's shoulders. What if Doug had been referring to something more ominous? What if Allison's suspicions that he was trying to kill her weren't merely the paranoid speculation of a depressed woman? As if sensing her unease, Cody reached over and threaded his fingers through hers. She gave him a wan smile in return. There was nothing more she could do until the show ended. With a grim resolve, she forced herself to stare at the ice for the remainder of the performance, the irritating lyrics of *The Show Must Go On* blasting over the rink like a mocking anthem. *Please be okay, Allison,* she repeated inwardly like a mantra.

When the spectacle eventually drew to a close, Sophia let out a weighty sigh of relief, clapping indifferently as the announcer introduced the cast of skating couples and the countries they hailed from. Usually, Sophia would have been leading the charge in the applause department, but at the moment she wanted nothing more than to make an early exit to beat the stampede. The sooner she knew that Allison was safe, the better. Cody could tell her she was being paranoid all he wanted, but when she got something stuck in her head, she couldn't rest until she resolved it.

At last, the lights came up and a seething herd of bodies began making the slow trek to the exits. Sophia fixed a frozen smile on her face as she shuffled slowly out to the aisle after Cody and Doug, trying to tune out the passengers around her raving about the extraordinary talent they'd witnessed from former Olympian and World ice-skating champions.

"That was really something," Doug said, when they finally made it out to the foyer.

"Mesmerizing," Cody agreed. "I'm not usually much of a one for shows like this, but the athleticism was extraordinary. Those jumps and spins were—"

"We shouldn't hold Doug up," Sophia cut in. "He needs to check on Allison."

"Yeah, get going, man," Cody said.

Doug gave a grunt of acknowledgement. "All right. Where do you guys want to eat dinner?"

"Sophia and I ate at Trattoria del Mare last night," Cody replied. "The food was superb. I wouldn't mind going back."

"Italian's Allison's favorite," Doug said. "I'll run that by her. If she gives me the green light, I'll make an early reservation for five o'clock."

"Sounds good," Cody said. "Text us. We'll wait to hear from you."

Sophia clenched and unclenched her fists, trying to steady her breathing as she watched Doug's departing figure.

Cody laid a hand on her shoulder. "Are you all right? You sound like you're hyperventilating."

"I'm worried about Allison," she choked out. "I can't help it. My gut's telling me something's not right."

"She's fine. Stop obsessing about her," Cody said. "You're driving yourself nuts for no reason. Doug's gonna text us any minute now. Do you want to walk around before dinner—build up an appetite? Not much point in going back up to the cabin."

"Let's go up to the pool deck," Sophia suggested. "I wouldn't mind catching some sun."

"Maybe I'll give that FlowRider a spin," Cody mused as they got into the elevator. "Doug mentioned it was a blast."

"We'll have to stop off at our cabin and pick up your swim trunks," Sophia said.

"Let's do it. Might as well make the most of our last day at sea."

They locked eyes for a brief moment, and Sophia knew they were both thinking the same thing. As long as they were still at sea, they were sheltered from the storm that was coming. But they were only keeping the ugly reality of their problems at bay temporarily. The minute they docked, they would reenter the world they'd left behind, a world she hadn't realized was teetering precariously on the edge of a cliff.

Cody's phone chirped with an incoming message. He

glanced at it and frowned. "It's Doug. Allison's not in the cabin."

Sophia's blood turned to ice in her veins. "Does he know where she went?"

"No. He's wondering if we've heard from her." Cody typed out a quick response and hit send.

The elevator stopped at their deck, but Sophia grabbed Cody's sleeve. "No! We need to go down to Doug."

"We can't just barge into their cabin," Cody protested.

"Watch me!" Sophia spat out, as she rammed the button for deck ten. "Something's happened to Allison. She wouldn't leave the cabin without letting Doug know where she was going. And she never responded to my text from earlier either."

Cody scratched his forehead. "What text?"

"Never mind," Sophia said, as the elevator dinged and came to a halt. She slipped out through the doors before they had fully opened and darted across the hall to cabin 10664.

"Doug?" she called out, thumping her fist loudly on the door. "It's Sophia and Cody." She raised her hand to knock a second time just as the door swung open.

A harried-looking Doug stood before her, his ordinarily groomed hair sticking up in unruly tufts. He ushered them both in and then sank down on the bed. "I've been calling and calling. Her phone keeps going to voicemail. It's not like her to take off by herself."

"Can you think of any place she might have gone?" Cody asked. "Did she mention picking up any last-minute souvenirs from the gift shops or anything like that?"

Doug studied the carpet for a moment before shaking his head. "No. She already bought her nieces and nephews some T-shirts and stuff."

Sophia ran a curious eye around the room. "Is her purse here?"

Doug blinked helplessly. "I … didn't think to look." He got to his feet and opened the nightstand on the other side of the bed. He frowned and then nodded. "It's right here. She keeps it here when we're in the room."

"That's good. That means she can't have gone too far," Cody said breezily.

Sophia's stomach knotted. "I don't know. It might not be a good thing."

"What do you mean?" Doug asked, his voice sounding small and frightened.

Sophia inhaled a calming breath. "Is her wallet in her purse—and her key pass?"

Doug opened and shut his mouth, the look on his face suggesting he was trying to wrap his head around the direction she was going with this.

His gaze followed Sophia's to the balcony where a lone black and silver flip-flop lay next to the railing.

25

ROB

Rob was leaning back at his desk daydreaming about Misty when a call came through on his radio from Dave. "This is Charlie two. Do you read me?"

Rob unclipped his radio from his belt and pressed the talk button. "Copy that. Go ahead, Charlie two."

"Possible Code Oscar. Location and time unknown. Allison Robinson. 10664. Captain alerted. CCTV review underway."

Rob shot up in his chair. The radio slipped from his fingers and skidded across the floor, crashing into the door. *Code Oscar. Man overboard.* It wasn't so much the code that had sent an electric shock through his system—he was trained for these kinds of situations—it was the name and the cabin number that had fear clawing at his chest. He dropped to one knee and fumbled with clammy hands to pick up the radio. Dave's voice grew more insistent. "Hello? Do you read me? Charlie one, are you there?"

Rob fought to pull himself together as he stammered a response. "Roger that. On my way."

Goosebumps spread over his skin like a battalion of fire

ants. Everything kept coming back to cabin 10664. It couldn't be a coincidence. The missing necklace, Allison Robinson, Misty. There had to be a connection. His legs felt like rubber as he exited the office and hurried to the crew stairwell. What in the world had Misty got herself tangled up in? Some kind of scam, or drug deal gone horribly wrong? Had Misty done the unthinkable? He shook his head free of the stomach-churning thought. It wasn't possible. Allison hadn't gone missing last night after Misty's visit. Unless Misty had returned to the cabin today, she couldn't have had anything to do with Allison Robinson's disappearance. Rob tightened his jaw. At least not directly. But it still left the possibility that she'd said something to Allison that had made her jump. But what?

Rob ran up two flights of stairs and then took the elevator the rest of the way to deck ten. Sweat trickled down in rivulets beneath the collar of his shirt. After taking a moment to compose himself, he knocked on the door of cabin 10664.

Seconds later, a man Rob didn't recognize opened the door to him.

Rob proffered a curt nod. "Afternoon. I'm Officer Benson. Is Doug Robinson here?"

"Yes, yes of course. Please, come in. I'm Cody Clark, a … friend of his. This is my wife, Sophia," he said, motioning to a petite, chestnut-haired woman punching out a text on her phone.

Rob dipped his head in her direction, his attention immediately drawn to Doug Robinson who was slumped in a deck chair on the balcony. Steeling himself for the difficult conversation ahead of him, Rob made his way to the sliding door, and rapped on it once to get Doug's attention before joining him. To Rob's annoyance, Sophia followed him out on the balcony and leaned against the railing, arms folded in front of her. He raised his brows in her direction. "It might be better if I spoke to Mr. Robinson alone."

Doug flapped a languid hand. "Let her stay. She's a friend. And please, call me Doug."

Rob kept his expression neutral, masking his displeasure at being overruled. "If you have no objections," he began, pulling out his notebook and phone. "I'd like to record this interview. I want to make sure I don't miss anything."

"That's fine," Doug replied, fingering a black and silver flip-flop in his lap.

Rob cleared his throat. "First of all, I want to assure you that the captain has been informed of the situation, and an emergency broadcast has been issued to muster the crew to search for your wife."

Doug opened his mouth to say something, but Sophia beat him to it.

"What exactly does that mean, Officer? Are we turning around?"

Rob fixed her with a reproving stare. If she was going to keep interrupting him, he'd insist she leave. "My colleague is reviewing the CCTV as we speak. Based on his findings, the captain will make a decision on whether or not to turn the ship around. In the meantime, we're conducting a thorough onboard search."

In truth, Rob already knew what the captain's decision would be. No one had seen Allison go overboard, and no one knew when she'd gone missing. Even if a Code Oscar could be confirmed, the captain wouldn't turn a ship containing over five-thousand passengers around to blindly search hundreds of miles of ocean in the hope of retrieving a body.

He coughed discreetly before turning to address Doug once more, "Can you tell me when you last saw your wife?"

Doug's brows twitched toward each other as if he was laboring to remember. "Right before I went down to the ice show. We made arrangements to go to the matinee with Cody and Sophia. At the last minute, Allison said she wasn't feeling up to it. She wanted to take a nap instead."

Rob scribbled a quick note. "Was she sick?"

Doug let out a sharp sigh. "No, not sick, per se. She was dreading the thought of going home."

"How would you describe her state of mind?"

Doug hesitated, shooting an uncomfortable look Sophia's way before answering, "She ... had a miscarriage last year. She's struggled with depression ever since."

Rob gave a practiced nod of understanding. "Was your wife taking any medication?"

"An antidepressant, and ... the occasional sleeping pill."

Rob made a note of the medications. "Has she ever tried to harm herself before?"

Doug curled his fingers into a fist. "Once. She swallowed some pills in the bathtub. Thankfully, I found her in time. They managed to pump her stomach."

Rob gestured to the flip-flop in Doug's lap. "Does that belong to your wife?"

"Yes," Doug answered, a despairing crack in his voice. "It was lying over there by the railing, right where Sophia's standing."

Rob walked over to the balcony and peered over it. Sophia stepped aside while he snapped a few pictures. He returned to his seat, keeping his gaze fixed on Doug, only too aware that Sophia was watching him intently. He sensed she was itching to butt in on the conversation again, but for now at least she'd taken the hint and was keeping her mouth shut. Her turn would come. He would have to question everyone in the room, including Sophia's husband, who'd had the decency to remain in the cabin while he conducted this interview.

"Where's the other flip-flop?" Rob asked.

"Missing, *obviously*," Sophia snapped. "How quickly are you going to be able to deploy search and rescue boats?"

Rob adjusted his cap and addressed her with an air of patient condescension. "It's not that simple. First, we need to confirm what we're dealing with here. If the CCTV footage reveals that Allison left her cabin, then it's possible she's somewhere on board. As we speak, I have crew checking all the bars, restaurants, and attractions. Trust me, it wouldn't be the first time a guest indulged in one cocktail too many and got hopelessly lost on board." He fixed a sympathetic smile on his face and then turned back to Doug. "Has your wife ever got confused or lost her way on the ship before?"

Doug met his gaze, a flicker of hope in his eyes. "Yes, once or twice. She got lost one day on the pool deck. And, she … misplaced her necklace, if you remember."

A wall of heat crept up the back of Rob's neck. At all costs, he wanted to steer clear of that topic. The necklace was an incriminating link between Misty and Allison; one that he'd much rather keep to himself.

Before he had a chance to respond, the slider door opened.

"There's someone here to see Doug," Cody said, stepping out on the balcony, along with a Bella Oceania crew member clutching a handful of brochures and pamphlets. She gave a pert nod in greeting to Rob before addressing Doug. "Mr. Robinson, my name's Ellen. I'm a member of the care team here on board. I'm here to offer you emotional support and make sure you get everything you need at this time."

"Emotional support?" Sophia blurted out. "He doesn't need emotional support. He needs answers. He needs boats deployed. He needs the crew to search the ship, and the water surrounding the ship. He needs the CCTV footage of—"

"I can see that you're in considerable distress," Ellen soothed. "I'm here to help. Are you a friend of Allison's?"

Sophia threw up her hands in disgust. "I'm sure you're a genuinely nice person, Ellen, but right now we have all the care people we need on this balcony. So why don't you leave us a brochure and go find someone more in need of your services."

"Calm down, Soph," Cody chided.

Ellen flushed crimson, a wounded expression on her face as her eyes zig-zagged between Sophia and Rob.

"It might be best if you check in with me later," Rob said. "I'll radio you if we need you."

Ellen studiously avoided eye contact with Sophia as she laid a brochure on the glass table. "It was nice to meet you, Mr. Robinson. Here's my card if you have any questions."

As soon as she left, Sophia let out a disgusted humph. "Nice to meet you? What does she think is going on here?"

Cody gave a reproving shake of his head. "She's only trying to do her job."

Rob threw Sophia a stern look before resuming the interview. "Doug, is this the first time your wife has gone missing on this cruise?"

He scratched the back of his head. "Yes, as far as I know—well, apart from getting lost on the pool deck."

"Have you noticed any other unusual behavior?"

Doug furrowed his forehead. "There was this one incident on Labadee."

"Go on," Rob encouraged him.

"Allison passed out in the water—she almost drowned. The paramedic on the scene asked if she was taking any medication." Doug's voice trailed off briefly. "The thing is, I thought she'd stopped taking her antidepressants. That's what she told me. But when I looked in her purse, three-quarters of her prescription was gone."

"That doesn't mean to say she took the pills," Sophia interrupted.

Cody laid a restraining hand on her arm.

"Anyone could have taken them out of her bag," Sophia went on, shaking off Cody's hand. "It was lying on the beach all afternoon beneath her lounger."

Rob flattened his lips. "If you don't mind, I'd like to finish up this interview with Doug. I'll get to you after that."

Undeterred, Sophia stared brazenly back at him. "Actually, I do mind. This is a critical situation. We need to act quickly. We don't have time to waste sitting around taking leisurely statements."

Before Rob could respond, Dave's voice came over the radio. "This is Charlie two to Charlie one. Do you read me?"

"Loud and clear, go ahead Charlie two."

"CCTV footage confirms Allison Robinson hasn't left her cabin since returning yesterday shortly before 5:00 p.m."

26

SOPHIA

Sophia bit back the whimper of shock that rose to her lips as Officer Benson clipped his radio back on his belt.

"What ... what does that mean?" Doug asked, his voice trailing off.

Officer Benson turned to him, a stiff grimace on his face. "I'm deeply sorry, Doug. Based on the CCTV evidence, there's a strong possibility your wife fell overboard."

Doug let out a strangled sob. His gaze met Sophia's, his face crumpling in grief. He dropped his head, squeezing Allison's lone flip flop to his chest.

Cody went over to him and laid a hand on his shoulder. "I'm so sorry, man."

Sophia pressed her back against the balcony railing, her heart thumping so hard she feared it would burst. Images of Allison free-falling to her death flashed to mind. It would be all too easy for a depressed person to throw themselves off a balcony. Not that she would have pictured Allison taking such a drastic step. She wasn't a gutsy person—she'd been terrified of riding the zip line before they'd talked her into it.

Maybe that was why she'd asked for some of Cody's sleeping pills—to make the jump easier.

Sophia's throat burned as she fought to hold back tears. In all likelihood, there would be no search and rescue—at the most an attempt to retrieve Allison's remains. But sharks would beat them to it. Sophia sucked in a ragged breath. She wanted to cry, but what was the use? Doug had already taken on the role of the broken-hearted, collapsing with grief right on cue. Someone needed to be Allison's advocate—find out exactly what had happened to her. It was the least Sophia could do—she was good at grabbing the helm when things got tough. Summoning her resolve, she turned to Officer Benson. "What happens now?" she demanded. "Will the captain deploy search and rescue?"

Benson's grip tightened around his pen. "All reasonable efforts will be made to locate her. You need to understand that we're in a difficult situation here. No one witnessed her going overboard, and we have a timeline of several hours to work with. That's a vast amount of water to cover."

Sophia narrowed her eyes at him. "What are you saying? *Reasonable effort* could mean anything. You have to try and find her, right?"

"The captain will make that decision." He pocketed his notebook and got to his feet. "I'd be happy to arrange for Ellen to come back and talk to you, Doug, if you want. She can make sure all your needs are taken care of, order food, handle calls, or anything else you might think of."

Doug shook his head, dissolving into tears again when he attempted to speak.

"My husband and I will take care of him," Sophia said.

"Absolutely," Cody added.

"All right. I'll need to take both your statements as well," Officer Benson said. "Probably best to handle it down in my office. As you're not relatives, you'll need to independently identify Allison Robinson on the CCTV footage."

"Cody, why don't you go first," Sophia said. "I'll wait here with Doug until you get back."

As soon as Officer Benson and Cody disappeared out the door together, Sophia sat down in the deck chair next to Doug, eying him with mixed emotions. She couldn't bring herself to offer him a hug, or even touch his hand. She wasn't sure yet what she'd witnessed—an impressive performance, or a broken man. The burner phone suggested Doug had been conducting some kind of secret life that Allison knew nothing about. If it was an affair, he was conveniently free to pursue it now. Sophia squeezed her hands in her lap, selecting her words carefully. If he had given a performance, she would have to do the same. The last thing she wanted to do was let slip what Allison had told her.

"I'm so sorry, Doug," she began. "I knew Allison was hurting, but if I'd had any idea she was that unhappy, I would have stayed in the cabin with her instead of going to the ice show."

Doug shook his head emphatically. "This isn't on you. It's my fault. I should have trusted my gut. I suspected she was abusing those antidepressants behind my back, but she kept denying it. I wanted to believe her—this was supposed to be our fresh start. No more lies." He let out a shuddering sigh. "I feel bad you and Cody got dragged into this. Of all the people you could have befriended, it had to be us. You should be having a good time celebrating your success this week. Instead, you're caught up in this mess."

Sophia averted her gaze. Evidently Allison hadn't mentioned their business woes, after all. "Don't worry about us. We're just devastated for you."

Doug set the flip-flop down on the table between them and wiped the backs of his hands over his eyes. "Allison loved those flip-flops. This must have fallen off when—" He broke off abruptly, a heart-wrenching moan escaping his lips.

Despite her reservations, Sophia felt compelled to do something to comfort him. She laid a hand on his shoulder. "Can I get you anything, Doug? I can order some food if you want."

He sniffed and shook his head. "I'm not hungry."

Sophia glanced at the time on her phone and got to her feet. "It's almost dinner time. I'm going to order you a burger and fries anyway. You should try and eat something."

She opened the slider door and wandered into the cabin to locate the room service menu. She might as well order something for herself and Cody too. They would likely end up keeping vigil with Doug for the next few hours at least. He didn't seem particularly keen on the preppy care team member, Ellen, not that Sophia blamed him. Anyone could serve up a pamphlet with a side of platitudes.

After placing an order, Sophia ducked into the bathroom under the guise of grabbing some tissues for Doug. She couldn't resist taking a quick peek in the drawers and the toiletry bags sitting on the counter. She rummaged hurriedly through everything, but there was no sign of the sleeping pills Cody had given Allison. On the surface, it only seemed to confirm what Sophia had feared—that Allison had taken them before she jumped. *Why, Allison why?* Sophia pressed her hands to her head as a wave of guilt assaulted her. Cody had a hand in this too, albeit unintentionally.

She stared numbly at her reflection in the mirror. She hadn't gotten a chance to relay to Allison what Cody had overheard.

I can't believe I did it.

Had Allison gone ahead and confronted Doug about the burner phone? Was it possible his answer had pushed her to the edge?

27

ROB

Inside his office, Rob gestured to Cody to take a seat. "Can I get you anything, a cup of coffee, a water?"

Cody shook his head as he sank into the chair opposite Rob. "No. I'm good, thanks. I just can't believe this is happening."

Rob propped his elbows on the desk in front of him and interlaced his fingers. "I'm sure this must be a terrible shock for you and your wife."

A haunted look crossed Cody's face. "It's certainly not the kind of thing you imagine happening to someone you know. Not that we knew them all that well. I mean, we only just met them when we were boarding. When we found out their wedding anniversary was the day before ours, we thought it would be fun to meet up for dinner to celebrate. It just sort of grew from there."

"So you spent a lot of time with them during the cruise?" Rob prompted, reaching for a legal pad and pen.

"Every day, except for yesterday." Cody frowned. "Actually, we only saw Doug today. Allison skipped the ice show. Doug said she wasn't feeling up to it."

Rob made a note of the information. "When was the last time you saw Allison Robinson?"

"We waved to her and Doug getting off the ship in Cozumel. They were in line ahead of us. They spent the day by themselves."

"And before that?"

Cody scratched his cheek, thinking it through. "It would have been at the Slow Vibes piano bar. Doug requested a special song to celebrate their wedding anniversary. The blonde singer performed it—I forget her name, Martina or something like that."

Rob shifted in his seat, forcing his features to remain expressionless. "Misty Murano?"

"Yeah, that's her. Doug managed to talk Allison into dancing with him and afterward they got a huge round of applause. Allison got a bit flustered, and she knocked her drink into her lap. We ordered another round while she went back up to the cabin to change. She ended up texting Doug to say she was tired and going to bed instead."

Rob averted his gaze, rubbing a finger over his upper lip. Allison hadn't gone to bed though. She'd had an unexpected visitor. Misty had slipped into the room after her and closed the door. Whatever had transpired between the two women in the cabin that night had triggered Allison's disappearance —he was sure of it. Misty was involved, somehow. And that terrified him. He would have to tread carefully in his line of questioning. He needed to make sure Cody and Sophia Clark were satisfied Allison had committed suicide. There could be no hint or suspicion of foul play in either of their statements, or the local police would launch a full investigation once they arrived back at Fort Lauderdale. Thankfully, Doug Robinson had confirmed his wife's depressed state of mind, and even her previous attempts to take her life. If Rob kept his wits about him, this would all blow over without involving Misty.

Rob checked his notes and then asked, "How long did you remain in the piano bar after Allison went up to her cabin?"

"I think around forty-five minutes or so. It was shortly after midnight when Sophia and I got to bed."

"I understand from Allison's husband that she had a history of severe depression. Did she exhibit any unusual behavior around you?"

Cody shifted position, a chagrined look on his face. "No, not really. I mean I was there on the beach at Labadee when she passed out in the water. It might have been my fault actually. I was pushing everyone to try those Labadoozies they're famous for. They were strong—heavy on the rum. I think it was just a mixture of alcohol and too much sun. I didn't know anything about her taking prescription medication. That probably didn't help either. But I'm sure it wasn't intentional on her part. Just a bad mix."

Rob frowned. He needed to steer Cody back to the theory that Allison had committed suicide. "Her husband said she tried to take her life once before, after the miscarriage. The incident at Labadee might have been another cry for help." He lowered his voice and added softly. "And when that didn't work, she resorted to a more drastic course of action."

Cody gave a skeptical shake of his head. "I don't know. She seemed to me to be enjoying the cruise. I can't imagine what would have driven her to take her life all of a sudden—and in such a horrific manner. It doesn't make sense."

Rob studied him over his steepled fingers. "Maybe not, at first glance. But as you mentioned earlier, you didn't know her all that well. Unfortunately, it's not the first time someone has jumped from a balcony on a cruise ship, especially after a night of drinking."

"She wasn't much of a drinker," Cody answered.

Rob raised his brows. "But she was taking prescription drugs—possibly abusing them."

Cody gave a half-hearted nod. "I see what you mean."

Rob pulled his keyboard toward him and tapped on it for a few minutes before turning the monitor so that both he and Cody could view the screen. "I'm going to ask you to watch this footage with me and tell me if you recognize Allison Robinson among the other passengers. If you could point her out to me, that would be great."

Cody pulled his chair in closer. A medley of bodies of all shapes and sizes, decked out in brightly colored beachwear, filled the screen. After watching the video for a couple of minutes, Cody spotted Doug and Allison disembarking from the ship at Cozumel.

"There," he said, pointing to Allison, right before the camera panned past her and Doug. "That's her."

Rob rewound the footage, froze the screen, and took a still picture, before turning the monitor back around. "Great, thank you, Cody. That's all I need from you for now. I appreciate your assistance and, on behalf of Bella Oceania, I'm truly sorry that you and your wife had to go through an experience like this on your cruise."

Cody dipped his head in acknowledgement. "Sophia and I will be fine—she's a strong woman. It's a raw deal for Doug, though. My heart goes out to the poor guy."

"I'll send someone up to Doug's cabin to fetch Sophia once I get your statement uploaded," Rob said.

As soon as the door closed behind Cody, Rob tossed his pen down on the desk, his shoulders sagging. Misty's name had come up, but, thankfully, Cody Clark hadn't said anything to implicate her. Evidently, he was unaware of her visit to Allison's cabin. He seemed like the pliable sort—genuinely gutted at what had happened, at a complete loss as to why or how. He'd pushed back a little on the suicide theory, which concerned Rob to some degree. He would be sure to minimize that in Cody's official statement.

Truth be told, it was Sophia Clark he was more worried about. He had a hunch she wasn't going to accept the official version of suicide until every other theory had been eliminated. And that could be a problem.

28

ROB

Rob sucked on a mint as he waited for Sophia Clark to make an appearance in his office. He'd just finished up a rather lengthy conversation with the captain, updating him on the details Doug and Cody had provided, and discussing how to handle the situation once they arrived back in port. As Rob had suspected, the captain was unequivocal in his decision not to turn the ship around for what was essentially a lost cause. They would be docking on schedule in Fort Lauderdale in the morning, and the local police would meet them to review the statements they'd taken and conduct their own interviews. At that point, it would be out of Rob's hands entirely. All he had to do until then was make sure no one caught a glimpse of the footage of Misty entering Allison's cabin. The most foolproof course of action would be to delete it, but he had a hankering to keep it as leverage, just in case Misty decided to walk away from him again.

A sharp rap on the door startled him. "Come in!" he called out, straightening up in his seat.

He set his expression to neutral as Sophia entered and sat

down opposite him. He proffered her a tight smile. "Thank you for coming down to—"

"Before we get started," Sophia said, cutting him off. "Has the captain made a decision yet? Is there or is there not going to be a rescue operation?"

Rob threaded his fingers together. "The captain confirmed a few minutes ago that we will be proceeding on course and docking in Fort Lauderdale early tomorrow morning as scheduled."

A determined glint hardened in Sophia's eyes. "Are you telling me you're not even going to make an effort to look for Allison? Can't Bella Oceania send out some tenders or something?"

"I'm afraid I don't make the policy on these matters," Rob responded. "The captain has weighed all the material factors and taken into consideration the safety of his crew. He came to the conclusion that there's nothing to be gained by an indiscriminate search of the water at this point."

"What about the police?" Sophia fumed. "Will they send out the Coast Guard once we get to Fort Lauderdale?"

Rob reached for the pen on his desk and twisted it between his fingers. "I'm very sorry for your loss, but you need to understand that there's virtually no chance your friend survived the fall, not to mention the hours she's been in the ocean."

"But the police will conduct an investigation into what happened, won't they?" Sophia persisted.

"I can't speak for the Fort Lauderdale police, but I can assure you that proper procedure will be followed by Bella Oceania. Part of that procedure requires me to take statements from everyone who was with Allison over the past twenty-four hours, which is why you're here." He set down his pen and consulted his notes. "I understand from your husband that the last time you spoke to Allison Robinson was two nights ago in the Slow Vibes piano bar. Is that correct?"

"Yes." Sophia said, with a resigned sigh. "She and Doug were dancing together."

"How would you describe her mood that evening?"

A tiny furrow appeared on Sophia's brow. "She seemed content. At least in that moment. But she had shared some things with me earlier that made me think she wasn't all that happy deep down."

"Go on," Rob urged, pleased at the direction the conversation was taking. The more information he could document about Allison's distraught state of mind, the stronger the case for suicide, and the less likely the police would be to pursue any other line of inquiry.

"She lost a baby about six months ago," Sophia said.

Rob gave a sympathetic nod. "Doug mentioned the miscarriage."

Sophia threw him an odd look. She opened her mouth to respond, then closed it again as if debating with herself about something.

"How did the miscarriage affect her?" Rob prompted.

"She suffered from postpartum depression. She said it drove a wedge in her relationship with Doug."

Rob gave a knowing nod. "It can drive some women to kill their own children, not to mention themselves."

A flash of anger darted across Sophia's face. She slid forward in her chair and pressed the palms of her hands on the desk. "You're missing my point. I'm not convinced Allison committed suicide. Things weren't all they seemed between her and Doug. She suspected he had been messing with her medication. What happened on the beach on Haiti was no accident—her drink was spiked."

Rob blinked across at her as he absorbed the impact of her words. This wasn't the direction he wanted the interview to move in. He'd intended to steer it to the inevitable conclusion that Allison had been a deeply unhappy woman who'd seized an opportunity to put an end to her misery. Sophia Clark was going to be an even bigger thorn in his side than he had predicted. Evidently, she was prepared to do and say whatever it took to stir the pot and make sure the Fort Lauderdale police launched an investigation of their own.

Sweat prickled on the back of Rob's neck. He couldn't allow her to go around spouting her suspicions. He needed to shut her down. But she wasn't the type you could easily put a lid on—in fact, it would likely only incense her more. He would have to find a way to placate her instead. She had bristled at every attempt he'd made to assure her that Bella Oceania was handling the situation in a professional capacity—maybe he should try a more personal approach.

"My sister had postpartum depression," Rob said, arranging a suitably pained expression on his face. "At one point, she was convinced her husband was trying to poison her." He gave a sad shake of his head. "It's not unusual to become paranoid of those around you who love you the most. It was an extremely tough time for our family, but she pulled through in the end. It was just a matter of finding the right doctor and the right medication. Sadly, Allison Robinson never got the chance."

"I still think the police need to consider the possibility that it wasn't suicide," Sophia said, jutting her chin out stubbornly.

Rob raised his brows. "Doug Robinson's going to carry the guilt of what his wife did for the rest of his life; wondering if he should have done anything differently, wishing he hadn't left her in the cabin alone, regretting not taking her to just one more doctor. By all accounts, Allison was a very troubled woman. I would caution you to be careful about adding to her bereaved husband's grief unless you have hard evidence."

Sophia shrank back in her seat and pressed her lips tightly together. She seemed to be considering what he'd said. He suspected she'd wrestled with the same thoughts herself deep down.

"Allison may not be here to speak for herself, but she confided her suspicions to me," Sophia said. "I wouldn't be able to live with myself if I didn't advocate for her. If I'm wrong, it's not as if I've lost Doug's friendship. I barely know the man. But if I'm right, then Doug Robinson doesn't need a grief counselor, he needs a pair of handcuffs and a prison cell."

"I appreciate your concerns," Rob said, masking his irritation and slipping back into professional mode. "I'll certainly make a note of them. Now, if you don't mind, I'd like to have you identify Allison Robinson in the CCTV from yesterday." He enlarged the footage he'd shown to Cody earlier, and adjusted the screen so that Sophia could view it.

She watched for a moment or two and then tapped a polished fingernail on the screen. "That's her, getting off the ship with Doug. Not a great angle—they're behind that couple in the matching shirts."

"Thank you," Rob replied, turning the monitor back around.

"Wait!" Sophia said. "How do we know Allison got back on board the ship later on that day? And that she went up to her cabin?"

Rob coughed discreetly, his mind racing. The last known footage of Allison showed her entering her cabin with Misty hot on her tail. He certainly couldn't share that with Sophia. But he needed to calm her down somehow. It wouldn't do any harm to let her see the clip of the Robinsons returning to the ship. He'd already tracked it down earlier to confirm that Allison had indeed re-boarded before they left Cozumel.

"Let me see if I can pull up that footage." Rob tapped on the keyboard and quickly located the file. "Ah, here we go," he said, tilting the monitor in Sophia's direction again. She watched, hawk-eyed, as a steady stream of passengers filed back onto the ship, laden down with beach bags and souvenirs.

"There's Doug and Allison," Rob said, pointing them out as the footage rolled.

Sophia leaned in closer, frowning at the screen.

"So you see they re-boarded *Diamond of the Waves* at 4:38 p.m.," he pointed out pleasantly.

Sophia shook her head. "Something's not right."

"What do you mean?" Rob asked, his eyes swerving between her and the screen.

"Rewind it!" Sophia insisted. "I want to watch it again."

Biting back his exasperation, Rob dutifully rewound the tape. Sophia's eyes were glued to the screen as Doug and Allison strolled arm-in-arm up the gangplank, Doug carrying a beach bag, Allison laughing at something he'd said, one hand on top of her hat as if to keep it from flying away.

"I know what's bothering me now," Sophia said, frowning. "It's the hat. See how she's trying to hold it on? It's too small for her." Sophia whipped her face to Rob, her eyes flashing an air of urgency. "That's not Allison Robinson!"

29

ROB

Rob hunched his brows together trying to grasp the significance of what Sophia was telling him. "I don't understand. What does her sun hat have to do with anything?"

Sophia tightened her jaw, the words spilling from her lips. "It's a Gigi Burris designer hat. Doug bought it for Allison for the cruise, but it was too big. She wore it the first day to keep him happy, but it kept slipping over her eyes. She complained about it the whole time and she hasn't worn it since."

Sophia tapped her fingernail on the frozen image on the computer screen. "That woman can't possibly be Allison. She's an imposter."

Rob scratched the back of his neck, his stomach knotting with rage. His frustration with the unrelenting Sophia Clark was mounting by the minute. She had got some kind of bee in her bonnet about the stupid hat, and he could tell she wasn't going to let it go. "Let's not jump to any wild conclusions. I can appreciate—"

"Do you have any other video of Allison after she boarded?" Sophia blurted out. "We can't identify her properly from this footage in the hat and oversized sunglasses. This could be anyone."

Rob grunted his skepticism. "She's got her arm tucked into Doug Robinson's. And he confirmed that he and Allison left the ship together and returned together."

"Exactly!" Sophia shot back. "We have only his word for it that this is Allison. But I'm telling you that hat's too small for her head. Play it again and I'll show you what I mean."

With an air of reluctance, Rob rewound the footage and watched for a third time as Doug Robinson and the dark-haired woman on his arm walked up the gang plank.

"See what I'm talking about now?" Sophia said, her voice rising with conviction. "She's trying to keep the hat from falling off her head the entire time."

"Uh-huh," Rob mumbled in response. But it wasn't the hat he was looking at anymore. It was the way the woman pulled out her key pass with a subtle flick of her wrist, elbow bent—a peculiar little gesture that Rob was oh-so-familiar with. He could feel the blood draining from his head as a clammy fog crept in to replace it. He hadn't been able to locate Misty on the ship all day yesterday. She'd finally responded to his texts and told him she was practicing with the band. Like a fool, he'd believed her. A white-hot anger sliced through his innards like a burst of lightning.

"Officer, are you all right?" Sophia's voice broke through his musings.

"Yes, absolutely. Just thinking this through," he replied, trying desperately to shift his focus back to the woman sitting opposite him and away from the woman on the screen. "There's probably a simple explanation for this. Maybe Doug bought his wife a new sun hat on Cozumel. You said yourself the old one was too big."

"Then ask him," Sophia said through gritted teeth. "Call

him up right now and ask him. Because if you don't, I'm going straight to the police once we dock at Fort Lauderdale, and I'll tell them what a lousy job you did of this investigation, and how you ignored me when I told you that woman with Doug wasn't his wife."

Rob swallowed down the bile creeping up his throat. At all costs, he had to keep Misty out of this. But the situation was rapidly spinning out of his control. He needed to do whatever it took to pacify Sophia Clark. His only option was to roll the dice and bet that Doug Robinson would lie through his teeth if he was put on the spot.

"All right. Let's talk with Doug and see if we can clear this up." Rob checked his notes and then dialed Doug Robinson's number. The last thing he wanted to do was talk civilly to the man right now—he'd sooner rip his head from his shoulders—but he needed to go through the motions to satisfy Sophia and get her out of his hair so that he could process what he'd seen and figure out what to do about it.

"Put him on speaker," Sophia said in no uncertain terms. "I don't want to hear this second hand."

Pulse thundering in his temples, Rob placed the phone on the desk between them. When Doug answered, Rob cleared his throat, "Doug, it's Rob Benson from security."

"Yes?" Doug's voice sounded thin and fragile, just like a grieving husband's voice should. Except of course he wasn't a grieving husband at all. That much Rob knew now without a shadow of a doubt.

"I'm in the process of taking the Clarks' statements," Rob replied. "Cody was here earlier, and I have Sophia in the office with me now—you're on speaker. Sophia was just reviewing the video footage of you and Allison disembarking the ship at Cozumel and then returning late afternoon. This is probably a minor issue, but she remarked that the sun hat your wife is wearing appears to be too small for her. Yet, she remembers it being too big for Allison—falling over her eyes."

"I'm not sure how this is relevant," Doug said in an aggrieved tone, "but, for what it's worth, Allison lost her hat on our jeep tour—it blew right off her head. I bought her a new one at a market stall." He gave a hollow laugh. "It was likely a child's size—but it was all they had."

"Do you still have that hat?" Sophia asked.

There was a brief silence before Doug responded. "No. We tossed it once we got back on board. It was just one of those cheap throwaways."

"Thank you, Doug. Sorry to bother—" Rob began before Sophia cut him off.

"Why was Allison wearing the hat if it didn't fit properly?"

Doug let out a heavy sigh. "She wanted the photographer to take our picture coming back on board."

"I see. Thank you for clearing that up, Doug," Rob said. "I'll call you back after I'm done here."

He hung up the phone and gave Sophia a look of admonishment. "Sounds like a perfectly reasonable explanation to me."

"I disagree," she countered. "I'm telling you he's lying through his teeth. That woman was wearing the sun hat to hide her face."

Rob tapped his fingers impatiently on the desk. "There's no reason to think he's lying. The woman on his arm has the same dark hair as—"

"It's not her!" Sophia retorted, getting to her feet. "You need to listen to me! That woman is not Allison Robinson! She was afraid Doug was trying to kill her. And now he's pulled it off. He staged this whole thing—all those incidents to make her look fuzzyheaded and depressed. But he won't get away with it. And Bella Oceania won't get away with covering it up either. I'm going straight to the police when we dock."

Rob clenched his jaw as Sophia stormed out and slammed the door behind her. He sank back in his chair, trying to collect his jumbled thoughts. He needed to figure out how to handle this, and quickly. No matter what, he had to protect Misty from prosecution. But she had betrayed him, and for that she would pay.

30

ROB

Rob was lost in his thoughts when a knock on the door made him jump. One of the junior security guards stuck his head inside. "I'm going to grab some coffee before I make my rounds. Want me to pick you up anything?"

"No, thanks. I'm good," Rob replied.

The security guard nodded, about to close the door, before clearing his throat, "By the way, did Misty ever get a hold of you?"

"No. I didn't know she was trying to reach me." Rob frowned, glancing down at his phone. "I don't have any missed calls or messages."

The guard cracked the door open a little wider, a curious gleam in his eye. "She stopped by earlier. Dave was here. I assumed she was looking for you." He injected a loaded pause before adding, "She stayed for a while. Might want to watch your back. I wouldn't put it past Dave to make a move on her."

Rob gave a terse nod by way of dismissing the guard, who was obviously keen to glean some tidbit of gossip—a morbid curiosity Rob had no intention of satisfying.

After the door closed behind the guard, Rob sat back and rubbed his tense shoulders. He wasn't afraid of Misty succumbing to Dave's advances—Dave didn't have a chance with her. But why had she come to the office? She must have wanted to talk to him. Was it about Allison? His heart thudded in his chest. He hoped she'd kept her mouth shut and not said anything to arouse Dave's suspicions. Rob was more convinced now than ever that she'd had a hand in Allison's demise. But he intended to put everything in place to make sure Doug Robinson took the fall for it—it was always the husband, after all.

He reached for the stress ball on his desk and squeezed it. Sophia Clark was not going to rest until the police opened an investigation. He would have to figure out a way to get Misty off the ship and past the port authorities as quickly as possible—and before anyone started asking awkward questions about the identity of the woman who'd accompanied Doug Robinson to Cozumel. As long as the footage of Misty entering Allison's cabin didn't come to light, there was no reason to suspect her. And he would take care of that. When this was all over and done with, Misty was going to owe him a lot more than she already did.

Rob hit the speed dial for Misty's number but, as he'd expected, it went straight to voicemail. "Hey, it's me. Call me as soon as you get this. It's important. We need to talk."

A flicker of self-doubt went through him as he ended the call. What he was planning to do was crazy—some part of him acknowledged that. Dave was right. He'd become obsessed with Misty Murano. Why else would he be willing to risk his job to help her? He doubted she'd actually pushed Allison overboard. He didn't believe she was capable of something so violent. But something she'd said had likely triggered Allison. She might have told her about the affair. Maybe she'd even told her that Doug was leaving her—or that she'd be better off dead. Rob's throat bobbed with fear. Nowadays, you could be prosecuted for talking someone into committing suicide, and Rob knew better than most that Misty Murano was able to talk anyone into anything. He had little doubt that Allison had died the night Misty had gone to her cabin. It was clever of her to impersonate Allison Robinson the following day. By the time Doug had sounded the alarm that his wife was missing, there was absolutely no chance she would ever be found.

He flinched when the door suddenly swung open and Dave strode in. He tossed Rob a wary look on the way to his desk. "Thought you'd be on break by now."

Rob straightened up in his chair and reached for the legal pad he'd been making notes on. "I haven't had a chance. The captain wanted me to take statements from the Robinsons' friends—that couple they've been hanging out with. Strictly protocol, of course. There's nothing to suggest it wasn't suicide."

Dave crossed his arms in front of him and pursed his lips. "Sad business. It's bad enough when it's accidental, but I hate the thought of some poor soul deliberately taking a dive from their balcony."

"Unfortunately, the evidence suggests that's exactly what she did," Rob replied. "Her husband found one of her flip-flops laying by the balcony railing. Apparently, she had a history of depression—she tried to kill herself before."

"Unlikely there'll be an investigation in that case. Never going to recover the body anyway," Dave muttered as he shuffled through some papers on his desk.

"I heard Misty stopped by earlier," Rob ventured.

Dave's head whipped up, and Rob read a flash of guilt in his expression. His heart slugged against his ribs. He'd wager a bet that Dave had tried to make a move on her.

"Uh ... yeah, that's right," Dave said with an awkward

chuckle. "She was gonna surprise you, but she got tired of waiting. You don't ever want to keep a lady waiting. It never ends well."

Rob balled his fingers into a fist beneath his desk. *You mean she got tired of you hitting on her.* "Did you tell her where I was?"

Dave nodded as he casually flipped open a folder. "Yeah, I told her what happened and that you went to the cabin to take the husband's statement."

Rob reached for a paperclip and began unwinding it as he scrutinized Dave, now bent over his paperwork, purportedly engrossed in some task. Dave was being evasive, but there was also an air of smugness about him that left Rob feeling hollow inside. Was there something else he wasn't telling him about Misty's visit? Anger prickled his skin. Dave had some smooth moves, but Misty would never willingly throw herself at someone with a belly and a receding hairline. If he found out Dave had laid a finger on her, he would make sure the man never worked again.

"You go ahead and take your break," Rob said. "I want to finish writing up this last statement for the captain."

As soon as Dave took off for the mess hall, Rob pulled up the security camera software on his screen. He needed to make a copy of the footage of Misty entering Allison's cabin for his own records, and then delete it from the hard drive. By the time they docked at Fort Lauderdale, there could be no record of any connection between Misty Murano and the Robinsons, especially now that Sophia Clark had made it her mission to trigger a full-blown investigation. Rob's copy of the tape would be the insurance he needed to keep Misty under his control—she wouldn't be able to walk away once she knew what he had on her.

He clicked on the three-hundred-and-sixty-degree camera in the corridor outside cabin 10664 and pulled up the time stamp he'd made a note of earlier. As he rolled the footage, a dull thud began in his chest. The clip of Misty slipping into the cabin after Allison was gone. He fast forwarded the video and watched in disbelief as the camera captured another passenger walk by less than a minute later—a passenger he hadn't seen when he'd watched it the first time. An icy shiver gripped his shoulders. It was too much of a coincidence to assume that the camera outside cabin 10664 had malfunctioned—or skipped forward in time. Someone had tampered with the video.

Rob thumped his fist on the desk. Misty had more gumption than he'd credited her with. She'd got to the footage before him and covered her tracks. It confirmed what he'd feared all along—that Misty was involved. Rob twisted his lips in rage. She couldn't have altered the video herself—she didn't have the know-how. It was no coincidence that he'd been out of the office when she'd stopped by earlier. She hadn't wanted to talk to him at all—she'd wanted to make sure he wasn't around. She must have recruited Dave to help her get rid of the incriminating clip. And no doubt Dave had been only too happy to ingratiate himself with her—especially if it meant getting back at him.

A cold sweat broke out over Rob's brow. Without the video, his plan was in tatters. He had nothing to hold over Misty now—no way of controlling her. Unless he did something drastic, he was going to lose her.

31

ROB

Rob paced back-and-forth in his office, his brazen plan percolating in his brain. The hardest part would be convincing Misty to go along with it now that he'd lost the leverage he'd been counting on. But he had an idea about how to handle that too. He would lie and say he'd made a copy of the footage of her entering Allison's cabin before Dave deleted it. Once she realized how much trouble she was potentially in, she would be putty in his hands. If he could get her off the ship and safely out of the port without any interaction with the police, he would figure out the rest of the details later.

When Dave returned from his break, Rob made a beeline for Misty's cabin. He knew her routine by now—she'd be putting on her makeup and dressing for the final evening's entertainment. His pulse hammered in his temples as he took the stairs two at a time down to the lower deck. Sweat dampened his armpits, not from the physical exertion, but from the mental strain of what he was about to do. It all had to go smoothly from beginning to end in order to pull it off. And for that to happen, he needed Misty to buy into his plan, at least the part he intended to divulge to her. The surprise would come afterward—an unpleasant one, but she had to be taught a lesson for betraying him.

Outside her cabin, Rob hurriedly smoothed down his hair and blew out a calming breath before rapping their special signal on the door.

Misty opened the door to him in a black satin strapless gown, hairbrush in hand. A puzzled look crossed her forehead. "Rob! What are you doing here? I'm getting ready for the show."

"I need to talk to you. It's urgent."

Without waiting for an invitation, he elbowed his way inside and then turned to face her, arms folded across his chest. "Close the door."

Her frown deepened. "You're scaring me, Rob. What's going on?"

With a stone-faced expression, he ran his eyes over her beautiful features as he'd done a thousand times before. For a long moment, he stood silently drinking in her full-lipped pout, her porcelain skin, and her captivating eyes, framed by those sweeping lashes, that had the power to wash some kind of an elixir over him, making him wilt in her arms. Forcing himself to get a grip, he refocused on the task at hand, determined to stick to his script and not get sidetracked. Time was of the essence. He unfolded his arms and softened his voice. "It's over Misty. I know what you did. You need to let me help you."

She cocked her head to one side, blonde curls spilling in a waterfall over her shoulder. "This sounds serious. Let me guess. I'm in trouble for not returning the cabin steward uniform to housekeeping. Don't you have more important issues to deal with?" She began to move the brush seductively through her blonde hair, baiting him as she so often did. But tonight Rob had other priorities. He needed to be meticulous about checking all the boxes and making sure there was nothing left that connected Misty to the Robinsons—like the dark wig she must have been wearing when she'd posed as Allison. Hopefully, she'd returned it to the costume room already. He made a mental note to search her room later when she was performing and make sure she hadn't left it lying carelessly around.

"This isn't about the uniform," Rob replied, his tone low and controlled. "I know you've got yourself mixed up somehow with Doug and Allison Robinson. You need to tell me what's going on."

Misty threw herself into the chair at her vanity desk and began pinning up her hair. "Are you talking about the poor woman who took her life?"

"It's way past time for playing games," Rob answered in a low growl. "How do you know her husband?"

Misty held out her hand in a gesture of bewilderment. "He requested a song. Lots of passengers do."

Rob took a step toward her, grabbing her by the arms. His breath came in short, sharp stabs at the heady scent of her, but he quashed the urge to bury his face in her hair. "What about Cozumel?" he snapped. "I'm willing to wager he wanted more from you there than a song."

With an indignant gasp, Misty tore herself away from him. "Have you completely lost your mind, Rob? What are you ranting about?"

"I know you impersonated Allison and left the ship with Doug Robinson that day." Rob swallowed the lump in his throat, forcing the haunting image of Misty with her arm tucked into Doug's from his mind. He would deal with that later. First, he had to make her understand how much trouble she was in.

"Misty, I only want to help you. If you had a hand in Allison's death, even if you just know something about it, you're equally as culpable as Doug. You're in way over your head. You could end up in prison for the rest of your life. You've got to let me help you."

Misty tossed her head, a piqued expression on her face. "I've heard enough. You need to get out now. I've got a show to get ready for." Turning her back to him, she began lining her lips in front of the makeup mirror.

Rob allowed a ponderous silence to settle in the air between them before he delivered the next blow. "Dave told me what you made him do."

Misty's bare shoulders tensed. She set down her lip liner brush and turned to face him, fluttering her lashes. "And what exactly does the deluded Dave think I asked him to do?"

"Alter the footage from the camera outside cabin 10664—Doug and Allison Robinson's cabin," Rob replied in a wooden tone.

Misty quirked an eyebrow. "Why would I ask him to do something like that?" She got to her feet and walked over to him, placing her palms flat on his chest. "Robbie, darling! We both know Dave has the hots for me. He wants to come between us, it's nothing more than that." She pouted her freshly lined lips at him. "Aren't you going to even try and kiss me? I know you want to. I can see it in your eyes."

He took her hands in his and brushed his lips gently over her fingers. "Misty, listen to me. I made a copy of the footage of you following Allison into her cabin before Dave deleted it. That was the last time anyone saw Allison Robinson alive. Do you understand what that means?"

She wet her lips, a momentary flicker of uncertainty in her face. Her eyes narrowed, her catlike reflexes weighing what he was saying. "Why did you do that?"

"Why did you ask Dave to delete the footage?" he shot back.

She sighed, letting her shoulders sag as she traced a finger along his jawline. "Okay, I admit I asked him to help me. I was afraid of what might come of it if the footage came to light—that it would make me look guilty."

Rob gripped her tighter and shook her. "What did you do to her, Misty?"

"Nothing! Like I told you already, I only went there to assure her I didn't take her necklace. When she disappeared, I knew I had to delete the footage. If anyone sees it, they'll think I had something to do with it." Her eyes widened and for the first time Rob saw a glimmer of fear in them. "I didn't do anything to that woman. I swear it. You have to believe me."

"I do believe you," Rob lied, kissing her fingertips again.

She rested her head on his chest, suppressing a muffled sob. "So you'll destroy the clip now, right?" she said in a tremulous tone. "I don't want to be implicated in anything."

Rob grimaced. "Even if I do, there's still the footage of you leaving the ship with Doug Robinson on Cozumel to worry about."

Misty tensed in his arms, catching a tear on the back of her finger, ever mindful of her makeup. She was a proficient actress, but Rob didn't mind—he was sold on whatever performance she wanted to give him, for now.

"That's why I kept a copy of the clip of you entering Allison's cabin," he said, forcing the words through his clenched lips. "Because you betrayed me with her husband."

Misty squeezed his hand, interlacing her long, delicate fingers with his. "Help me, Robbie. I don't know what to do. You're right. I did spend the day with Doug Robinson on Cozumel. I had messed things up with you, I know that now —and I was lonely and confused. He said his wife wasn't feeling well and she backed out of their plans at the last minute. I was flattered when he invited me to accompany him. He's a very handsome man—any woman would be gratified by his attention. But, as it turns out, he's also an arrogant jerk." She hesitated, a perfectly sculpted pucker on her forehead. "And he might be a murderer too."

Rob gripped her more tightly. "What are you talking about? Did he say something about wanting to get rid of his wife—anything at all?"

"No ... not directly. But he complained a lot about how depressed she was all the time and how he wished it could just be over." She sucked on her bottom lip. "Do you think he might have killed her?"

"I don't honestly know." Rob released her and ran a hand through his hair. "Listen to me, Misty. There's still a chance this incident will be written up as a suicide and not investigated any further. But if the police find out Doug was making comments like that, they will launch a full-blown investigation."

"But it won't be a problem, will it?" Misty batted her eyelashes at him. "I'm not going to say anything. And you're not going to turn over the footage to the police, are you?"

"Of course not. But we have another problem. Allison's friend, Sophia Clark, knows someone impersonated Allison on Cozumel. She's like a bloodhound when it comes to details. She watched the footage and noticed the sun hat was too small for you—you had one hand holding it on the whole time while you were shielding your face from the camera."

"Can't you delete that footage too?" Misty asked.

Rob shook his head. "It's not that simple. It would raise some major red flags. The clip in the corridor outside your cabin was relatively easy to tamper with. Only a handful of people walk around that late at night. But thousands of people disembarking and re-boarding the ship—there's no easy way to edit that video."

Misty shrank back from him. "I'm so scared, Robbie. I only wore the stupid hat and wig because Doug said he didn't want his friends to see me with him. I don't want to get caught up in anything he might have done."

Rob pulled her toward him again and kissed her, reveling in the way she melted into him, willing and compliant once more. "You won't. Not if you do exactly what I tell you to do."

32

SOPHIA

Sophia leaned over her state room balcony and inhaled the fresh, briny scent of the air as she observed the bustling Fort Lauderdale docks below. Cody joined her and handed her a coffee. "Did you sleep at all?" he asked.

She took a quick sip and shook her head. "I kept going back through every single minute of every day of the cruise in my mind, combing through all our interactions with Doug and Allison. It was almost like I was straining everything through a sieve to try and find something critical I might have missed. Some clue to tell me what was actually going on beneath the surface."

Cody squeezed her shoulder. "You've got to let it go now, Soph. This isn't our fight anymore. We've got our own battle waiting for us at home, and it's going to take all of our energy and attention to win it. The best you can do is give the police your statement and leave it to them to figure out what happened."

Sophia frowned. "I don't care what that security officer,

Rob Benson, thinks—I know that wasn't Allison boarding the ship with Doug in Cozumel."

Cody shrugged. "Even so, it doesn't mean that Doug killed her. One thing could have led to another. Maybe her depression about returning home, combined with his philandering ways, triggered her to finally go through with taking her own life."

"He kept telling us about how this was the start of a new beginning for him and Allison," Sophia mused. "Was it wishful thinking, or was it all an act, knowing full well he would be rid of her by the end of the cruise? Maybe the new beginning was all about him."

Cody shook his head slowly. "Who knows what the truth is? He had some gall spending a day with another woman right under Allison's nose—I'll give him that. I wonder how he hooked up with her."

Sophia let out a contemptuous snort. "Every woman on the ship has been eyeballing him since day one. I imagine it wasn't too hard to find some female company for the day."

The phone in their cabin rang, and Sophia darted back inside to answer it. She was waiting on a call from the cruise line with instructions for this morning's order of events. All she'd been told so far was that she, Cody, and Doug, would be given priority disembarkation status and escorted off the ship ahead of the other passengers. The Fort Lauderdale police would be waiting to meet them and take their statements. After that, they were free to return home. Sophia inhaled a sharp breath. The next couple of hours were critical. She had to do whatever it took to convince the police that they needed to conduct a thorough investigation—she couldn't let Allison down.

Sophia reached for the handset and pressed it to her ear. "Sophia Clark speaking."

"Good morning, this is Anna from Guest Services. I'm

calling to let you know that we're sending someone up to your room right now to escort you and your husband off the ship."

"Great, thank you," Sophia replied. "What about our bags?"

"You'll need to bring those with you at this time."

Sophia hung up and relayed the instructions to Cody. After wheeling her bag over to the door and setting her purse on top, she checked the bathroom and under the bed one last time to make sure they hadn't forgotten anything. She felt sick to her stomach at the thought of Doug going through the same motions in the cabin below them, packing up Allison's belongings, preparing to leave the ship without her. She didn't feel sorry for him in the least. Even if he wasn't a murderer, he was still a cheat.

Moments later, there was a knock on their cabin door. Cody opened it and a young man with a broad smile introduced himself as Carlos from Guest Services. "Let me take your bag for you, ma'am," he said to Sophia.

"Thank you," she said, handing it to him before following him out of the room.

Sophia largely ignored the small talk Cody and Carlos exchanged as they rode down in the elevator together. Ordinarily, she was the one to carry on conversations with strangers, but today her mind was fully preoccupied with thoughts of Allison, leaving room for little else. When they exited the elevator on deck four, Rob Benson was waiting for them, along with a throng of restless passengers already lining up to disembark. Benson tilted his head in their direction. "Morning, Mr. and Mrs. Clark. I'll be escorting you off the ship."

Sophia raised her brows discreetly at Cody. Officer Benson had unambiguously injected distance into his greeting, his tone considerably chillier than the day before. Sophia suspected he held it against her that she'd insisted the woman in the footage wasn't Allison Robinson. No doubt, he was eager to do everything he could to prevent the incident from blowing up into anything more than a regrettable act of suicide. Bella Oceania had a reputation to preserve after all. Murder at sea was not the kind of headline that boosted business.

Carlos wheeled her bag over to her, beaming when she handed him a twenty-dollar bill. "Thank you, ma'am. Have a safe trip home."

"Don't jump down my throat about the tip," Sophia muttered to Cody. "I know it was frivolous, but I didn't have anything smaller and I don't want to look like a cheapskate in front of all these people."

Cody harrumphed. "Get used to it. The minute we step off this ship, we're broke. Time to start acting like it."

After turning in their key cards, they followed Officer Benson past the line of passengers—some of whom threw them curious, or mildly resentful looks—down the gangplank, and onto the dock. Sophia darted a glance around the area, wondering where they were supposed to meet the police. The port was a hive of activity, vehicles pulling in and out, porters milling around piles of luggage, dock workers calling to one another, cranes and other machinery cranking in the background.

Next to the Uber pickup location, Sophia spotted the bass player for Misty's band, Dimitri, standing at the curb with his belongings. As she watched, a white van pulled up alongside him, and a middle-aged, curly-haired woman climbed out. They embraced and kissed, before loading his double bass case into the back of the van and driving off. There was no sign of Misty Murano, or any of the other band members. Sophia hadn't spotted Doug Robinson anywhere either, even though she'd been keeping a watchful eye out for him. It was possible he'd been whisked off to the police station ahead of them.

"Mr. and Mrs. Clark," a deep voice boomed. "I'm Detective Mendoza."

Sophia turned as a tall, broad-shouldered man stuck out a hairy hand to Cody and pumped his arm before gesturing to an unmarked car. "My partner, Officer Lee, is waiting for us. We're going to take you down to the station now to give your statements, and then I'll have one of my officers drive you back to your vehicle."

"How long is this going to take?" Cody asked, climbing into the back seat. "We're eager to get back to our kids."

"I can appreciate that," Detective Mendoza replied in a soothing tone. "We'll do our best to make this whole process as expedient as possible. I understand this must be a difficult situation for you."

"It's certainly not the way we envisioned ending our cruise," Cody agreed. "It's hard to believe we were talking and laughing with Allison just the day before she took her own life."

"*If* that's what she did," Sophia corrected him.

33

DETECTIVE MENDOZA

Detective Mendoza checked his messages and slurped on a bitter coffee as he waited in his office for his partner, Officer Lee, to join him. They'd arranged for Doug Robinson to give his statement first. After that, they would interview Cody Clark, followed by his wife, Sophia. Rob Benson, the ship's Chief Security Officer, had also consented to come down to the station and give a statement as soon as all the passengers had disembarked, which Mendoza estimated would probably take a couple of hours.

Based on what he'd gathered from Rob and the cabin steward he'd spoken to briefly, the Clarks and the Robinsons had been pretty tight from the first day of the cruise. If all their statements lined up, this would be an open and shut case as far as Mendoza was concerned. On the surface, there was nothing to indicate foul play, and everything to indicate that Allison Robinson had been a very unhappy woman with a history of depression and a predisposition to suicide.

Lee rapped on the glass panel on his office door. "Ready when you are, boss."

Mendoza got to his feet, his chair clicking as it released

his weight. He'd been piling on the pounds for the past year and, according to both his wife and his doctor, it was time he did something about it. But finding the time was proving to be a challenge. With four busy teenagers at home, he was no longer master of his own schedule, and retirement was still a way off.

In the interview room, Mendoza introduced himself to Doug Robinson and expressed his condolences before sitting down opposite him at the small metal table backed up to the wall. Officer Lee busied himself setting up the recording system. Overhead a fluorescent tube light flickered. Mendoza ran a critical eye over it, making a mental note to let the janitor know it needed to be replaced. He didn't like distractions when he was conducting interviews. It was a lot easier to extract the truth in a controlled environment where he commanded the sole attention. He nodded discreetly to Officer Lee, who switched on the recorder and stated the date and names of those present.

Mendoza opened his notebook and printed the date neatly at the top of the page before fixing a searching gaze on Doug Robinson. He was never in a rush to begin an interview. He'd discovered that a strained silence at the outset often did more to prod a witness into talking than a volley of questions. Doug Robinson was unquestionably *easy on the eye* as his wife would put it. In fact, Mendoza had heard a couple of the female officers in the break room giggling about him when he'd fetched his coffee earlier. But he'd learned a long time ago in this business not to let appearances color his opinion of a person one way or the other. Good looks could hide a multitude of sins.

Mendoza cleared his throat. "Let me begin by saying again how sorry I am for your loss. We appreciate you coming down to the station."

Doug inclined his head in acknowledgment, his chiseled jaw taut with apparent grief. "Thank you."

"Can you tell me when you last saw your wife?"

"It was around 1:40 p.m. yesterday, right before the ice show." Doug braced his elbows on the table in front of him, his voice echoing the anguish in his eyes. "She was supposed to go with me—with us, Cody and Sophia had tickets too—but, at the last minute, she said she wasn't feeling well."

"What were her symptoms?"

Doug gave a despairing shake of his head. "Honestly, I don't think it was a physical thing. She was feeling depressed about going home after the cruise." His voice quieted to a whisper. "We lost a baby about six months ago. To be honest, it's been a rough road ever since."

"Rough for her or for you?"

Doug threw him a flustered look. "For both of us, in different ways."

"How so?"

"We dealt with our grief differently. Allison suffered from severe postpartum depression. She tried to take her life once before. She was on antidepressants." Doug faltered, rubbing his hands over his face. "I did everything I could to help her, but it was never enough. She was always teetering on the precipice."

Mendoza jotted down *undercurrent of resentment* as he waited patiently for Doug to continue. If the man was hoping to elicit some morsel of sympathy from him, he would be sorely disappointed. That wasn't Mendoza's style. He never allowed a witness to prompt a response from him. Instead, he intended to let Doug ramble on. Allowing him enough rope to hang himself would be a more effective strategy of getting to the truth than giving him a shoulder to cry on. It was the same way Mendoza parented his teenagers. His wife thought he was too hard on them at times, but she would thank him one day when their sons graduated into society as resourceful, independent citizens with big hearts and strong backbones.

"It's been extremely difficult for me," Doug continued, clasping his hands in front of him. "Mainly because I never knew how to help her. Nothing seemed to work."

Mendoza exchanged a fleeting glance with Officer Lee. Referring to his wife in the past tense was not a check mark in Doug's favor. But not enough to incriminate him either.

"Did you ever get frustrated with your wife when she was struggling with her depression?" Mendoza asked.

Doug sputtered, an injured expression on his face. "Of course, all the time. I was frustrated with her, and frustrated with myself, and frustrated with the doctors for not being able to fix her. I loved my wife very much, Detective. It was painful to see her suffering and not be able to do anything about it."

Mendoza gave an understanding grunt as he wrote *narcissist* on his notepad and underlined it. The guy was hard to read, extremely polished. There was something about Doug Robinson he didn't like, but he wasn't getting a strong feeling either way when it came to whether or not he'd killed his wife in an act of premeditated murder.

Mendoza tapped the end of his pen on his notepad, trying to decide if he should dig a little deeper into Allison's frame of mind. Maybe he could nudge Doug into overplaying his hand and contradicting himself in the process. He planted a stoic gaze on him once more. "Did you notice any shift in your wife's mood from the previous day?"

Doug rubbed his chin in thought and then gave a grim nod. "I would have to say, yes. To all appearances, she seemed happy on Cozumel. We tooled around on the beach for a while, went on a jeep tour, shopped at the local market, had a seafood lunch." He pulled his brows together, his face creasing. "But I could tell she was struggling. I think it was the realization that we were going home soon—back to the place where she'd suffered unbearable loss and heartache. It hit her doubly hard after having such a fun time on the cruise away from all the memories. She just can't let it go. She still has boxes of unused baby clothes and toys. I keep telling her to get rid of the stuff—donate it or whatever." Doug leaned back and ruffled a hand through his hair. "We even talked about selling the house when we got back and moving to a new area. I thought maybe that would be a solution, a fresh start. She seemed excited about the idea. But she could be that way sometimes—act happy, and then come crashing down to a new low."

Mendoza fired him a challenging look. "Ever get resentful of all her mood swings?"

He detected a tiny flicker of anger in Doug's eyes before he answered in a tone of forced civility, "I wouldn't say resentful, more like frustrated. I'm a guy. I like to fix things."

"Frustration often turns to resentment when you can't fix something," Mendoza said, cocking a smile. He had to give Doug credit. He was taking the interrogation in his stride, wearing a suitably pained expression on his face. No doubt he'd come down to the station expecting, as the grieving widower, to be pandered to instead of grilled. But Mendoza saw himself as a surgeon of sorts when it came to crime, using his scalpel to carefully cut to the heart of a matter. Sophia Clark's words nagged at him: *if that's what she did.* Sophia wasn't convinced Allison had taken her life, and there had to be a reason why. His gut told him to keep digging.

"I realize you're only doing your job, Detective," Doug said, his gaze swerving briefly to Officer Lee and back. "But as you can appreciate, I'm in a lot of pain right now and I have a difficult job ahead of me breaking the news to Allison's family. If you have no other questions, I'd like to go home now."

Mendoza gave a solemn nod. "Of course. You're free to leave. Our condolences once again to you and your family."

He motioned to Officer Lee to end the interview, then got to his feet and walked Doug to the door. "We'll be in touch. I'm sure we'll have some more questions as the case proceeds."

Doug's brows shot up. "Case? I assumed your next step would be to declare my wife dead."

Mendoza stretched a polite smile over his face. "I've never been one to put much stock in assumptions."

34

DETECTIVE MENDOZA

"What's your take on the husband?" Officer Lee asked, as he and Mendoza made their way back to the coffee machine for refills.

"I'm conflicted," Mendoza admitted. "If he had a hand in his wife's demise, it's not going to be easy to prove. There's a lot of evidence to back up the picture he painted of her."

Lee poured two fresh coffees and handed a steaming cup to Mendoza. "He appeared a little shaken when you told him you'd be in touch. I got the impression he thought he would give his statement and that would be the end of it."

Mendoza grunted in assent. "You never know what's in a suspect's head until you give him a good rattling and observe what rolls out. Something about him isn't sitting right with me." He glanced at his watch. "Let's see what the Clarks have to say about him."

Mendoza greeted a nervous-looking Cody Clark with a cursory handshake while quietly evaluating his witness. He wasn't a bad-looking man in a clean-cut sort of way, but he had an air of restlessness about him that suggested he wasn't entirely comfortable being there. And the mounds beneath his eyes indicated that he'd been running on too little sleep for quite some time. If Mendoza had to take a stab at it, he'd say the man was burdened with a few problems of his own.

"I appreciate you and your wife allowing us to whisk you straight from the dock down to the station," he began. "We'll do our best to have you on the road home to your family shortly. Obviously, this is a sad situation for everyone involved—certainly not the vacation you signed up for. I understand you and your wife befriended Doug and Allison and spent a lot of time with them during the cruise."

"Yes. We met them during the boarding process," Cody said, rubbing his knuckles in an agitated fashion. "We got talking and discovered our wedding anniversaries were only a day apart. Someone suggested getting together for dinner that night—probably my wife, Sophia. She's the outgoing one. She loves meeting new people."

Mendoza made a note of the information. "How would you describe Doug and Allison?"

Cody folded his arms, his face rigid with concentration. "They were fun to hang out with. Well, Doug was—he was the life-and-soul-of-the-party type. Allison was quieter, sweet-natured, a bit absent-minded. Almost delicate in a way. Sophia and I both liked her."

"What do you mean by delicate? Was she sick, pregnant?"

"I don't think so. She had a miscarriage a few months back. Doug said it shook her up emotionally. I guess she was very depressed about it." A disquieted look crossed Cody's face. "She was on medication for it."

Mendoza allowed a thoughtful pause to pass before nodding. "Yes, Doug mentioned that. Did you pick up on any conflict between him and Allison?"

Cody shook his head. "Can't say I did. They were pretty affectionate as far as I could tell. Doug was always very attentive to Allison, protective of her, in tune with her needs.

Although—" He broke off, darting a hesitant glance at the recording device.

"Go on," Mendoza nudged.

"Sophia seemed to think Doug was a bit of a player. I guess she caught him flirting with one of the female entertainers at the Robo Bar one evening. Although, it could have been the other way around—women were always ogling him. But he only had eyes for Allison any time I was with him."

"Do you happen to know the name of this entertainer?"

"Misty Murano. She's a singer. Doug put in a song request with her for his and Allison's wedding anniversary."

"So, it's possible that's what Doug and Misty were discussing at the bar?"

Cody gave a dubious nod. "That's what he told us. Sophia's not convinced though. And once she gets an idea in her head, there's no talking her out of it."

Mendoza asked a few more questions and then signaled to Officer Lee to wrap up the interview. "Thank you, Cody. We appreciate you taking the time to come down to the station. We'll be in touch if we have any additional questions. If you don't mind waiting around a few more minutes until we take Sophia's statement—we'll get you back to your vehicle after that."

As soon as Cody exited the room, Mendoza turned to Lee. "Seems Allison's loving husband might be a bit of a player, after all. I'm sure we're about to hear all about it from Sophia Clark."

They looked up at a sharp knock on the door. The front desk clerk stuck her head in, a perturbed look on her face. "The security officer from the ship is wondering if you can interview him next. He says he has a pressing matter to attend to. He's been pacing up and down the hallway ever since he got here. Sophia Clark says she doesn't mind waiting."

Mendoza and Lee exchanged a circumspect look.

"Sure," Mendoza responded. "Send him in."

"Pressing matter—who's he kidding?" Lee remarked. "What's more pressing than a suicide on his watch? He's probably just sick of hanging around the station. Apparently, he thinks he outranks his passengers, cutting in line like that."

"You know how self-important some of these security officers can be." Mendoza curled his lip in disgust. "All right, let's find out why he's in such a hurry to get out of here."

A short time later, the door opened, and Rob Benson entered the room still dressed in his crisp white Bella Oceania uniform. He nodded in greeting to Mendoza and Lee and then sat down stiffly in the chair Cody Clark had vacated moments earlier. "Appreciate you pulling me ahead in the schedule."

"My colleague mentioned you had some important matter to attend to?" Mendoza responded, raising a questioning brow.

A flicker of irritation glinted in Rob's eyes. Clearly, he hadn't expected Mendoza to pry. But Mendoza had a knack for it. And he wasn't one to waste an opportunity. You never knew what you would find when you began to peel back the layers.

"It's my mother's seventieth birthday today," Rob said in a testy tone.

"Congratulations to your mother," Mendoza replied, casually flipping open his notebook and noting down Rob's first lie. He would bet his paycheck that Rob wasn't hurrying off to attend a birthday party. "In that case, let's dive right in so we don't keep you from the festivities any longer than we have to." Mendoza nodded to Officer Lee and waited until the requisite information for the interview had been recorded before launching into his first question. "When did you learn that Allison Robinson was missing?"

"My Deputy Security Officer, Dave O'Reilly, radioed me a Code Oscar about—."

"Remind me what that means again—the code," Mendoza interrupted, holding up a questioning finger. He was pandering to the man's arrogance, but he was banking on getting more out of him that way. He knew Rob's type. Small-man-in-a-uniform syndrome. Stroke his ego enough and he'd open right up.

"Code Oscar is the vessel emergency code when someone falls overboard," Rob preened. "It's mainly used in the cruising industry."

"Got it," Mendoza said, making a point of writing it down. "Carry on."

"Allison's husband, Doug Robinson, contacted security to report his wife missing after he got back from the ice show matinee. Dave took the call and radioed me. I went straight to the Robinsons' cabin to meet with Doug. The Clarks were there with him."

"Do you know why Allison didn't attend the show with her husband?"

"I believe he said she wasn't feeling well."

Mendoza jotted down *the husband said* and underlined the words, before asking, "What made you think his wife had gone overboard?"

Rob exhaled a slow breath as if to soften the impending blow, "I was told she had a history of severe depression following a miscarriage last year. Apparently, she was taking anti-depressant medication and might have overdosed a couple of days earlier in Haiti. A paramedic was called to the beach." He ran the tip of his tongue along his lips. "From what I understand, it wasn't the first time she'd tried to take her own life."

"Was there any physical evidence to suggest she'd gone overboard?"

Rob nodded gravely and pulled out his phone. He scrolled through some photos and then passed the phone to Mendoza. "One of her flip-flops was lying next to the balcony railing. The other one's missing."

Mendoza scrutinized the picture. "So you spotted this flip-flop by the railing when you got there?"

Rob's eyes bulged, his self-assured manner momentarily slipping. "No. Doug had already picked it up by the time I got to the cabin."

"What about Allison's purse?" Mendoza asked, handing the phone back to Rob.

"It was still in the cabin, along with her key pass. The crew searched the ship for her from top to bottom. And we had a team review all the elevator and stairwell CCTV. There's no indication she ever left her cabin that day."

Mendoza tapped the end of his pen quietly on the desk, a steady gaze fixed on Rob. Something about the security officer's demeanor was setting off alarm bells. Not to mention the sweat on his upper lip that was at odds with the chilly temperature in the room. On the surface, his rendition of events was seamless. No doubt his colleague, Dave, could back him up, as could the Clarks who'd been with Doug in the cabin. By all accounts, Rob had done everything according to the book. So why was he getting a bad feeling about this?

"I take it you interviewed any crew members who interacted with the Robinsons on a daily basis?" Mendoza continued.

Rob gave an emphatic nod. "I talked to their cabin steward and the wait staff who served them."

"Did any of them mention witnessing any kind of disagreement between Doug and Allison?"

"No, nothing of that nature," Rob said, fleetingly averting his eyes. Mendoza's curiosity was instantly piqued. He suspected the security officer had picked up on something amiss between the couple, but, for whatever reason, he was holding it close to his chest. Maybe the CCTV had captured Doug and Allison in some kind of altercation. Was Rob trying to protect the cruise line—and, ultimately, his job? A suicide was bad publicity, but a murder at sea would be an even bigger blight on Bella Oceania's record that would have far deeper ramifications.

Mendoza consulted his notes before continuing. "Cody Clark seemed to think that Doug might have been a bit of a player—supposedly he'd been flirting with one of the entertainers on board, a Misty Murano. Do you know her?"

Panic pooled in Rob's eyes before he composed himself, "Uh, yes, she's one of the singers, I believe."

Mendoza rubbed his chin thoughtfully. Interesting addendum. *I believe.* A clumsy attempt to distance himself from the woman. But why would Rob need to do that?

Mendoza let an awkward silence unfold as he took stock of the man's discomfort. He hadn't missed the barely perceptible tremor in Rob's voice, or the slight sheen on his forehead indicating that his heart was palpitating a little more than it should.

He picked up his pen and circled the name Misty Murano.

35

DETECTIVE MENDOZA

The minute Rob exited the interview room, Detective Mendoza tossed his pen on the table and threw Officer Lee a charged look. "The mysterious Misty Murano is the connecting piece of the puzzle. She and Doug Robinson had some kind of interaction in the Robo Bar. My guess is that Rob Benson's trying to keep her out of this for some reason or another."

"Maybe he has a thing going with her himself," Lee observed. "He sure got hot and sweaty under the collar once her name came up."

Mendoza scrunched his eyes shut and pinched the bridge of his nose, releasing the pressure that had built up over the course of the back-to-back interviews. "Better bring Misty in for an interview too. Call the cruise line and get her contact info ASAP. I'm going to take a quick break to stretch my legs and get the blood flowing. I'll meet you back here."

Ten minutes later, Sophia Clark sat down in the chair Mendoza gestured to and planted an unflinching gaze on him, which impressed him right off the bat. At six-foot-three and two-hundred-and-fifty pounds, he could be an imposing figure to some women—which often worked against him when interviewing female witnesses. He'd wager a bet that Sophia had more spunk than any of the men he'd interviewed so far this afternoon. Not to mention a woman's intuition. If there was a thread to unravel in this convoluted plot, Mendoza had no doubt she'd already been picking at it. He nodded to Officer Lee to begin recording.

"Sorry to keep you waiting so long," he began. "The security officer from the cruise line had some pressing obligation he needed to attend to."

Sophia flapped a dismissive hand. "I just hope he told you the same thing I'm here to tell you."

Mendoza drummed a finger lightly on his notepad, hoping she'd come straight to the point. "Which is?"

She scooted forward in her chair. "I'm not convinced Allison took her own life. Doug Robinson didn't spend the excursion day on Cozumel with his wife. He lied about who he was with."

Mendoza hefted an encouraging brow. "Oh?"

"Rob Benson called me down to the security office to identify Allison on the CCTV. He showed me a clip of Doug with a dark-haired woman on his arm boarding the ship at Cozumel. She was holding Allison's designer sun hat on top of her head to stop it falling off—it didn't fit properly. My hunch is the only reason she had it on in the first place was to hide her face."

Mendoza scratched the stubble on his cheek. "I'm afraid I don't follow. You're saying you don't think it was Allison because she was holding her hat on? Isn't that a normal thing to do when it's windy—she was at the port, after all?"

Sophia shot him an impatient look. "Doug bought her that hat for the cruise. It's a Gigi Burris—very expensive. But it was too big. It kept slipping over her eyes, so she stopped wearing it after the first day."

"Interesting." Mendoza set his pen down on the table and interlaced his fingers over his belly. Sophia Clark had a keen eye for detail, as well as being tenacious, and intuitive—a winning combination in his line of work. He had a hunch her statement would do more to help him get to the bottom of what had really happened to Allison Robinson than anything he'd heard up until this point. "All right, let's start at the beginning. You said you're not convinced it was suicide. I take it you're basing that on more than an ill-fitting hat."

Sophia gave a sharp nod. "I've been combing through everything that happened from the moment we met the Robinsons. Right off the bat, I could tell we'd have fun hanging out together. Doug was extremely outgoing. I liked Allison too, especially as I got to know her more—though she seemed a bit fuzzy-headed at times. But as the cruise got underway, several things struck me as odd."

Mendoza picked up his pen again. "Such as?"

"To begin with, Doug gave Allison this expensive necklace for their ten-year wedding anniversary at dinner on our first night. Supposedly, the lock on the safe in their room wasn't working properly, so she ended up stashing it in her suitcase while they attended a show with us. When she looked for it later that evening, it was gone." Sophia tucked a strand of hair behind her ear, allowing a moment for that to sink in before continuing. "She and Doug turned their cabin upside down, but they couldn't find it anywhere. Allison insisted on calling security and reporting the theft. She thought the maintenance guy who'd gone into their cabin to repair their safe while they were at the show must have taken it."

Mendoza shot a look Officer Lee's way. "Doug didn't mention anything about a theft, did he?"

Lee shook his head. "Not that I recall."

Sophia arched a brow. "That's because later on that night, the necklace showed up again in the pocket of a Bella

Oceania robe hanging in the closet. Doug insisted that Allison was just forgetful, but she was convinced she hadn't put the necklace there."

"You did say she came across as fuzzyheaded at times," Mendoza pointed out.

Sophia gave a measured nod. "At first, I thought it was because of the antidepressant medication Doug said she was taking. The day we went to Labadee she passed out in the water. She wasn't drunk—she'd only had one cocktail. The paramedic on the beach asked if she was on any medication and Doug pulled her prescription out of her purse to show him. The bottle was almost empty." Sophia allowed a dramatic pause to ensue, before going on, "Allison told me afterward that she didn't remember taking any of the pills. I wrote it off as forgetfulness on her part, but it niggled at me."

"Anything else bother you?" Mendoza prodded, scribbling down a couple of notes.

"One other day we were on the pool deck, and Allison went to look for a restroom. While she was gone, Doug insisted we move to the hot tub on the opposite side where we wouldn't be in the shade. He said he'd told Allison to meet us there." Sophia puckered her forehead. "It was ages before she came back. She said she'd been looking all over for us. Doug laughed it off, as if she'd simply forgotten what he'd told her. We'd all been drinking cocktails and getting silly, so I didn't think much of it at the time. But later on, when I lined it up against all the other incidents, I questioned whether Doug had really told Allison we were moving, or whether he'd deliberately left her hanging."

"So you think he might have been setting her up during the cruise to make her look scatterbrained."

"In retrospect, I'm sure of it." Sophia narrowed her eyes. "Allison even asked me if I thought Doug had tried to kill her by spiking her cocktail that day on the beach at Labadee. She suspected he was having an affair—said he'd been traveling for work a lot. And she found a burner phone hidden beneath his clothes in their cabin."

Mendoza tapped his fingertips together for a long moment, weighing the information. Clearly, Sophia had a keen sense of when things didn't add up. He was inclined to trust her instincts. He glanced down at his notepad and scanned through what he had written. "What about this woman, Misty Murano? Your husband mentioned that you saw Doug Robinson flirting with her in a bar."

Sophia twisted her lips. "It looked that way to me. Two peas in a pod. He had women ogling him all the time, and Misty got more than her fair share of attention too—from passengers and crew alike."

"Is it possible Doug was with Misty Murano on Cozumel?"

Sophia blinked, considering this for a minute. "The woman in the CCTV footage had dark hair, like Allison. I suppose she could have been wearing a wig. Now that I think of it, Misty probably has access to all sorts of costumes as a performer."

"Even if Misty did accompany Doug to Cozumel, it still doesn't prove he killed his wife," Mendoza said, scratching the back of his head thoughtfully. "Did you see Allison at all that evening after Doug got back?"

Sophia shook her head. "Doug texted to say they were wiped out and going to order room service."

Mendoza drew his brows together. "If Allison didn't spend the day on Cozumel with Doug, it means she could have died a day earlier." He glanced across at Lee. "How are we coming on the contact details for Misty Murano?"

"Bella Oceania emailed me everything they had on file," Lee replied. "She's not answering her phone. I've left a couple of messages. I'll keep trying."

Mendoza pursed his lips and turned back to Sophia. "You said Misty got plenty of attention from passengers and crew alike. Did you notice her hanging out with any crew members in particular?"

"I saw her with the Chief Security Officer, Rob Benson, in the Robo Bar. He's the one who responded to the situation when Allison went missing." Sophia huffed in disgust. "He's a waste of time. He took Doug's statement, snapped a few pictures, and left. I got the impression he wanted to hurry up the process and label it a suicide so he could close the case as quickly as possible. I suppose a suicide is marginally better than murder when it comes to bad cruise line publicity."

Mendoza gave a nod of acknowledgment. "You said earlier that Allison called security to report her necklace missing. Do you know who she spoke to about it?"

Sophia rolled her eyes. "That was Rob Benson too. He took the report and did a cursory search of the cabin."

"Got it," Mendoza said, setting down his pen. "Well, I think I have all I need for now. You've been extremely helpful, Sophia, and I know you're eager to get home to your kids."

Sophia got to her feet and rested her fingertips on the metal table. "Just promise me you won't let Doug Robinson get away with this."

"I don't make promises, especially when 'this' has yet to be defined," Mendoza responded, locking eyes with her. "I prefer to sift through the evidence and trust the process."

"Then let's hope that's enough to nail him, because Allison didn't deserve this," Sophia retorted, slinging her purse over her shoulder.

After she retreated out the door, Mendoza sank back in his chair and folded his hands behind his head. "Tell me, Lee, are you any good at equations?"

"It's been awhile. What have you got?" Lee asked, powering down the recording device.

Mendoza gazed up at the white-tile ceiling."Rob times Doug, minus Allison."

Lee let out a snort of laughter. "You got me stumped, boss."

"That's because we're missing the variable we need to solve it."

"And what would that be?" Lee asked, blinking in bewilderment.

"*Who,* not what." Mendoza rubbed his palms on his pant legs and got to his feet with a heavy grunt. "It's time we had a conversation with Misty Murano. My hunch is that once we do, this house of cards will come tumbling down."

36

DETECTIVE MENDOZA

"Are you sure this is the right address?" Detective Mendoza asked, as he and Lee pulled up at a dilapidated trailer parked on an overgrown lot. Twenty-four hours had gone by since they had first tried to contact Misty Murano and they still hadn't heard anything back from her despite leaving numerous messages.

"It's the address Bella Oceania emailed over to me," Officer Lee affirmed, checking his phone.

Mendoza grunted, peering through the windscreen of their unmarked sedan. "Doesn't look too promising. No vehicle in sight, no lights on, no sign of any activity. Wait here. I'll check it out." He climbed out of the car and slammed the door shut before picking his way through the weeds to the trailer.

"Anyone home?" he called out, banging his knuckles on the door. He waited for a minute or two then hammered more insistently a second time. "Police! Is anyone there?"

When no one answered, he walked around to the side of the trailer, tenting his hands over his eyes to peer through a small crack in the miniblinds. It was impossible to make out much other than one corner of a well-worn, tan-colored couch with a checkered cushion leaking stuffing. He shook his head in disbelief. If this was all Misty had to look forward to on her time off, she was better off staying on the cruise ship. He returned to the front door and tried the handle, caught off guard when the door swung open. He motioned to Lee that he was going in, then peered cautiously around the doorframe, reaching for his weapon. He quickly scanned the space, documenting in one practiced sweep several alarming anomalies. A shattered glass vase and a bouquet of trampled flowers lay strewn over the mangy carpet. The table sported an abandoned coffee mug, a half-eaten slice of toast, and a lidless jar of strawberry jelly over which a fly was buzzing with manic anticipation.

Mendoza gritted his teeth and holstered his weapon. There was no way Misty had left her home like this voluntarily, or the door unlocked. Something foul had gone down, and the odds were that either Doug Robinson or Rob Benson was involved. He lumbered down the trailer steps and jogged back to the car where Lee was waiting, a questioning look on his face. "No sign of her?"

"None. Doesn't look right at all," Mendoza replied in a clipped tone as he started up the engine. "There's a half-eaten breakfast on the table, and a vase of flowers smashed on the floor. And the door was left unlocked. Misty Murano didn't leave here of her own free will. We need a photo ID ASAP."

"Already got it. Check this out." Lee held out his phone for Mendoza to take a look. "There's your linchpin to unraveling this fiasco—Misty Murano. Helen of Troy, baby. That's the kind of face men duel over."

Mendoza scowled as he put the car into gear. "You mean the kind of face that gets a woman thrown overboard."

"Possibly. And that's not all," Lee continued, scrolling through his phone. "I dug up some pictures of the *Diamond of the Waves* crew on Facebook. Looks like Misty Murano and our Chief Security Officer, Rob Benson, were an item. I came across one of them looking pretty cozy at a Christmas party last year."

Mendoza shot Lee a sidelong glance. "Could have been just drunken antics."

"It's a little more than that as it turns out. I talked to Rob's colleague, Dave O'Reilly—he's the Deputy Security Officer on board. He says Rob and Misty have been dating on and off for a year-and-a-bit. Apparently, she broke it off with him recently. And get this, Dave says Rob couldn't accept it. He's completely obsessed with her, watches her all the time on the ship's CCTV."

Mendoza let out an aggravated grunt. "Call the station and get an address for Rob Benson, and Doug Robinson too while you're at it. I'm willing to wager one of them knows where Misty Murano is and the other one's looking for her."

TEN MINUTES LATER, they pulled up outside Rob Benson's property, a single-story residence with a wraparound porch, located only a few miles from Misty's trailer. They sat in the car and waited for a short while to see if they could spot any sign of movement.

"I'm guessing this is where Misty spent most of her time off the ship," Mendoza said. "This place is a lot more appealing than her digs. Neat as a pin."

"Pretty private set up he's got here," Lee observed. "Looks like a three-acre lot."

"All fenced in," Mendoza added. "Which means he might have a dog. Better take precautions, just in case."

"If he's home, his car must be in the garage," Lee remarked, tilting his chin at the oversized detached garage a short distance from the house.

"Let's check the main building first," Mendoza said, climbing out.

They unlatched the gate at the foot of the path and strode up to the front door. Mendoza rang the bell, then stepped back to wait for Rob to answer it. "Don't hear any barking. Maybe he's taken his dog out for a walk."

"I'll take a quick stroll around to the back of the house and see if I can spot anyone," Lee suggested.

He reappeared a few minutes later. "No one home, as far as I can tell."

Mendoza motioned to the detached building. "Let's see if his car's here."

They made their way over to the garage and peeked in the window of the attached apartment, but it was impossible to see anything through the blinds.

"I'm guessing this is a guest apartment, or maybe an office or something," Lee said.

They walked around to the back of the building and knocked on the access door. After waiting for several minutes, they knocked again, to no avail.

"Doesn't look like he's here. Keep trying his number," Mendoza said, casting a lingering glance around the manicured property. "Let's go pay Doug Robinson a visit in the meantime."

As they turned to go, a muffled thump from inside the building caught their attention. Mendoza exchanged a silent nod of understanding with Lee, his hand automatically reaching for his weapon. He knocked sharply on the door again. "Police! Anyone home?"

Seconds later, they heard a loud crash.

"That's it, we're going in," Mendoza muttered to Lee.

"Police! I need you to step away from the door," he yelled, rattling the handle.

Gritting his teeth, he raised his weapon and fired off two

shots, splintering the wood around the lock. Gun drawn, he kicked open the door and edged slowly around it, searching for a figure in the gloomy space. A black trash bag was taped over the blinds covering the solitary window they'd tried to peek through. No wonder they hadn't been able to see inside. Whatever Rob had stashed in here, he didn't want anyone spotting it. Mendoza's gaze flitted over the miscellaneous shadowy shapes huddled around the room: a heavy wooden desk, a stack of metal filing drawers, and a small refrigerator. His gaze came to rest on a closet door in the far wall. Silently, he gestured to Lee to back him up. Gun at the ready, he padded across the floor and twisted the handle. Inching the door open, his eyes widened at the sight of a duct-taped figure writhing helplessly on the floor.

"It's okay! We're here to help," Mendoza said, dropping to his knees and peeling the duct tape from the woman's mouth. I'm Detective Mendoza and this is my colleague Officer Lee. Can you tell me your name?"

The woman winced as the tape ripped several blonde hairs from her head. "Misty … Murano," she choked out. "Water, please."

Officer Lee hurriedly retrieved a water bottle from the refrigerator in the corner of the room and held it to Misty's lips while Mendoza worked on freeing her bound hands and feet.

After she'd drunk her fill, she let out a long shuddering sigh. "Thank you. I thought I was going to die in there. It's so hot." She dabbed the back of her hand to her moistened lips and then tensed. "Do you see my phone anywhere?"

Mendoza cast a searching glance around the small storage room filled with self-assembly shelving that Misty had evidently been kicking and knocking items from in an attempt to alert them to her predicament.

Following his gaze, Misty said, "I heard you thumping on

the door. I thought I was imagining it at first." She groaned, as if in pain, her eyelids fluttering closed. "I ... don't feel so good."

"Get a medic coming," Mendoza muttered to Lee, as he put an arm around Misty.

He escorted her over to a nearby office chair, then switched on a floor fan and pulled it closer to her. "The ambulance is on its way. I need to ask you a couple of questions in the meantime. Can you tell me how you ended up here?"

Misty dropped her head into her hands and shook it. "I really need my phone."

Mendoza bit back his frustration at her inability to focus on what was important. "I want to help you, Misty," he assured her. "What happened to you was a crime. Can you tell me who tied you up?"

"He did," she said looking up at him through tear-filled eyes."

"Who's he? I need a name," Mendoza responded.

"Rob Benson," Misty said in a plaintive whisper. "This is his house."

"Okay." Mendoza nodded encouragingly. "Why did he tie you up?"

She blinked solemnly, her lustrous eyes latching onto Mendoza in distress before they rolled back in her head. "Because I killed that woman."

37

DETECTIVE MENDOZA

"I want a BOLO out on Rob Benson's vehicle and undercover agents watching the house twenty-four seven until he's picked up," Detective Mendoza relayed to Officer Lee, just as the wail of an ambulance reached their ears. "Radio it in right away."

Moments later, two paramedics came through the door. Mendoza got to his feet and stepped out of their way while they checked a semi-conscious Misty's vitals before lifting her onto a stretcher trolley and transporting her out to the waiting ambulance.

Officer Lee directed a meaningful look at Mendoza. "Was that a confession?"

Mendoza dismissed the idea with a grunt. "Don't count on it. We haven't got to the bottom of this yet. She was so dehydrated she didn't know what she was saying."

"Or she could be covering for someone."

Mendoza pursed his lips. "We need to find Benson. Now that he's facing kidnapping and hostage charges, I reckon he'll be a lot more cooperative."

"Do you want to head to the hospital and finish questioning Misty first?" Lee asked.

"Let's hang about here for a bit—keep an eye on the place from a distance. I have a hunch Rob wasn't planning on leaving Misty alone for too long in that closet. With a bit of luck, he'll come driving up any minute."

They pulled their unmarked sedan around the corner onto a cross street, rolled down the windows, and sank down in their seats to wait. Less than thirty minutes later, they heard the sound of an engine approaching the property, then slowing down. They quietly exited their vehicle and watched from a safe distance as a blue Subaru Outback pulled into the garage. Seconds later, the rolling metal door clattered shut.

Springing into action, Mendoza and Lee jogged around the corner, and across the lawn to the detached garage. "Police! Put your hands where I can see them!" Mendoza growled, kicking open the access door at the back of the office.

Rob Benson, stood frozen mid-stride, zigzagging a confused look between Mendoza and the open closet door as he slowly raised his hands above his head.

"Rob Benson, you're under arrest for the unlawful kidnapping and false imprisonment of Misty Murano," Officer Lee said, cuffing him as he read him his rights.

"It isn't what you think," Rob protested. "I was only trying to protect her."

"You can tell us all about it down at the station," Mendoza replied, nudging him toward the door.

For the second time in the space of two days, Mendoza found himself seated opposite Bella Oceania's Chief Security Officer, Rob Benson. Only this time, Rob had a lawyer seated at his side—an angular woman in her fifties with tight gray curls, a long, thin face, and a nasally voice that Mendoza was trying hard to tolerate.

The update he'd received from the hospital was that Misty had had a panic attack and been given something to calm her down. Apart from being dehydrated, it appeared she was unharmed. Mendoza had asked the hospital to hold off on discharging her until he was through with this interview. He wanted to hear Rob's side of the story before he tackled Misty. She had passed out cold immediately after her bombshell confession, and Mendoza hadn't even had a chance to confirm who the woman was that she'd killed—presumably Allison Robinson.

"Why don't you begin by telling us what the nature of your relationship with Misty Murano is?" Mendoza said.

Rob's eyes skated briefly to his lawyer's impassive face before he responded in a faltering tone. "Misty's ... my girlfriend."

Mendoza stared intently at him. "Any reason why you didn't tell us that in the last interview when her name came up?"

Rob scowled. "You didn't ask."

"You acted as if you barely knew her."

"We were discussing the disappearance of Allison Robinson, not my personal life," Rob answered with a sullen shrug.

Mendoza stared coldly back at him. "Why did you kidnap Misty Murano and detain her against her will."

"I didn't kidnap her. She came to my house voluntarily."

"And why did she do that?"

"She wanted to stay with me."

Mendoza raised an eyebrow. "Any particular reason why?"

Rob huffed in aggravation. "There doesn't have to be a reason. She stays with me whenever she wants—which is most of the time. Her trailer's a dump."

Mendoza threw him a cutting glare. "The thing is, Benson, the evidence suggests Misty didn't leave her trailer of her own free will. Which makes me think she didn't arrive at your house of her own free will either, nor did she have any desire to stay there. In fact, the duct tape is kind of a dead giveaway, wouldn't you say?"

A deep flush crept up Rob's neck. "She wasn't thinking straight. I needed her to calm down before she did something rash. I was only trying to protect her."

"Protect her from what exactly?"

Rob crossed his arms in front of him, his face closing over.

"You need to understand you're looking at some serious charges here, Rob," Mendoza lowered his voice to a conspiratorial level. "I'm trying to help you. It would be better for you in the long run if you cooperate fully."

Rob stole a furtive glance at his lawyer. She pinched her brows together and gave him a crisp, no nonsense nod in return.

Rob wet his lips, shifting nervously in his seat. "It has to do with what happened on the ship."

"Go on," Mendoza prodded.

"I'm pretty sure Misty had something to do with Allison Robinson's disappearance."

"Why do you think that?"

Rob passed a shaking hand over his forehead. "I was hoping it wouldn't come to this."

"What did Misty do, Rob?" Mendoza asked, an ominous undertone creeping into his voice.

"She ... she followed Allison Robinson into her cabin the night she vanished. I saw it on the CCTV. I was afraid she might have ... you know—" He stopped talking abruptly and wrinkled his forehead.

Mendoza shot Lee a quick look. If Sophia Clark's hunch

was right that Allison hadn't accompanied her husband to Cozumel, then the timeline suggested she had been killed the night before. Which meant Misty Murano could have murdered her.

"I'll need to see that CCTV footage," Mendoza said.

Rob gave a glum nod. "The file's on my phone."

Mendoza braced his elbows on the table and leaned forward. "Rob, it's important for your sake that you tell me everything. What is it that you think Misty did?"

"I don't think she actually *did* anything," he said in a slightly panicked tone, his eyes flicking from Mendoza to his lawyer. "She might have said something to upset Allison, that's all. It wouldn't have taken much. Allison Robinson was unhinged—completely paranoid. She accused one of our staff of stealing her necklace. Turned out it was in her room the whole time." He stared dismally down at the table. "And then Sophia Clark saw Doug talking to Misty in the Robo Bar one night. She got the wrong end of the stick and told Allison they were flirting. Maybe that's why she jumped. She was already depressed, on medication for it. She had some kind of overdose episode on Haiti, and her husband said it wasn't the first time she'd tried to do herself in."

"What makes you so sure the conversation between Doug and Misty was innocent?" Mendoza asked, watching Rob's reaction intently. "Maybe Sophia was right and there was something going on between them."

Rob gave a shrug that came across as more angry than nonchalant. "All the guests flirted with Misty. She's a beautiful woman—she drives men wild with longing and women green with envy."

Mendoza took note of Rob's increasingly rapid tone and the glistening sweat on his forehead. Apparently, he was one of the men Misty Murano drove wild.

"So explain to me exactly how you were *helping* Misty by tying her up," Mendoza asked, tapping a finger on the desk.

Rob's lawyer leaned over and whispered something in his ear. Rob scratched his cheek distractedly. "I suspected Doug might have done something to his wife. I was afraid Misty would get caught up in it—if it turned into a murder investigation. I was trying to keep her from saying anything to incriminate herself until it all blew over."

Mendoza raised a skeptical brow. "Sure you weren't trying to punish her for a dalliance with Doug Robinson?"

"I don't know what you mean," Rob spluttered.

"Duct taping your girlfriend and locking her in a closet sounds more to me like you were trying to punish her. Was there anything you thought she needed to be punished for, Rob?"

His lawyer cleared her throat. "You're intimidating my client."

"Was she even your girlfriend?" Mendoza continued, undeterred, allowing a mocking note to creep into his voice. "Your colleague in the security office seems to be under the impression that she dumped you."

Rob slammed his fist down on the table, half rising out of his seat before his lawyer laid a restraining hand on him. "She was *mine* before he stole her from me."

Mendoza painted on a look of abject sympathy. "Who stole her from you?"

"Doug Robinson," Rob said through gritted teeth. "He killed his wife so he could be with Misty."

38

DETECTIVE MENDOZA

Detective Mendoza and Officer Lee headed back to the interview room to wait for Misty Murano's arrival. She had been discharged from the hospital a short time earlier and two officers had been sent to pick her up and bring her down to the station—under the guise of taking her statement so they could prosecute Rob for kidnapping and unlawful imprisonment. Of course, they were investigating a lot more than that at this point, but it was proving to be a tangled web. Although Mendoza still hadn't ruled out the possibility that Allison had taken her own life, he was growing more convinced with every new development in the case that she had been murdered. The question was whether Misty was behind Allison's death, or whether she was protecting someone. Doug might have bumped off his wife, as Rob maintained, but then again Rob might be trying to pin Allison's murder on Doug in a desperate bid to keep Misty out of it. He might even have masterminded Allison's death himself, intending to pin the blame on Doug to punish him for stealing Misty. All options were on the table as far as Mendoza was concerned.

There was a knock on the door and the desk clerk escorted a pale and visibly shaken Misty inside. She seated herself in the chair opposite Mendoza and Lee and tucked a strand of glossy blonde hair behind one ear with shaking fingers. Mendoza eyed her appraisingly. She wasn't wearing a scrap of makeup, but her natural beauty was enough to take a man's breath away. He knew this because Lee had stopped breathing the minute she sat down, his jaw locked in drop-down mode. Mendoza cleared his throat, throwing him a reproving look. "Ready?"

Lee fumbled with the recording device, his cheeks reddening.

"Thanks for coming down to the station to give us a statement, Misty," Mendoza began. "How are you feeling?"

"Better, thank you. A little weary." Her voice had a honeyed, sultry tone, reminding Mendoza that she was a professional singer, and by all accounts, a good one. She leaned forward in her chair, a slightly frenzied look in her eyes. "Did you find my phone yet?"

"I'm afraid not," Mendoza said. "But once we secure a search warrant for the property, we'll look for it more thoroughly."

"I really need it," Misty said, dragging in a sharp breath. "Please let me know right away if you find it."

"Absolutely." Mendoza consulted his notes briefly. "I'd like to go back to where we left off earlier, before you passed out. Do you remember how you ended up on Rob Benson's property?"

She wrung her hands and gave a shallow nod. "He stopped by my trailer. He said he needed to talk to me. One thing led to another and we got into an argument. The next thing I knew he was duct taping me. Then he put me in the trunk of his car and drove me to his place."

"What were you arguing about?"

Misty's eyelashes fluttered downward. "He ... accused me of cheating on him. I've been trying to break it off with him for some time, but he's not getting the message. He's very controlling—he's been growing increasingly obsessive over the past few months. He scares me sometimes."

"Before you passed out, you told us Rob tied you up because you killed a woman," Mendoza said, quieting his voice. "Who were you referring to?"

"No one. I didn't kill anyone," Misty protested, giving a frantic shake of her head. "He thought I did. But he was mistaken."

Mendoza exchanged a skeptical look with Lee. "Okay, who did he *think* you killed?"

Misty squeezed her hands together, darting a wary look at the recording device. "Allison Robinson."

"And what led him to believe that?"

"He saw me on the CCTV, following her into her cabin. I didn't realize quite how obsessed he'd become until recently. Dave says he's been watching me on the ship's CCTV for months."

Mendoza made a couple of notes on his pad. "If you didn't kill Allison, why did you follow her into her cabin?"

There was a beat of silence before Misty mustered a response. "I wanted to explain to her what really happened with her necklace."

"And what was that?"

Misty studied a polished fingernail for a long moment before letting out a beleaguered sigh. "Doug took it from her suitcase. He gave it to me and asked me to return it while they were out of the cabin."

"Is that the kind of favor you normally do for passengers?" Mendoza hefted a questioning brow as he waited for her answer, sensing the case was about to unravel. Lee shifted uncomfortably in the chair next to him.

Misty looked directly at Mendoza, a flicker of understanding in her brooding blue eyes. "I know what you're thinking, but it wasn't like that. I met Doug Robinson at a cocktail lounge in Miami last year. I was on a month-long break between cruises and singing in clubs to make some extra money. He came in one night with a couple of business associates. I noticed him right away, of course, like every other woman in the bar. He stayed on after his associates left. He bought me a drink and we ended up talking all night. We had this instant connection. He wanted all the same things out of life that I did. He was passionate, funny, outgoing, driven—everything I admired in a man. When I went back to work on the cruise ships, he would fly to different ports to meet me. He had a ton of frequent flyer miles and he traveled all the time for business anyway."

"Were you still dating Rob Benson at the time?"

Misty gave a guilty nod. "I wanted to end it. I felt trapped in that relationship. It was different with Doug. He wasn't possessive, or jealous, or controlling."

"Did you know he was married?"

Misty blinked back a tear. "He lied about that. He told me he was separated and going through a difficult divorce."

"Did he give you any details—why they were divorcing?"

Misty pulled a tissue from her purse and twisted it in her fingers. "They had a daughter, Ava. She was only a couple of months old at the time. Allison was struggling with severe postpartum depression. He couldn't handle it any longer. He said she wasn't anything like the woman he'd married."

Mendoza turned a page and scribbled down a few more notes. "Why didn't they go through with the divorce?"

"Their baby died all of a sudden. Allison couldn't accept it. Her depression spiraled out of control and she tried to take her life. Doug said he felt guilty about leaving her after that, he was afraid of what her family would think of him. He didn't want to lose his company—Allison's father had put up the money to start it, you see. Doug wanted to wait until things stabilized, as he put it."

Mendoza leaned back and studied her over his steepled fingers. She was talking freely now, and it all sounded plausible, but the frustrating part was that he still felt like he was missing something obvious. "How did the Robinsons end up on the cruise with you?"

"It was Doug's idea," Misty answered. "He told Allison he'd booked a cruise to celebrate their ten-year anniversary. It would be a fresh start for them. He told me it would be an opportunity for us to spend time together—that Allison would probably stay holed up in her cabin all day every day." She hesitated. "He was playing us both."

"What do you mean by that?"

Misty drew her delicately arched brows together. "Doug kept insinuating that Allison would end her life, given the right circumstances. He wanted to know if I would be there for him when the day came. I suppose deep down I knew what he was hinting around about. I mean, why else would you take your suicidal wife on a cruise and book a cabin on the tenth floor?"

39

DETECTIVE MENDOZA

Detective Mendoza tapped his foot softly up and down beneath the table, weighing up Misty's credibility. A sixth sense told him he was watching a performance—flawlessly executed. Had she even had a panic attack before she'd been hauled off to the hospital? He didn't know what to believe anymore. As for her confession, it was useless. A feverish, dehydrated hostage could say almost anything, and it wouldn't hold up in court. Undoubtedly, she was a masterful storyteller, but his years of experience told him there was something she was skating around. Was she trying to protect herself, or Rob, or Doug, or some combination of the three? Had Allison's death been a terrible accident they were trying to cover up?

Mendoza laid his pen down on the table in front of him and pinned a quizzical gaze on Misty. "Are you suggesting Doug Robinson thought his wife would commit suicide on this cruise?"

"Yes." Misty blinked solemnly back at him. "But it didn't go as he'd anticipated. He hadn't expected her to actually start enjoying herself. They met this other couple—the Clarks—and Allison hit it off with the wife. That wasn't how Doug wanted things to go, even though he was pretending to be a devoted husband. He'd planned on Allison isolating herself in the cabin, like she did at home. It ticked him off to no end that she was making an effort to socialize again, but he decided to use it to his advantage. He fed the Clarks stories about how Allison was self-medicating and out of it at times."

"How do you know all this?" Mendoza asked. "Did you meet up with him during the cruise?"

"He had a burner phone he used to talk to me," Misty explained. "It was hard to find much time to be together—a few stolen minutes here and there. Like I said, Doug hadn't anticipated Allison even wanting to leave the cabin. He was hoping she would see an easy way out by jumping overboard, leaving him free to be with me."

"And when that didn't go as planned, how did Doug react?"

Misty pulled her lips into a pout. "Not well. I could tell he was growing increasingly desperate. He thought ... he thought he might have to help her along."

"Help her along?" Mendoza echoed, catching the startled look Lee shot his way.

Misty grimaced. "He wanted it to be quick. His plan was to ply her with alcohol and pills so she wouldn't experience any fear when he pushed her off the balcony. It all sounded so logical when he explained it to me at first—maybe because I so desperately wanted to be with him that I didn't allow myself to acknowledge what he was actually planning to do. Initially, I pretended to go along with the idea. He wanted me to help him—you know, with the necklace and some other ideas he'd dreamed up to make her come across as loopy and forgetful. He needed to make it look like she was abusing antidepressants and mixing her pills with alcohol. That way, no one would question it when she jumped."

Mendoza tightened his jaw. As sick as it sounded, he could picture the debonair Doug plotting this. The hard part would be proving it without a body, or any real evidence. "Tell me about Cozumel. Was that you who accompanied Doug?"

Misty's startled gaze careened between him and Officer Lee. "How did you know about that? Let me guess, Rob told you."

"As a matter of fact, it was Sophia Clark. When Rob asked her to identify Allison in the CCTV footage, she knew right away something was wrong."

"How could she tell?" Misty asked with a curious lilt to her voice.

"It was the hat that gave you away. Sophia noticed that it was too small on you. But she said it was too big for Allison —she only wore it one day because it kept slipping over her eyes."

Misty sighed, a faraway look in her eye. "I wish I had a friend who paid that much attention."

Mendoza cleared his throat, eager to straighten out a few more pieces of the puzzle before she grew too tired to continue. "The thing that's not making sense to me in all of this, Misty, is why you're willing to rat out Doug Robinson, the man you supposedly love."

A solitary tear trickled down Misty's cheek. She dabbed at her face with the tissue before crushing it in her hand. "I do love him—did love him. But something's been on my conscience for a while now. It's the reason I can never be with Doug any more than I can be with Rob. I don't know why I pick the men I do—although I admit I like the money and the gifts they shower on me. I've been taking stock recently and I realize I need to start doing things differently.

None of the men in my life are good for me. Quite the opposite. Rob's controlling and possessive, and Doug's a cold-blooded murderer."

Mendoza pressed his fingertips together, training his gaze on her. "That's a strong accusation. Are you sure he killed her, and she didn't jump?"

Misty blinked blankly at him. "I'm not talking about his wife. I'm talking about his daughter."

40

DETECTIVE MENDOZA

A nerve pulsed in Detective Mendoza's neck as he fought to keep his expression neutral. It took a lot to throw him off kilter, but Misty had delivered a bombshell that had kicked him in the teeth and left him spinning. Just when he thought the plot couldn't thicken anymore, she had introduced a disturbing twist to the already sordid tale. After twenty plus years on the force, he had a strong stomach for murder, but it never got any easier when there was a child involved. His own four sons were almost grown now, but he would willingly lay down his life for any of them in a heartbeat. He'd never understood how a man could even consider hurting anyone weaker than himself—let alone a child.

After exchanging a loaded look with Officer Lee, Mendoza returned his attention to Misty. "Are you accusing Doug Robinson of killing his baby?"

Misty swept her hair from her face with a graceful flick of her hand. "I'll leave that up to you to figure out—you're the expert, after all. But I'll tell you what I do know." She propped an elbow on the table and rested her chin in her hand, her distraught expression only making her all the more alluring. "His baby died two days after I told him I wasn't interested in having children."

Mendoza knit his brows together. "What else do you recall from that conversation?"

Her lips twitched into a melancholic smile. "We were talking about a possible future together. I told him I wanted to travel the world—that was the whole reason I started working on cruise ships to begin with. Entertainers are allowed off the ship during the day to see something of the ports we stop at. We typically only work evenings on board. Anyway, I said to Doug that I didn't see how it could work for us as I wanted to start a travel blog and I didn't want kids —they would only tie me down." She fell silent, staring down at her hands as she rubbed her thumb slowly over her knuckles.

"And then what happened?" Mendoza prodded.

She released a soft breath. "Two days later, I got a text from Doug saying their baby had died."

"Are you sure of the timing?"

Misty nodded solemnly. "It totally freaked me out. At first Doug told me Ava—his daughter—died from SIDS, but then the coroner came back with some suspicious findings. There were signs that she'd been suffocated. Doug said Allison had taken an extra dose of antidepressants that day and that the coroner suspected she'd rolled over on their daughter in her sleep."

Mendoza twisted the plastic pen in his hand. "Did you suspect Doug of having anything to do with it at the time?"

Misty shook her head, a haunted expression on her face. "No. It never even occurred to me until he started dropping hints about how much better it would be if Allison would just end it and put them both out of their misery so he could finally be with me. That's when I realized he was as obsessed with me as Rob, in his own way. Only Doug was far more dangerous. He drugged Allison that day on Labadee—I'm convinced of it. I think he drugged her the day their baby died too. I don't think she rolled over on their daughter at all —I think Doug suffocated her." Misty pulled her lips into a tight line. "He's a monster."

Mendoza held her gaze in a forbidding stare, trying to read what lay beneath her alluring face. Was she telling him the truth? Had Doug Robinson acted alone? Or had Misty conspired with him to eliminate Allison? The only way to know was to turn up the heat and watch what happened. He clicked his ballpoint pen a couple of times and then cleared his throat. "As far as the investigation goes, this is all speculation on your part. The only physical evidence points to your involvement, and I have more than enough at this point to detain you. You were the last one seen with Allison the night she disappeared, which makes you a person of interest."

Misty straightened up in her seat, a fire in her liquid eyes that Mendoza hadn't seen yet. "I know what it looks like. But that's not what happened. That's why I want to help. I'll wear a wire and meet with Doug if you want. I'll do whatever it takes to prove to you that he killed his wife *and* his baby."

Mendoza flexed his fingers into a fist beneath the table as he thought it over. If Misty Murano had killed Allison Robinson, it was unlikely she would offer to assist in the investigation—even going so far as to wear a wire. If Doug was the real killer, Mendoza would welcome any help to get the man to confess to a crime that would be almost impossible to prove otherwise.

After a ponderous silence, he expelled a sharp breath. "All right, I'm willing to wire you up in order to hear what Doug has to say for himself."

"I have one condition," Misty countered. "If he confesses to the crime, then you won't pursue any charges against me. I wasn't a willing accomplice—he duped me into returning the necklace to his cabin."

"Agreed. But without his confession, all bets are off."

Misty gave a terse nod. "I understand."

Mendoza leaned back in his chair and motioned to Officer Lee to end the interview.

"Is there any word on my phone yet?" Misty asked, reaching for her purse. She'd posed the question as a casual afterthought, but Mendoza could feel the palpable tension radiating off her as she waited on his response. Why was she so desperate to recover her phone?

"Not yet," he replied, flicking his notebook closed. "When we do find it, forensics will need to process it."

A streak of panic lit up Misty's face before she looked away. It irked Mendoza that she wasn't coming clean with him, despite her offer to help with the investigation. His years of experience told him he couldn't trust her. He would use her to set up the sting, but he would be prepared for anything. If she was thinking about using the opportunity to make a run for it, he would be ready for her, and he wouldn't hesitate to slap a pair of handcuffs on her no matter how provocatively she arched her penciled brows at him.

"Let's get you set up with that wire," Mendoza said, getting to his feet.

Misty locked eyes with him. "Before I meet with Doug, there's something I need to show you at my trailer."

41

MISTY

Misty stuffed her hands deep into her coat pockets to keep them from shaking as she walked down the street to the Dogfish Brewery on the far side of town where she'd arranged to meet Doug for a celebratory drink, as she'd dubbed it. Detective Mendoza had driven her out to her trailer earlier, but she hadn't found what she'd been looking for—the one thing that would have made all this unnecessary. For now, she would have to keep up the facade. She couldn't come clean with Detective Mendoza until she knew for sure everything had gone according to plan—that there was no possible way she could be charged with Allison's murder.

Outside the brewery, Misty sucked in a shallow breath, wondering if the wire was sensitive enough to pick up on the nuances of her breathing. She slid a curious glance at her surroundings. Somewhere in a nearby parking lot, Mendoza was waiting in an unmarked van to listen in on her conversation with Doug. This would have to be the greatest performance of her life. Her freedom depended on it. The police suspected Allison hadn't committed suicide—that she had in fact been murdered and someone had covered it up. They were on a mission to find her killer, and, right now, Misty was in their crosshairs. Mendoza hadn't minced his words—she was the last person seen with Allison. It was time to shift the focus off herself and move Mendoza's attention to Doug.

When she'd called Doug earlier to set up this rendezvous, he had given her an earful. He'd been frantic about not being able to get a hold of her in the two days since *Diamond of the Waves* had returned to port. She'd had to reassure him over and over again that she hadn't been with Rob—that she'd simply wanted to be careful about being seen with him too soon. After all, they didn't want to arouse anyone's suspicions—particularly not Sophia Clark's in light of what she was telling the police. Thankfully, Doug had bought that logic.

Misty pushed open the heavy brass and wooden door to the brewery and looked around the dimly lit, wood-paneled space. Despite everything, her heart leapt when she spotted Doug sprawled in a corner booth, one arm draped along the leather seat back, his dark hair undulating in effortless waves. His face lit up when he caught sight of her weaving through the tables toward him. He leapt to his feet to embrace her, but she ducked and slipped into the bench opposite him. "Easy, handsome," she chided with a mischievous wink. "You're still the grieving widower and I'm the seductive lounge singer, remember? A classical crime pairing. Highly suspect."

"Like anyone on this side of town knows us." He pushed a Daiquiri across the table to her. "I took the liberty of ordering for you." He quirked a crooked grin and extended a hand across the table, palm upturned, inviting her to reciprocate. She twisted her lips disapprovingly. "Don't! We need to be careful."

"I don't want to be careful. I want to celebrate." He leaned toward her and lowered his voice. "It's done, baby. And the best part about it is that I'm home scot free."

She flipped him a weak smile, darting a glance around at the other patrons.

"What's wrong?" Doug asked, picking up on her agitated demeanor.

"The thing is," she said, pulling at a thread in her coat. "I'm not sure you did get away with it."

Doug's eyes bored into her. "What are you talking about?"

"The detective," she replied in a breathless whisper. "I don't think he believes you."

"Mendoza?"

Misty pressed a fist to her lips and nodded, before remembering the wire. "Yes, the one who took your statement."

Doug let out a disdainful snort. "It doesn't matter what he thinks. He doesn't have a shred of evidence."

Misty swallowed hard, her eyes latching onto Doug's. He still hadn't said anything that would hold up in court. It was time to make him sweat a little—hopefully, he'd slip up in the process. "He says he has evidence, Doug. Supposedly, from another passenger."

"What kind of evidence?"

"I don't know," Misty conceded. "He took their statement."

"Did he say who it was?"

"He wouldn't tell me."

"I'll bet it's Sophia Clark," Doug said, his voice dripping with malice. "I don't know what all Allison confided to her, but she started looking at me funny a couple of days into the cruise."

"You might be right," Misty agreed. "She didn't seem too friendly that night in the Robo Bar."

Doug's grip on his glass tightened. "I can find a way to shut her up."

Sensing her opportunity, Misty widened her eyes in alarm. "You shouldn't talk like that. It's bad enough what you did to Allison."

A sneer of contempt formed on Doug's lips. "It was what she wanted. All I did was help her finish what she started."

Misty ran a shaking finger around the rim of her untouched drink, allowing a beat of silence between them. "I feel so guilty. We should have told the police the truth—we still can."

Doug let out a sharp breath and gripped her arm so hard she winced. "Don't say that. Allison wanted out—she couldn't take it anymore. I did her a favor. You know how depressed she was. It wasn't the first time she tried to do herself in."

Misty stared at him. "Was she truly that depressed? Or did you just say that so I'd help you?"

Doug's expression grew testy. "You know as well as I do, she was clinically depressed. Her medical records prove it. After Ava died, Allison was completely distraught over what she'd done. I've had to live with a suicidal wife for months on end. Do you have any idea how miserable it's been for me?" He broke off, slipping his fingers into hers before she had a chance to pull away. His grip tightened with a ferocity that took her breath away. "You're the best thing that ever happened to me, Misty. And now I'm finally free, we can begin our life together."

Misty leaned a little closer, reverting to the silky tone that had always served her well when she wanted something. "If we're going to be together, I need you to tell me the truth about everything. Did Allison really smother Ava?"

"Yes," he answered, a look of bored unconcern in his eyes. "No one knows for sure if it was accidental or if she had some kind of psychotic break."

Misty twisted a strand of hair around her finger. "It's just ... odd that it happened right after we had that conversation about me wanting to travel, and not wanting kids. Two days later, Ava was dead."

Doug gave a languid shrug. "Sometimes things work out the way they're meant to be. It would have been worse if Allison had checked out and left me stuck raising a pint-sized version of herself."

Goosebumps pricked the back of Misty's neck at the hint of amusement in his voice. She shrank back, admiration for the man she'd once loved souring to the point of revulsion. "How can you talk about your daughter like that?"

Doug pressed her fingers to his lips, his eyes drilling into her in a way that no longer lit a flame of longing inside her. "Let's not talk about her. I only care about you."

Misty snatched her hand away. "If you really love me, then tell me the truth. I don't want to start out our life together keeping secrets from one another. Did you kill Ava?"

"Of course not!" he snapped back, before dropping his voice to a coaxing tone. "Baby, I'm not a monster. What kind of a man do you take me for?"

"The kind that drugs his wife and shoves her over a cruise ship balcony into the depths of the ocean." After a heartbeat she added softly, "Did you drug her the night Ava died too?"

Doug flashed her a startled look. "Okay, I admit I may have given her an extra dose of antidepressants. All she did was lay around and cry all day. I was only trying to help. How was I supposed to know she would roll over and smother her own child?" His shoulders sagged and he shook his head. "Maybe I was just hoping she would fall asleep and never wake up again."

Misty cast a harried glance around at the other patrons. "You do realize you could be held criminally responsible in your daughter's death too if it comes to light that you drugged Allison? I could even be dragged into it if they find out about us—they might try to charge me as an accomplice to murder." Her voice trailed off on a plaintive note. "What are we going to do? I'm so scared, Doug."

"Don't be," he reassured her. "No one knows what happened to Ava or Allison other than you and me. "You're safe now. You're out of that obsessed kook Rob's clutches. I'm going to take care of you from now on."

Misty chewed on her lip. "I didn't want to tell you over the phone, but Rob came by my trailer the other day."

Doug scowled. "What did he want?"

"He thinks I killed Allison." Misty let a few tears trickle down her cheeks. "He's been watching me on the CCTV. He saw me going into your cabin."

Doug leaned across the table and gripped her by the shoulders. "Is he blackmailing you?"

She shook her head. "No. It's worse than that. He forced me into his car and took me to his place. He locked me up—said it was for my own protection. He was afraid I would say something to incriminate myself. I might still be there if Mendoza hadn't come looking for him. He's been charged with kidnapping and unlawful imprisonment. But he's out on bail. I'm afraid he's going to come after me again."

Doug's eyes grew hard with rage. "I should have thrown him overboard too when I had the chance."

42

DOUG

Doug drove home from the Dogfish Brewery feeling oddly disconcerted. He hadn't been able to get a good read on Misty. When she'd called earlier, he'd been both relieved and ecstatic to hear her voice. But the celebratory drink she'd proposed had turned into more of a downer than he'd anticipated. She'd been acting strangely—akin to the polished persona that took over when she was performing. Some parts of their conversation had felt contrived. But her tears had been real. And she'd been telling the truth about Rob holding her hostage. She'd even pulled out a copy of the police report from her purse. Doug's knuckles tightened around the steering wheel. Rob was turning out to be another problem that wouldn't go away—like Sophia Clark.

He blew out an aggravated breath as he pulled off the freeway. Everything had become more complicated than he'd expected. Allison's suicide on *Diamond of the Waves* should have been an open and shut case, but he hadn't counted on that sick puppy Rob spying on Misty on the CCTV and catching her entering their cabin. Doug couldn't stomach the thought of him stalking Misty now that he was out on bail. She had assured him she was staying with a friend for the next few nights, as a precaution. He wished he could have brought her back to his place. He'd wanted to, now that he was free to pursue her unhampered by a wife and child. He'd even suggested it, knowing she would turn him down.

Despite his disappointment, he understood the need for them to keep their distance, for the time being at least. If they were seen together, it would raise a red flag or two. Not that he had any reason to think they were being watched. Still, Detective Mendoza, with his wooden-faced expression that rarely cracked, was not a man to be underestimated. He didn't come across as if he were particularly well-endowed in the cerebral department, but he had an unnerving way of blinking like a reptile, slow and steady, as though building up to a deadly strike. Judging by the barrage of terse, biting questions he'd grilled Doug with, Mendoza considered him more of a suspect and less of a grieving widower. Doug didn't like the man, and he didn't trust him. He suspected the feeling was mutual.

Turning into his driveway, he hit the garage door opener, and pulled in next to Allison's maroon Volkswagen SUV. He switched off the engine and scowled across at the hulking vehicle—the one she'd insisted on buying the minute she'd gotten pregnant. Ideally, he'd like to list it and get it out of there, but he was pragmatic enough to know that getting rid of her stuff too soon wouldn't be seen as befitting the actions of a grieving spouse. He'd resigned himself to putting the brakes on a lot of what he wanted to do until the funeral was over and the dust had settled. With a discontented sigh, he climbed out of his BMW and made his way inside the house.

"Hello Doug," a familiar voice whispered.

He froze in the mudroom, one hand reaching toward the wooden coat rack. Blood roared in his eardrums. Had he really just heard her voice? *Don't be stupid!* He scrunched his eyes shut, willing himself to get a grip. Maybe it was the murmuring of a guilty conscience. He was losing it—imagining her ghost whispering to him from the watery depths.

His hands curled into fists as another thought struck him. *Misty!* Had she come here after all, mimicking his dead wife like she used to do, flaunting her skill as a performer? It wasn't funny anymore. With a disgruntled air, he turned and strode into the kitchen, ready to confront her, but came to an abrupt halt.

Allison was seated at the kitchen table, unmoving, like a wax figure, her color anything but. His throat closed over. For a long moment, he couldn't speak—couldn't formulate a thought. His knees shook and he took an unsteady step backward. He blinked, wondering if the alcohol was playing tricks on him. But he hadn't drunk that much—their cocktails largely forgotten as he and Misty had bickered over their situation.

"You look shocked to see me," Allison said, uncrossing her legs and slipping off her coat. "I wonder why?"

He sucked in a jagged breath. "I ... I thought you were ... dead."

Allison let out a mirthless laugh that seemed to echo around the space. Her voice when she spoke had an edge of steel to it that he didn't recognize. "*Hoped* I was dead, you mean." She eyed him with an air of sad disdain. "You always did entertain such high hopes. I just wasn't part of them anymore."

The room began to spin around him as Doug sought to make sense of what was staring him right in the face. He reached out a hand to steady himself on the granite countertop behind him—the one he and Allison had picked out together. His fingers curled around the cool beveled edge. This was really happening. He was in his own house—awake, not dreaming. His wife was sitting at the table in front of him —not a ghost, not even wet. But how was that possible?

He'd killed her, hadn't he? He'd pushed her over their state room balcony. Granted, he'd been inebriated after a few drinks at the Robo Bar, and the details were a little hazy, but the CCTV footage confirmed she hadn't exited their cabin afterward.

His brain raced to assemble his memories of how it had all gone down. He could recollect some of the details from that evening, but other parts were foggy. The plan had been to take Allison out on the balcony to enjoy the view for their last evening, and then set her up on the railing and encircle his arms protectively around her—right before shoving her overboard. He clearly remembered her scream—a piercing shriek that had burned in his ears like fire.

In the silence that followed, Misty had whispered to him, her voice laced with pride and satisfaction, *You did it!* He frowned, suddenly unsure of himself. Had Misty been there? No, Allison would have seen her. He was getting confused. He'd texted Misty afterward to let her know he'd done it— he'd read the text the next morning.

"I can see you're burning up with questions for me. Take your time," Allison said, a cool smile on her lips. "I'm not going anywhere. This is my home, after all."

Doug took a sharp breath that stung the lining of his throat. He was desperately trying to figure out where it had all gone wrong. Something was missing from his discombobulated thoughts. Something was eluding him that he couldn't put his finger on. He ran through the sequence of events in his head again, gasping when it hit him. *The splash!* He hadn't heard a splash when Allison hit the water.

Goosebumps tingled over the back of his neck. Would he have heard anything from that height? He hadn't thought much about it at the time. He'd been too intoxicated for rational thought. He shouldn't have drunk as much as he did that night—he hadn't intended to, but somehow he'd ended up plastered.

He remembered peering over the railing, but he didn't recall seeing Allison bobbing in the dark water below. He'd assumed she'd died instantly, like they say you do when you hit the water from a great height—like hitting concrete. He'd read up on it beforehand to make sure. He passed a shaking hand over his jaw. Could Allison have tumbled to the deck below, and survived? But how?

His eyes roved disbelievingly over his resurrected wife. By all appearances, she was uninjured. How could she possibly have survived a fall from such a height without breaking every bone in her body? He plowed his fingers through his hair, increasingly agitated as the enormity of it hit him.

"You're finding it hard to look at me, aren't you? Your dead wife returned home intact." Allison kept her gaze fixed on him. "What do you think it's like for me having to look at the face of the man who tried to toss me overboard like a piece of garbage—the man who killed our child."

Doug locked his hands into fists at his side, rage bubbling up inside him. "I didn't kill Ava."

"Technically, no. Legally, yes," Allison shot back. "You drugged me that night. And then you put Ava in the bed next to me. You knew what would happen."

"You're crazy!" Doug yelled. "You're the one with the shrink."

"I did have a problem," Allison agreed. "A problem I sought help for. It's not something I'm ashamed of. Anyone with murder in mind has much bigger problems." She got to her feet and walked over to the kitchen window, staring out at the backyard. "I love this yard. We talked about filling it with children one day. You even picked out the spot where the swing set would go."

Doug's gaze darted around the room, random thoughts flitting through his mind. He could make a run for it—jump in his car and disappear before she called the cops. But that would make him look guilty. He could take a knife and kill her right now. But he despised the thought of all that blood. He'd wanted to make a clean break in every sense of the word. The cruise had seemed like the perfect solution—the ocean would have swallowed her whole.

He could force her into his car at knifepoint and drive her to some remote location. It wasn't ideal, but he had to finish what he'd started. He slid a furtive glance over the kitchen counter, his stomach knotting when he noticed the knife block that normally sat in the corner was missing. Allison had planned this meeting meticulously. In a shocking twist, she was one step ahead of him. His heart knocked against his ribs. It was unsettling to be thrown off-balance by a woman whom he'd despised for her weakness.

As if sensing the turmoil playing out in his head, Allison stepped away from the window and turned to face him. "Let me help you reconstruct the events of that night, as I know you can't remember squat. The thing is, Doug, two can play at your game. I spiked your drink at the bar with sleeping pills—Cody was kind enough to give me a fistful of his. When we got back to the cabin, I let you lead me out onto the balcony. You made an attempt to shove me over the railing, but I struggled and screamed. You could barely stand by then, and you passed out moments later. Afterward, I dragged you inside the cabin, sent a quick text to Misty to let her know you'd done the deed, and then left. When you got up the next morning, you read the text, saw that my purse was still in the room, found the flip-flop, and convinced yourself that you'd pulled it off."

Doug gave a bewildered shake of his head as he sank down in a chair. "I don't understand. Where did you go? How did you get off the ship undetected?"

A conspiratorial smile spread across Allison's lips. "I had help with that part."

"Who?" Doug spat out. "Sophia and Cody?"

Allison's phone dinged with an incoming text. She glanced down at it before answering. "See for yourself. My accomplice just pulled up outside."

43

DOUG

A horrified gasp ripped from Doug's throat when he saw who was standing in the doorway. The blood in his veins ran cold. *No!* It couldn't be Misty who had betrayed him. She was the whole reason he had done what he had done—or tried to. He got to his feet unsteadily. Something fearsome sparked in her eyes when she met his gaze. She had never looked more beautiful to him, in a dangerous sort of way. He didn't know whether he wanted to rip her limb from limb or ravish her. He forced air in through his nostrils, trying desperately to remain calm, willing the raging bull inside him to show restraint. There had to be an explanation for this. She was on his side; they were a team.

"Hello again," she said, as she brushed past him.

"Misty!" he croaked, shock crystallizing in his throat. "What are you doing here? What's going on?"

She perched on the edge of a bar stool and crossed her long legs. "I came to my senses in time, that's what."

Doug pressed his hands to his head. "This isn't making any sense."

"It's not that complicated," Misty responded. "The truth is,

I couldn't go through with it. I couldn't help you murder your wife and I couldn't stand back and watch it happen either. So, I went to visit Allison. I confessed to the affair and warned her about your intentions." Her voice softened momentarily. "I loved you, Doug. I thought I'd finally found the right man in you. I was so desperate to move on from Rob and his controlling ways that it blinded me to who you really were. I believed every word that dripped from your tongue. I felt sorry for you. I cried in my cabin every time I thought about how you were forced to live with a severely depressed wife day in and day out. It sounded like such a miserable existence the way you described it." She paused as Allison joined her at the island, arms folded in front of her.

"You told Misty you couldn't divorce me because you didn't want to lose the company you'd built up during our marriage," Allison said. "But that wasn't the real reason you tried to kill me, was it, Doug?"

He made an incoherent sound before Misty cut him off. "After I talked to Allison, everything became a lot clearer. She suspected you'd been messing with her medication. And she'd figured out you were responsible for Ava's death. You were afraid she would take her suspicions to the police. So you had to get rid of her. You didn't want to be investigated and risk going to jail."

"You've got it all wrong," Doug sputtered. "Allison's crazy. You can't believe anything she tells you. She's manipulating you."

Misty tweaked an impossibly arched brow even higher. "You're wasting your time trying to convince me of your lies, Doug. Like I said, I've finally come to my senses. It's always been the men in my life who were using me, trying to control me. First Rob, then you. Once I understood you were serious about making sure Allison didn't return from the cruise, I knew I had to do something. I thought she was too fragile to help herself, let alone spike your drink. Turns out she was stronger than either of us realized."

A chill snaked its way down Doug's spine. "You were in on all of it—drugging me, the text from my phone, faking her death?"

Misty shrugged. "I'm a performer. It's what I do best."

"How did you pull it off? I don't … understand. Allison didn't leave the cabin."

Misty flexed her polished fingers. "Rob's colleague, Dave, was only too willing to oblige me by altering the security footage to make it appear as if Allison never left your state room that day. I hid her in my cabin until we docked at Fort Lauderdale."

Doug slumped back down in his chair and rubbed a hand across his jaw. His eyes jerked toward Allison. "How did you get off the ship without anyone seeing you?"

"Dimitri, the base player, hid me in his double bass case."

"Up until that point, it all went very smoothly," Misty chipped in again. "Dimitri's wife met him at the dock, and they drove Allison back to their house. I was supposed to pick her up there later that night and take her to my trailer. But then Rob came by. He suspected I had something to do with Allison's disappearance. He wasn't thinking straight—kept rambling on about how we needed to disappear south of the border. He forced me into his car and took me back to his place."

"I waited all that night and the next morning for Misty's call," Allison went on. "I knew something must have gone wrong, but I didn't know what. I left Dimitri's house and checked into a hotel. I was afraid to go to Misty's trailer. I was worried she might have chickened out and told you what she'd done. I was afraid she would lead you straight to me." She threw Misty an apologetic look. "In my defense, I didn't know you all that well."

Misty swatted a hand dismissively. "Fortunately for me, Detective Mendoza stopped by my trailer and realized immediately something was wrong. He had a hunch Rob was involved. When he knocked on the door, I started kicking at shelving and knocking over anything that would make a noise. Mendoza heard me, and broke in. I didn't have my phone, so I still had no way of contacting Allison to let her know I was all right. Thankfully, she called Dimitri later that day and got the message I left with him."

"I think that should just about answer all his questions, don't you think?" Allison said, glancing at Misty.

Misty nodded and stood. "We're done here."

Allison pulled out her phone and tapped on the screen.

"What are you doing?" Doug growled through gritted teeth.

"Letting Detective Mendoza know you're all his."

Doug vaulted to his feet. "You've ruined my life, Allison. You never were anything but a sniveling doormat!" He spun and glowered at Misty. "And you—you're nothing but a pretty face. You're never going to amount to anything off the ship. You don't have what it takes." He strode across to the door and flung it open.

Detective Mendoza's burly frame filled the doorway. "Going somewhere, Doug?"

His eyes flicked to the French doors at the far end of the kitchen, a burst of desperation traversing through his veins.

"Don't waste your time," Mendoza drawled. "Officer Lee's stationed outside. If he has to take you down, he won't hesitate to incapacitate you."

Doug swung back around and shook his fist at Misty. "How could you do this, after everything I promised you?"

Misty gave a sad shake of her head. "You think you know a lot about women, Doug. But what you don't know is that we don't like to be played against each other."

44

THREE WEEKS LATER

"Thanks for having us over to meet your boys. You and Cody are very blessed," Allison said, dipping a chip into a dish of homemade salsa at the picnic table in Sophia's backyard.

"I don't know where they get their energy from," Misty marveled, reaching for a piece of watermelon.

Sophia sipped on her glass of Sauvignon, smiling as she watched her twins, Gavin and Will, tearing up and down the garden shooting at each other with water guns, shrieking each time they scored a hit. "They wear me out some days, but I can't imagine life without them." She motioned to Cody, manning the grill on the patio. "Not to mention my superstar husband who's been working from dawn 'til dusk since we got back from the cruise."

"Is your business going to make it?" Misty asked with a slight hesitation in her voice.

Sophia gave a thoughtful nod. "I'm optimistic. Our accountant helped us work out a repayment plan with the IRS." A wry grin appeared on her lips. "It doesn't allow for any cruises for the next five years at least, but I can live with that. We're spending more time with the boys as a family, doing simple things like taking the dog for a walk, fishing off the pier, or having a picnic at the beach. They're happier than they've ever been."

"How about you, Misty?" Allison inquired. "Have you made any plans yet?"

Misty grinned, deepening the hollows of her cheeks. She looked like she'd lost weight. No doubt the strain of worrying about whether Rob would show up on her doorstep again was taking its toll.

"As a matter of fact, I've started my travel blog and submitted some articles to magazines," Misty said. "I'm also writing my own songs again. I'm tired of singing covers."

"Good for you," Allison responded. "I can't wait for your first hit single. Then I can tell everyone that I know a celebrity."

Misty threw back her head and laughed, her long, blonde hair rippling in the sunshine. "Don't hold your breath. Whatever comes of it, I couldn't be happier. I'm finally going after my dreams. I've wasted enough time trying to fit into other people's plans for my life."

"Speaking of which, what's going on with the obsessed security officer?" Sophia probed. "Any updates?"

Misty pursed her lips. "Rob's agreed to plead guilty. He'll serve a year or two at most. But he'll never work in security again, that's for sure." She tilted her head toward Allison. "How are you doing?"

"I'm back in therapy and that's helping." She dropped her gaze and picked at a splinter in the wooden tabletop. "I'm trying to move on. The hardest part is not knowing for sure what happened to Ava—whether Doug smothered her, or I rolled over on her after he drugged me. Either way, I know now that he was responsible. I can honestly say I'm living free of that heavy feeling of guilt for the first time in a long time. I'm actually looking forward to the future now—something I never thought I'd say."

"Burgers are up!" Cody called from the grill.

He strode across the lawn to the picnic table with a tea towel hanging from his waist and a plate of burgers balanced on his fingertips. "Chef Cody at your service."

At the mention of food, the twins came tearing up from the bottom of the garden in a flurry of limbs, sweaty and disheveled. After assembling their burgers, which consisted of slathering a patty with ketchup, and disposing of the lettuce leaf Sophia had surreptitiously added, they climbed up into their treehouse to eat their food.

"So, Allison, are you back working at the real estate office?" Cody asked as he sat down at the picnic table.

"For now," she said, swallowing a sip of wine. "But I've decided I'm going to get my real estate license and open my own business. I practically run the office already—advertising, contracts, social media. Why be the executive assistant when I can run the whole show?"

"I'll drink to that," Cody said, raising his glass to hers.

Misty clinked glasses with them. "You're more than capable, you've proven that after what you came through."

"I have to be now that I need to support myself," Allison said.

"What's the latest with Doug?" Sophia asked, joining in the toast.

"He's officially been charged with attempted murder," Allison said. "Last I heard, he fired his lawyer. He can't accept the fact that he's going to end up serving time. He's refusing to plead guilty."

She dabbed at her mouth with her napkin. "I wish for his sake he would take the plea deal his lawyer negotiated. If he goes to trial and loses, he'll be looking at a much longer sentence."

Sophia pressed her lips together in a disapproving line. "His arrogance will be his downfall. He can't walk away from this. It's time he faced up to what he did and took responsibility for his actions."

"It can be a hard thing to do," Cody commented. "I know all about digging myself into a hole and having to swallow my pride and face the consequences in order to climb back out."

Sophia rubbed his arm affectionately. "That's different. You messed up, but you're not a monster. You wanted to give me and the boys everything. That's forgivable in my book."

Cody threw her a sheepish grin. "I don't deserve a woman like you, Sophia Clark."

"What man does?" She chuckled as she reached for her burger. "I guess God was feeling generous on the sixth day."

AFTER FINISHING their meal and hugging the Clarks goodbye, Misty and Allison walked out to their respective cars parked on the street.

"I can't thank you enough for giving me the courage to go through with it," Allison said, unzipping her purse. "I couldn't have done it without you."

Misty pressed the key fob to unlock her car. "Do you think Mendoza suspects?"

Allison shrugged. "If he does, he's not going to investigate any further. Thanks to you, we have a recording of Doug confessing to attempted murder. He can whine to Mendoza all he wants that we drugged him that night, but it's his word against ours. In light of his track record of drugging me, he's hardly credible."

"Good thing we managed to get him to the cabin after he passed out in the elevator," Misty said. "He never even questioned that he'd gone through with tossing you overboard when he woke up."

"I think reading the text he thought he sent you on the burner phone convinced him. I'm glad you came up with that."

"He gave me the idea," Misty replied. "Part of his plan all along was to use your phone to text Sophia and convince her you were still alive for another full day. By the time the alarm was sounded, he thought for sure you would be shark chum. Instead, he gets to be the pretty boy behind bars now."

Allison shuddered as she pulled out her keys. "He's not going to fare well in prison. I hope we did the right thing."

Misty reached for Allison's hand and squeezed it. "Don't second-guess yourself. He fully intended to kill you. He'd have tried again. Putting him away was the right thing to do. But what we did has to stay our secret. Pinky promise me you'll take it to your grave."

"I promise." Allison hugged her and gave her a grateful smile in parting. "Thanks to you, it won't be the watery one Doug had in mind after all."

THE CLASS REUNION

Ready for another thrilling read with shocking twists and a mind-blowing murder plot? Check out my psychological thriller ***The Class Reunion*** on Amazon! Releasing December 2020.

You can run but I will find you.

Working as a successful PI in Los Angeles, Heather Nelson hasn't seen any of her high school classmates from Iowa in over a decade. When she makes a last minute decision to attend her class reunion, she and her once tight-knit group of friends are surprised at dinner by a delivery of an elaborate forget-me-not floral arrangement. But the accompanying card contains an ominous message: *you deserve to die*—a message they brush off as an elaborate prank at first.

When several of the group come close to death in the following weeks, they begin to suspect that the sender of the message has deadly intentions. One-by-one the friends contact Heather to divulge secrets from their past, convinced that the skeletons they are hiding put them at risk. Fearing for their lives, they beg Heather to return to Iowa and track down the person they believe is trying to kill them. But her friends only think they know her. Heather is hiding an explosive secret of her own.

Is she really an intended victim in a deadly game of revenge, or a twisted killer?

- An unputdownable, brilliant psychological thriller with a mind-blowing murder plot! -

---

Do you enjoy reading across genres? I also write young adult science fiction and fantasy thrillers. You can find out more about those titles at **www.normahinkens.com.**

A QUICK FAVOR

Dear Reader,

I hope you enjoyed reading ***The Cabin Below*** as much as I enjoyed writing it. Thank you for taking the time to check out my books and I would appreciate it from the bottom of my heart if you would leave a review, long or short, on Amazon as it makes a HUGE difference in helping new readers find the series. Thank you!

To be the first to hear about my upcoming book releases, sales, and fun giveaways, sign up for my newsletter at **www.normahinkens.com** and follow me on Twitter, Instagram and Facebook. Feel free to email me at norma@normahinkens.com with any feedback or comments. I LOVE hearing from readers. YOU are the reason I keep going through the tough times.

All my best,

Norma

BIOGRAPHY

NYT and USA Today bestselling author Norma Hinkens writes twisty psychological suspense thrillers, as well as fast-paced science fiction and fantasy about spunky heroines and epic adventures in dangerous worlds. She's also a travel junkie, legend lover, and idea wrangler, in no particular order. She grew up in Ireland, land of make-believe and the original little green man.

Find out more about her books on her website.
www.normahinkens.com

Follow her on Facebook for funnies, giveaways, cool stuff & more!

ALSO BY N. L. HINKENS

Head to my website to find out more about my other psychological suspense thrillers.

www.normahinkens.com/books

- The Silent Surrogate
- I Know What You Did
- The Lies She Told
- Her Last Steps
- The Other Woman
- You Will Never Leave
- The Cabin Below
- The Class Reunion
- Never Tell Them

BOOKS BY NORMA HINKENS

I also write young adult science fiction and fantasy thrillers under Norma Hinkens.

www.normahinkens.com/books

The Undergrounders Series - Post-apocalyptic

Immurement
Embattlement
Judgement

The Expulsion Project - Science Fiction

Girl of Fire
Girl of Stone
Girl of Blood

The Keepers Chronicles - Epic Fantasy

Opal of Light
Onyx of Darkness
Opus of Doom

Follow Norma:

Sign up for her newsletter:

https://books.normahinkens.com/VIPReaderClub

Website:

https://normahinkens.com/

Facebook:

https://www.facebook.com/NormaHinkensAuthor/

Twitter

https://twitter.com/NormaHinkens

Instagram

https://www.instagram.com/normahinkensauthor/

Pinterest:

https://www.pinterest.com/normahinkens/

Made in the USA
Coppell, TX
15 May 2021